DELIVER US FROM EVIL

CONRAD JONES

CHAPTER 1

The whirring sound of a power saw woke him from his sleep. He couldn't tell where it was coming from – above or below. The flats were well soundproofed, but the high-pitched sound of the saw travelled through the structure, grating on his nerves. He checked his watch: it was three o'clock in the morning. What type of idiot would use a power tool at that time? One without a job, that's who. A lot of the flats were occupied by wasters now. It hadn't been like that when he'd moved in. The landlords had since dropped their standards and allowed the unemployed to rent apartments next to hard-working residents. Some of the newer families were African and Eastern European, and they all seemed to work hard. It was like the United Nations in the lifts, but they all had jobs. The jobless were the problem. He didn't think of himself as a snob, but the unemployed had lowered the standards in the tower block; it was noisier, dirtier and more dangerous. No one had used power tools in the middle of the night until the landlords allowed the unemployed to move in. The sound pierced the night again, louder this time. He tried to pinpoint where it was coming from. Below him, someone shouted angrily in a foreign language. A baby started crying, followed by more shouting. The saw whirred again, provoking more angry protests from below. He swore beneath his breath and threw the quilt off. He couldn't sleep through that nonsense. Enough was enough.

Paul Skelton was angry. He was angry most of the time. Life was one monotonous pile of bullshit. Stupid people made him mad, and most of the people he met were very stupid. People who used power tools at night were incredibly stupid. He switched on the light and swung his legs out of bed. The saw had stopped, momentarily. He paused and listened; the baby downstairs had settled down and the angry voices were muffled and less frequent. He thought about climbing back into bed when a sudden thud on the ceiling made him jump;

it was followed by the sound of something heavy being dragged across the floor. It wasn't directly above his bedroom, but it was close. His heart quickened and he held his breath. Another thump rattled him.

'You're taking the piss, stupid idiot,' Paul muttered. 'That's enough.'

He struggled into his tracksuit pants and pulled a vest over his head. The dragging sound began again. Then another thump. He stuffed his feet into his trainers and padded over to the door, muttering to himself about what he was going to do with that saw and where he was going to shove it. Then the lights went out.

'I don't believe this,' he said, searching for the door handle.

His hands touched the cold metal and he opened the door, feeling his way through the darkness while his eyes adjusted. A yellow glow filtered through the blinds from the streetlights below. The power cut was localised to the tower block – it happened in the building quite a lot. Too often. The last time it had happened, it was off for over an hour. He reached the kitchen and fumbled his way to the bits-and-pieces drawer. There was a torch in there, somewhere amongst the adapters and old phone chargers. The baby started crying again, joined quickly by another. A man and woman started arguing on the floor below in a language he didn't recognise. Getting to sleep tonight was going to be difficult. He found the torch and switched it on. The beam cut through the night and he aimed it at the ceiling. A circle of light shimmered. The knife block caught his eye and he thought about taking one, just in case, but dismissed the idea just as quick. A blade glinted in the light, its edge cold and sharp. Taking a blade to a noisy neighbour was a touch over the top. He would ask them politely to be quiet. If that didn't work, he would give them a slap. Nothing too heavy, just a jab on the nose. Make their eyes water and they would think twice about building an extension in the middle of the night. Another heavy thump from above steeled him on. The idiots were not giving up on whatever project they had started.

Paul walked to his front door and unlocked it. He opened it and the cold night air rushed in, touching his exposed flesh with icy fingers. Goose bumps appeared on his arms and he felt a sense of dread growing inside him. He looked across the landing at the city below. The lights twinkled like yellow jewels on a sea of black ink. A gust of wind whistled along the landing, blowing a polystyrene cup towards the stone stairwell. It tumbled over and over before disappearing into the dark. He listened as it clattered down the steps. A deep chill made him shiver, his mind searching for excuses not to step out of the warmth into the darkness.

It occurred to him that the power cut would silence the saw. He thought about not going upstairs, about going back to bed and trying to sleep despite the noise. The saw whirred again and the hairs on his neck bristled. Obviously, they had a battery-powered tool. That was it. The final straw. He shone his torch towards the stairs and tried to close the door quietly behind him, but the wind caught it, slamming it loudly. The noise echoed through the building and he froze to the spot, waiting for a torrent of abuse to be shouted from the neighbours below. None came. He took a deep breath and moved down the landing.

The stairwell was pitch black and looked like the entrance to the underworld. He shone the torch up the stairs and the beam of light illuminated the concrete steps. Black blobs of chewing gum stained them and there were dark patches in the corners. The reek of urine drifted to him. He whispered a curse that was carried away on the wind. The entire block was turning into a giant toilet. He was going to make a complaint to the estate managers directly. There were so many landlords in the building that nothing got done unless they were bypassed. Another gust of wind urged him up the first tier of steps; the cold made the task more pressing. He turned on the landing and took the steps two at a time. The wind was stronger as he climbed, funnelled along the balcony by the angle of the roof. The stench grew stronger and it was darker on the top floor – the power of the streetlights became diluted as he climbed.

He moved quickly from the stairwell along the landing using the torch to light the way. The windows in the first flat were boarded up. Scorch marks reached from the top of the lintels to the roof. The flat had caught fire in suspicious circumstances months ago. Paul heard the wind whistling through the handrails. It was then that he caught the smell of cooking: garlic, onions, pork. He glanced at his watch again. Three fifteen. What was wrong with these people?

Paul marched past two more empty properties and stopped outside the door of number ninety. The curtains were clean and tidy and drawn. Everything was quiet. He wasn't sure where the noise had been coming from, but he knew it was above his flat somewhere. That meant it was either ninety or ninety-one. He walked to the flat next door and looked in through the window. The kitchen inside was stripped, only the sink remained. Electric wires hung from empty sockets and a pile of copper pipes were leaning in the corner. Tins of contract paint were stacked near the door. Paul could see it was being renovated and ruled it out as the source of the noise. The flats beyond were all boarded up. That meant that the occupants of number ninety were the culprits. He walked back and listened outside the door. Someone was gently humming. He recognised the tune but the name of it eluded him. The sound of the saw whirring made him jump.

'Shit!' he hissed. He knocked on the door and waited. Nothing happened. He knocked again, louder this time. Nothing. 'Don't pretend you're not in,' he muttered as he knocked again. There was no response.

Paul moved from the door and looked in through the windows. He aimed his torch through the cracks in the curtains, but he couldn't see anything – the light was reflecting on the glass. He went back to the front door and opened the letter box. The odours of cooking drifted to him, making his mouth water. His hunger added insult to injury. He pointed the torch through the narrow gap and searched the hallway. There was no sign of life. He noticed some dark spots on the door near the kitchen that looked like fingerprints.

'Hello!' he shouted through the letter box. A clatter from the kitchen echoed up the hallway. Then it was still again. 'Hello?' he shouted again. He heard footsteps but it was impossible to make out where they were coming from. 'I've come to ask you to keep the noise down,' he shouted. 'Using power tools at this time of night is ridiculous, mate!' Paul looked through the letter box again. The beam of light scanned the walls, but nothing moved. 'I know you can hear me,' he shouted. Another clatter came from the back of the flat. 'You can talk to me, mate, or you can talk to the police. Make your mind up.'

There was no reply. Paul went back to window and tried to penetrate the blackness inside with the torch. It was impossible. The glare on the glass was blinding. He heard the front door open and he turned around.

'About time,' Paul said, angrily. The man stepped out and looked around. 'You've woke up the whole building, mate. What do you think you're playing at, using tools at this time of night?'

The man looked at him blankly. His eyes looked as black as the night. Paul felt uneasy. The man smiled and Paul saw dark smudges on his teeth. He was about to take a step backwards when, too late, a flash of dull metal registered. The hammer hit him upside the temple. He felt his knees buckle as the man swung again. A strong arm came from behind him, choking him. He felt himself being dragged inside the flat, but he couldn't shout for help. There were two attackers. One of his shoes became snagged on the sill and he kicked out to free it. The front door slammed closed and Paul knew he was in dire trouble. He struggled desperately to release the grip on his throat, but his attacker was too strong. The first man raised the hammer again and brought it down on the top of Paul's skull; there was a blinding flash. White-hot bolts of pain shot through his brain. This time, the lights went out completely.

CHAPTER 2

Detective Superintendent Braddick reached the top of the stairs and caught a whiff of garlic on the breeze – garlic tainted with something rotten. It was a familiar smell… burnt flesh. He had attended enough fatal fires to recognise the odour in an instant. Braddick nodded to the uniformed officers on the cordon and was handed a white forensic suit by his detective sergeant, Laurel Stewart. Her ginger hair was blowing behind her, a mass of curls. She pulled up her hood to stop it flapping in the wind and smiled at him.

'Welcome back,' Braddick said. 'I thought you would be as big as a house. You look well.'

'I was pregnant, not fat,' she said, frowning. 'But thank you anyway. It's nice to see you.'

'It's nice to have you back on the team. How is little Aimee?' Braddick asked.

'Not so little. She's growing every day,' Laurel said. 'Leaving her this morning was such a struggle. Rob was very supportive, bless him, but I felt like crying.'

'How is he?' Braddick asked.

'He's amazing.'

'Amazing?' Braddick said, raising his eyebrows. 'You used to call him a knob. Has motherhood made you soppy?'

'He is a knob sometimes, but he's my knob. Today he was amazing,' Laurel laughed.

'Don't stress. It will all be over in the blink of an eye. She'll be grown up, spending your money at university and having your grandchildren before you know it.'

'How would you know?' Laurel said, frowning. 'You don't even have a goldfish.'

'Just a thought, that's all.'

'Thanks for that thought.'

'You're welcome. Is this as bad as I'm being told?' Braddick asked, putting on his overshoes. His black skin looked darker still in contrast to the white plastic suit.

'Worse,' Laurel said. She grimaced. 'Much worse. I don't think I've seen Dr Libby so quiet.'

'Dr Libby is quiet? It must be bad,' Braddick said. 'Who called it in?'

'It was an anonymous call from a mobile phone with a withheld number. They reported that a homeless woman had been seen going into the flat on Tuesday and she hadn't been seen since.' Laurel leaned towards the balcony and gestured to a huddle of onlookers. Some of them were clearly unkempt and living on the streets. 'There seems to be a small community sleeping rough in the stairwells.'

'It looks like it,' Braddick agreed.

'Uniform sent a unit to the flat to make enquiries and the smell made them suspicious. They called it in and forced entry was made at one o'clock.'

'Okay, let's have a look,' Braddick said. He noticed DS Barlow approaching. 'Ian, I'm glad you're here. I need you to supervise the door to door. Start on the floor below and work down.'

'No worries, guv,' Ian said. He took out his mobile and headed down the stairs.

'Good man, thank you.'

Braddick glanced over the balcony. It was a long way down and he wasn't comfortable with heights. The crowd of onlookers was growing, and a raft of mobile phones were being pointed at the police activity. The residents of each floor were gathering and gossiping. Camera flashes blinked from every landing. Braddick knew the images would be posted to Facebook and Instagram already. It was a panoramic view from the ninth floor. He looked south, towards the river. A mile away, the St John's Tower was silhouetted against the grey waters of the Mersey, and both cathedrals dominated the skyline. He walked to the front door of number ninety and sniffed the air. The stench of decay drifted to him. All the garlic in the world couldn't mask the smell of a rotting human. Laurel handed him a small jar of tiger balm and he smeared some beneath his nostrils – it made his eyes water a little. He stepped inside and saw bloody fingerprints on the kitchen doorframe. Someone had put up a fight, trying not to be dragged inside. As he looked around, he tried to imagine what had happened.

The hallway was tastefully decorated and well-kept. He peered into the first doorway on the left. Two CSIs were on their knees, working, in the living room. A plasma television was fixed to the wall and a leather corner sofa dominated the room. It looked expensive. The CSIs were dusting a coffee table and a soup bowl for prints. There were no personal touches or clues about the person who lived there; no pictures or photographs. Braddick stepped into the room and watched the forensic officers working. The bowl held the remnants of a congealed amber liquid and a spoon. A rotten smell radiated from it. He could see prints on the metal handle, highlighted by the dust. There were also prints on an empty glass that looked like it had contained milk.

'You've found plenty of prints?' Braddick asked.

'Yes,' one of the forensic officers said, without turning around. His attention was on the bowl. '"Plenty" is an understatement.'

'There are dozens of them,' the second officer added. He looked up at Braddick. 'You shouldn't have a problem matching them to a suspect. Most of them are perfect.'

'That's good news,' Braddick said, looking around. There were no signs of a struggle. The sweet, sickly stench permeated the air. It clung to the carpets and curtains making the atmosphere toxic.

Braddick turned and headed for the kitchen; Laurel followed him closely. The prints on the doorframe were smeared blood. It had dried and turned dark brown. He stepped inside and looked around, analysing the scene. The table had been set for one person; crockery and cutlery had been used to eat and left when they had finished. At the centre of the table, matching salt and pepper mills were standing next to a bottle of West Indian hot pepper sauce and a bottle of vinegar. It was an ordinary scene except for the smell of death. It was rank. He walked around the kitchen towards the stove. The worktops were clean and tidy.

There was a blender, half full of dark sludge. He peered closer and got a whiff of rotting meat. He glanced at Laurel and grimaced. She nodded that she understood.

'Someone was making smoothies,' Braddick muttered. Laurel didn't respond. He looked at her for her opinion.

'I don't think it was a smoothie. I think it was stock,' Laurel said. She nodded to the stove.

'Stock?'

'For the soup.'

Braddick reached the cooker and studied two huge stock pots. He recoiled, looking at Laurel before looking back. The pot held an amber liquid, which had congealed. A severed female head looked back at him, the eyes boiled white. Slivers of onion and carrot floated in the soup. The second pot contained a much darker concoction that resembled chilli con carne. He could see kidney beans mixed into the mince and sauce. The smell of decaying human was overpowering. A chopping board had half an onion and some garlic cloves on it. They had been sliced thinly by someone with a talent for cookery. Braddick picked up a box of vegetable stock cubes and shook his head. He looked in the bin and scanned its contents: carrot tops, onion skins, an empty jar of chilli con carne sauce and some used sachets of herbs and spices.

'I'm struggling to comprehend what I'm seeing,' he said, turning to Laurel.

'It's not your average murder scene. Not by a long way.'

'I'll give you that,' Braddick agreed. 'It doesn't feel right to me.'

'In what way?'

'The scene should be chaotic, but it isn't.'

'I don't follow.'

'This kitchen is spotless, yet it looks like someone has used a head to make a chilli and some soup?'

'Not just a head,' Laurel said. 'Check out the fridge.'

Braddick opened the fridge. At first glance, it appeared to be the well-stocked appliance of a normal suburban household: yoghurts, cheddar cheese, bacon, butter, milk and orange juice. Anything opened was labelled in

Tupperware pots or sealed containers. On the middle shelf, he could see a thick fillet of meat wrapped in clingfilm, the skin and hair still attached. It was too hairy to have been taken from a female. Next to it, on a saucer, was a kidney. A small pool of blood had formed around it.

'We have a male victim, too?' Braddick said, closing the door.

'We have two victims, one female, one male,' Laurel said. 'There are no signs of their bodies yet.'

Dr Graham Libby walked into the kitchen. He said hello to Braddick.

'Just when you think you've seen it all, eh?' he said. His forehead wrinkled as he spoke. Braddick noticed grey hairs sprouting from his ears. He looked old and tired.

'It never ceases to amaze me what people can do to each other,' Braddick said.

'I overheard your comment,' Dr Libby said.

'Which one?' Braddick asked.

'About chaos.'

'And?'

'You're right,' Dr Libby said, crossing the kitchen. 'It should be chaotic.'

'Why isn't it?'

'It is, but we can't see it.'

'It is?' Braddick asked, frowning.

'It's better if I demonstrate what I mean,' he said, closing the blinds. The kitchen became dark. 'Watch this.' Dr Libby switched on a UV light. Smears of blood appeared everywhere, highlighted by luminol. Braddick looked around. Every surface was smeared with bloodstains. Splatter patterns ran up the cupboards to the ceiling. The floor around one of the chairs was heavily stained, the other two were unmarked. 'You were right, Braddick. It was chaotic, but someone spent a long time cleaning this place down. It's been wiped and mopped repeatedly.'

'That is a lot of blood,' Braddick said.

'It is, and some of it is much older than the rest,' Dr Libby explained. 'It wasn't spilled or cleaned at the same time.'

'So, it *is* chaotic,' Braddick said, studying the splatter.

'I would go so far as to say frenzied,' Dr Libby added. 'The kills were frenzied but whoever lives here has an organised mind.' He pointed to the cupboards. 'Open one of them.' Braddick opened one. Tins of beans and soup were lined up, uniform, in neat rows with the labels facing the same way. All the cereal packets faced the same way and anything that had been opened was repackaged in airtight containers.

'They do have a tidy thing going on,' Braddick agreed.

'Try the next one,' Dr Libby said. Braddick closed the cupboard door and opened the next one. It was full of cups and plates, stacked neatly in piles, handles pointing in the same direction. 'Whoever lived here was OCD and couldn't tolerate mess or disorder. I would be very surprised if they did this alone. They tried to clean up after the killings because the mess bothered them, not because they are forensically aware.' Dr Libby opened the blinds and gestured for the detectives to follow him. 'This is very interesting,' he said, pointing to a brown substance wrapped in cling film.

'What is that?' Braddick asked.

'I can't be sure yet but, from the smell of it, I would say it is compressed mushrooms,' Dr Libby said. Braddick looked confused. 'Psilocybin mushrooms to be precise.'

'Magic mushrooms?' Laurel asked.

'Exactly,' Dr Libby said. 'In this compressed form it can be eaten or turned into tea. It is a very powerful hallucinogenic.'

'Powerful enough to make you think boiling someone's head was okay?' Laurel asked.

'They're powerful enough to make you think it was a great idea,' Dr Libby said, nodding. 'Obviously, their effect would vary from person to person, but they would certainly loosen their grip on reality.'

'What are we looking for, Dr Libby?' Laurel asked.

'A raging psychopath with OCD,' he replied. 'Probably with a friend who has a similar mindset.'

'How long has she been there?' Braddick asked, taking another look at the head in the stock pot. She looked to be an older woman – her hair was grey. Patches of skin had fallen from her skull to reveal her teeth. They were a mixture of yellowed natural molars, and false dentures that were stained with tobacco. Parts of her scalp were still clinging to the bone, some hair still attached.

'From the state of decay, I'm guessing they were cooked a few days ago – three, maybe four at the most.' The doctor shrugged. 'The muscle in the fridge is still relatively fresh,' he said, grimacing. 'Excuse the inference. Obviously, it has been refrigerated but there is no discolouration yet.' He walked to the fridge and opened the door. 'I think it was harvested about the same time. Four days ago, maximum, would be my guess.' He pointed to the milk in the fridge. 'The milk still has four days on it. The occupant went shopping recently. Once we get everything back to the lab, I'll have a better idea.' He paused and raised his forefinger. 'Come and see this.'

Braddick and Laurel followed him out of the kitchen and into the bathroom. It was compact and had a shower above the bath. The smell of bleach was prevalent.

'Step in and close the door, please,' Dr Libby said. He switched off the light and turned on the UV torch. Blood smears covered the tiles and there was a tidemark of blood around the bath. The taps and toilet bowl were stained. 'Your killer, or killers, showered and bathed.'

'They were in no rush,' Braddick said.

'No. There are stains around the toilet bowl, I am guessing they disposed of some of their victims down the toilet.'

'They chopped them up and flushed them away,' Laurel said, shaking her head.

'Probably. They cleaned the rooms for cosmetic purposes, not forensic ones.'

'So, they cleaned up, moved the bodies, and then one killer showered and the other bathed?' Braddick asked.

'It looks that way,' Dr Libby said. 'Although there are some contradictions. There's only one setting at the table and the luminol shows a lot of blood pooled beneath one of the chairs. That would suggest one killer and a victim to me. What about you?'

'It would explain the blood pattern beneath the chair,' Braddick agreed. 'What else have you found?'

'I'll show you,' Dr Libby said. He turned on the light and opened the door. Braddick followed him into a small bedroom. A double bed dominated the room. It had been stripped and the mattress scrubbed. Dark stains and watermarks covered the material. 'There are no towels or bedding in the flat. I think they used them to clean up and then disposed of them with the bodies.' He waited until the detectives were in the room, closed the door and turned off the light. The UV torch revealed blood stains on the mattress, carpets and walls, and splatter on the ceiling. 'There's a lot of blood in here, too.'

'No one is losing that much blood and surviving,' Laurel said.

'Someone was killed here and someone else was killed in the kitchen.' Dr Libby shrugged. 'I think.' Braddick nodded that he agreed in principle. Dr Libby opened the wardrobe door. Clothes hung neatly pressed, colour coordinated, and separated into his and hers. 'The women's clothes are all the same size – they're a ten. The men's clothes vary in size.'

'Any clues who lives here?' Braddick asked, thumbing through the garments. 'Have we confirmed with the landlord whose name is on the tenancy?'

'We're struggling to contact her so we're not a hundred per cent,' Laurel said, shaking her head. 'The council tax has been paid up to date and the owner is registered as Victoria Theresa May.' Braddick frowned. Laurel grinned. 'Not that one,' she added.

'Are we sure?' Braddick asked. 'Our victim has short grey hair.'

'I saw her on the telly this morning,' Laurel said. 'Unless it was a recording, she's not the prime minister.'

'Has anyone spoken to her?' Braddick asked.

'The prime minister?'

'No. The landlady.' Braddick hid a smile.

'I've sent local uniform over to her house,' Laurel said. 'She lives in Cheshire.'

'We've looked through the post. There are two letters, which arrived yesterday,' Dr Libby said. 'Both are addressed to Fabienne Wilder. Fabienne is a female name and we have dresses and shoes in the wardrobe.' Pointing to the wardrobe, he added, 'There are no men's shoes. A male visited here but I don't think they lived here.'

'Agreed,' Braddick said, nodding. 'What do we know about Fabienne Wilder?'

'Nothing yet,' Laurel said. Braddick frowned. 'There is no record of Fabienne Wilder living here. It seems she is either new to the country or she lived beneath the radar.'

'Find me the remains of the victims and I'll tell you what happened here and when they died,' Dr Libby said.

'We're looking for them,' Laurel said. 'They're nearby, I'm sure of it. There's no way the killer moved two bodies down ten floors without being seen, even if there were two of them.'

'Did they use the refuse chutes?' Braddick asked. 'It's the only other way to get the bodies out, unless they were tossed over the balcony.' He paused. 'I assume we have searched the roof space?'

'They're being searched,' Laurel said. 'If they were hidden, rather than disposed of, we'll find them.'

'Do we know when the council collect the skips?'

'The day after tomorrow,' Laurel said. 'If they used the chutes then they're still here.'

'Good. If they disposed of body parts down the toilet, we need to search the drains, too,' Braddick said.

'I'll put forensics on it,' Laurel agreed.

A knock on the door interrupted them. Two uniformed officers stepped in wearing overshoes. One was the assistant chief constable. Braddick had wondered how long it would take him to arrive. He was paranoid about bad press. Boiled head soup and human chilli would not make for comfortable reading in the newspapers. There would be Hannibal the Cannibal headlines splashed all over them.

'Detective Superintendent Braddick,' the ACC said, offering his hand. Braddick shook it and smiled thinly. 'What the bloody hell has happened?'

'We have two victims, one male, one female,' Braddick said, walking into the kitchen. The officers followed him; he gestured to the stock pots. 'We could have more than one killer, but we can't be sure yet.'

'You think there are two victims?'

'There are male and female clothes in the bedroom. We could assume they belong to the suspects, or we could assume the tenants are the victims,' Braddick explained. 'Either way, the killer cooked them and ate them.' He shrugged. 'We don't have the victims' identification yet.'

'Bloody hell,' the ACC said. 'We need to ID them quickly.'

'Unfortunately, we don't have their bodies,' Dr Libby said.

'Who are the occupiers?' the ACC asked.

'We don't know yet,' Braddick said.

'Are they local people?'

'Local? What difference does that make?' Braddick asked. He cringed at the question – the headlines would be easier to bear if the killers were immigrants. He knew exactly what the ACC was thinking. The ACC blushed.

'Just a question.'

'You might want to keep that question to yourself,' Braddick said. He paused. 'The post is addressed to Fabienne Wilder, but we don't know anything about her.'

'Nothing at all?' the ACC asked, frowning.

'No. We have no information about her, yet, but the registered owner of the property is a lady, called Victoria Theresa May. She's been difficult to contact. We've sent uniform to speak to her—'

'What did you say her name was?'

'Victoria Theresa May. We don't think it's the PM. She lives in Cheshire,' Braddick explained. 'Uniform are on their way to her address as we speak.'

'Victoria Theresa May,' the ACC said, rolling his eyes.

'It's unfortunate, at best,' his uniformed colleague said. Braddick recognised him as a press advisor. *Good luck with that one.*

'Can you imagine the headlines?' the ACC muttered, shaking his head.

'I haven't given them much thought, to be honest,' Braddick said.

'Don't let this get blown out of all proportion, Braddick.'

'I'll leave all the press releases to you, sir,' Braddick said. He was about to add something about being more interested in detective work than politics, when a uniformed officer shouted him. *Saved by the bell.*

'We've found something in the bin chute, sir,' he said.

'Excuse me,' Braddick said, squeezing past the officers. 'I'm needed downstairs.'

'Of course, carry on, Braddick.'

'If you're going to look around, you need to suit up,' Braddick added. The ACC looked embarrassed. 'CSI haven't finished yet, so if you don't mind …'

'Yes, of course.'

Braddick met Laurel at the front door and stepped onto the landing. The balcony wall was waist height and made from brick. It offered some protection against the drop but did little to ease his fear of heights. He stayed away from the wall as they headed for the stairwell and ducked beneath the cordon.

'Google just called,' Laurel said. 'He has traced the owner of all the flats on this landing. They all belong to Victoria May. Apparently, she owns a large portfolio of property across the country, mostly the north-west and North Wales.'

'Did he find out anything about who Fabienne Wilder is?'

'There is a Fabienne Wilder on the PNC,' Laurel said. Braddick raised his eyebrows in question. 'He said he would call me back with the details when he had them all.'

'Why hasn't he got them?' Braddick frowned. They walked down the concrete stairs; their footsteps noisy in the stairwell. 'I don't understand, unless it's a juvenile record and it's sealed?'

'Maybe,' Laurel agreed. 'He'll call back when he knows.'

When they reached the third floor, uniformed officers and suited CSIs were cordoning off the landing. Braddick watched as they carefully removed black bin bags from the chute.

'What have you got?' he asked.

'Some bright spark has thrown an armchair down the chute,' a CSI said. 'It's jammed between the second and third floors. I can see your male victim, but he's buried beneath a few days of refuse. It'll take us a short while to get him out of there, but we'll get him out. He's not going anywhere.'

'Okay, good.' Braddick walked down to the next landing and looked beneath the stairwell. There was cardboard and bedding stashed in the corner. It looked like the occupant was out and about. He wondered who they were and how they'd ended up sleeping rough. It was an increasing blight on a city that prided itself on compassion and diversity. 'There are eyes under all these stairwells,' he said. 'We need to speak to as many of them as we can without scaring them away.'

'I've spoken to uniform. They'll use the tea and sympathy approach,' Laurel said.

'We've got something down here,' a voice shouted from below. 'Is Superintendent Braddick up there?'

'Tell him I'm on my way down,' Braddick said. They set off down the next flight of stairs. 'You were right about the bin chutes, Laurel.'

'There was no other way to get two bodies out,' she said. She was struggling to keep up with Braddick, who was taking the stairs two at a time.

'It was a risky option,' Braddick said.

'I've been thinking about that,' she said.

'What?'

'About why they used the chutes.'

'Go on,' Braddick said, looking at her.

'They had no choice. They took their time with everything they did,' she explained. 'They prepared everything carefully; they thought about everything else but rushed the disposal. Why the rush to get rid of the bodies and dump them in a place where they would obviously be found?'

'Because they had no choice,' Braddick agreed. 'We need to work out why.'

They reached the bottom of the stairwell and headed for the bin room. The large double doors were wedged open and eight skips had been wheeled out and searched. The contents had been inspected and separated. A crowd of onlookers was being held back by uniformed police at the entrance to the building, but multiple camera flashes told him the story would be all over the evening news reports and the internet.

'There's no way the ACC is going to keep a lid on this,' Braddick said. 'No matter how hard he tries, this is a big story.'

'Not a chance. He can't hush this up,' Laurel agreed. 'I'm not too bothered. Managing the press is why he gets paid the big money. It's his problem.'

'Over here, sir,' a CSI called. Braddick approached and saw a plastic sheet with three bin bags on it. 'I wanted you to see this before I send them to the lab.' He paused. 'They all contain body parts.'

'Good work, everyone,' Braddick said. 'Let's have a look.' The CSI opened the first bag. A forearm and elbow were clearly visible. The skin was grey and wrinkled with age – liver spots marked the skin. A second bag contained the upper thighs, the cuts straight but the edges jagged. 'What do you think they used to dismember the body, a power saw?'

'Something like that, yes.'

'Is she all here?' Braddick asked, looking at the bin bags. It felt desperately sad to him. She appeared to be elderly – a woman fallen on hard times, consigned to living on the streets. Her death was a final, terrible act of violence, her disposal an afterthought, thrown down a bin chute with the rubbish. 'Poor bugger.'

'We think so but, until I get her to the lab, I can't be a hundred per cent.'

'Do what needs to be done. Get her to the lab. I want to know everything about her, and I need to know yesterday,' Braddick said. 'The ACC is upstairs, and I think he's about to go into meltdown.' He nodded to the growing crowd. 'The press is all over this already. This is going to be big news until we catch someone.'

'No problem. I'll call you as soon as I have anything.'

'Thank you,' Braddick said as DS Barlow approached.

'They've recovered the male victim on the second floor, sir.'

'Okay, thank you,' Braddick said. He looked at Laurel. She smiled thinly and they headed back up the steps. 'What do you think went on?'

'I don't know,' she said, shrugging. 'Are both victims connected, or do we have two separate murders?'

'Guv,' Ian said from behind them. Braddick turned to face him. 'I just heard you talking to the CSI. Is it right that you think the killer used a power saw?'

'It looks that way, why?'

'I've been canvassing some of the neighbours and a few of them have mentioned a disturbance a few nights ago. Some said it was Tuesday, some said Wednesday, but they all agreed it was around three o'clock in the morning.'

'What did they say had happened?'

'They said that there was a racket coming from the upper floors, probably the top. They all heard the sound of a power tool being used. It woke a lot of the tenants up and caused a lot of shouting and the like.'

'That would tie in with our timeline,' Braddick said. 'I want to know if everyone who lives in the building is accounted for; we need to know if anyone is missing.'

'I'm not sure I follow, guv?'

'The victims could be residents,' Braddick explained. 'Make a list of everyone who has not been spoken to. Ask the residents if they have seen their neighbours since Wednesday. If someone is missing, we need to know.'

'That makes sense, will do, guv.'

'Keep talking to them. Good work.'

Ian went back down the stairs; Braddick and Laurel went upwards.

'The female victim was in the skips at the bottom of the chute, so we can be certain she was disposed of first – before the armchair was dumped,' Braddick said. 'The male was dumped much later.'

'So, they dismembered the female with a power tool at three o'clock in the morning and woke the neighbours?' Laurel asked.

'It sounds that way.'

'Why attract attention to yourself making all that noise?'

'Maybe they had to dispose of them quickly. Did they panic?' Braddick asked.

'What could have panicked them at that time of night?' Laurel said.

'Something imminent. Something they thought would happen the next day, maybe.' Braddick shrugged. 'Something they couldn't stop from happening.'

They reached the second floor and navigated a mound of bin bags. The smell of rotting refuse hung heavy in the air. A naked male corpse was being processed on a plastic sheet, the skin looked waxy and unreal. Braddick approached the men processing the body.

'What have you got?' he asked.

'He's about forty, well built, local – I would say,' the CSI said, pointing to a Liverpool FC tattoo on the forearm. 'There are restraint wounds on the ankles and wrists. He was tied up tight. He's missing a significant chunk of both thighs, and a kidney.' The CSI noticed a head wound. 'He's a big guy and wouldn't have been easy to control unless he was unconscious. He could have been disabled by this blow to the head, but we won't know if that happened before or after he died until we get him back to the lab.'

'Can we get a picture of his face to show around the residents?' Laurel asked. 'We can ask if any of them recognise him.'

'No problem. I'll do it now.'

Braddick noticed a deep wound on the upper arm. It resembled the letter 'h'. The man had suffered before he died, that much was obvious. He wondered if he had watched the killer making a chilli con carne with his thigh, or if he had bled to death beforehand.

'We have the bodies but we're not really any wiser.' He paused and studied the body. 'It matches what we've seen in the kitchen: one male, one female. All we need to do now is find out who they are.'

'It should be simple, but it won't be,' Laurel said.

'You know that,' Braddick agreed. 'I need you to coordinate with Ian and uniform, Laurel. I want to sit down with Google and find out what we have on Fabienne Wilder. The fact that he can't access her information is bothering me. We need to know who she is. I'll see you back at the office.'

CHAPTER 3

Constable Evelyn Hughes was pissed off. She always got the crap jobs, crap shifts, and crap officers to partner with. Today was about as crap as it could be. She'd been teamed up with Sergeant Boyle, who was a fat, misogynistic pig. He stunk of sweat and thought it was funny to fart in the car. It smelled like a rat had crawled up his arse and died. To make matters worse, he had a thing about her. He had been bothering her for months, offering to leave his wife and kids for her. Evelyn couldn't think of anything worse. She would rather be the oldest spinster on the planet than wake up next to a pig like Boyle. He promised to give her the moon and stars and treat her like a princess, but she wanted nothing from him. On the Christmas night out, he'd begged her to have an affair, but she was having none of it. Boyle had been very drunk and wouldn't take no for an answer. She had tried to be as diplomatic as possible, after all, he was her senior officer and could make her life a misery, but when he had followed her into the toilets and asked her for sex, she had lost it. She'd told him to fuck off in no uncertain terms, in front of at least six female officers who had staggered into the toilets. They had witnessed the entire scene and it didn't go down well. The following morning, the entire division had heard about it. Boyle was summoned by HR and cautioned, and Evelyn had been moved behind a desk while an investigation went on. It had taken months for things to settle down and he still held a grudge against her. She had asked for a transfer but was told that, if she had a problem working with Sergeant Boyle, she should resign. *Equal opportunities my arse.* The force was as male dominated as it always had been. There had been times when she'd thought that giving the fat pig the odd hand-job in the car wouldn't be as bad as being sidelined, but she knew it would never stop there. Men like Boyle never backed off. The thought of letting him anywhere near her made her want to puke. She was still ambitious and decided to stick it out. One day she would be *his* superior, and then she would make him back off.

'This is the place,' Boyle grunted. He was looking at a large detached house set back from the road. It stood alone on a green belt of land, surrounded by sparse woodland and an orchard. 'The driveway is around this bend on the left.'

Evelyn slowed the vehicle and indicated left. It was a remote spot in leafy Cheshire, and the real estate was worth more than she would earn in her working life. That pissed her off too – being reminded of how poor she was in comparison to the Cheshire set – who she protected – made her feel inadequate. It was a crappy errand to be sent on. The quicker they could get it over with, the better. As she steered the police car along the driveway, she got the sense that something was wrong.

'That's odd,' she said. 'All the downstairs curtains are drawn.'

'Why is that odd?' Boyle scoffed, disinterested.

'Because it's dinner time, for one, and we're in the middle of nowhere, for another. Why would you close the curtains, anyway? There's no one looking in.'

'She might be at it with the gardener on the settee,' Boyle chuckled.

'Are you always such a pervert?'

'Or, she's bent over the kitchen table with the postman giving her a delivery.'

'You make me sick,' Evelyn said, shaking her head. 'Do you think about anything else?'

'Football and beer,' he answered.

'That figures,' Evelyn said.

'And you, of course. I often think of you,' he added.

'That Ford Focus parked in front of the house,' she said, ignoring him. 'It doesn't belong in this picture. Something isn't right.' She pulled up next to the Ford and looked around.

'What's that?' Boyle snorted. 'Women's intuition?'

'No,' Evelyn said. 'Basic police work. That is a fifteen-year-old motor parked outside a three-million-pound property, the curtains are closed when it's daylight, and a particularly nasty murder recently occurred at one of her properties. That's why we're here, remember?'

'You're making assumptions,' Boyle said, yawning.

Evelyn turned off the engine and climbed out of the car. It didn't feel right: the sun was shining, and it was warm, yet every curtain on the ground floor was drawn and every window was closed. She approached the Focus and looked in. It was tidy inside; its keys were still in the ignition. Evelyn opened the door and took a closer look. There was a brown stain on the key fob – it looked like dried blood. She spotted a partial footprint near the pedals but couldn't be sure if it was mud or not.

'This could be blood on the keyring,' she said, pointing to it.

'It could be a lot of things,' Boyle said, unconvinced.

Evelyn walked to the front of the car. She felt the bonnet, but the metal was cold. The vehicle had been standing for some time. She looked around and wondered if she was being overcautious. Victoria May could be away on holiday. The Focus could belong to an employee or a friend. Cheshire was hardly crime central. Leaving the keys in the car was not an issue in an area like that.

'What are you doing, Sherlock?' Boyle asked, sarcastically.

'Grow up, sergeant,' Evelyn muttered.

'What did you say?'

Evelyn ignored him and walked around the Ford.

'Let's just knock on the door and get this done, shall we?' Boyle said.

'You knock on the front door and I'll check the back,' she said. Boyle rolled his eyes skyward. 'I'm just going to take a look around the back, what is the problem?'

'You *are* the problem,' Boyle said. He hitched up his trousers, but his beer belly wasn't cooperating.

'If there's nothing wrong, she'll open the door and you can tell her what she needs to know.' Evelyn shrugged. 'It isn't a big deal. You knock on the front, I'm going to check the back of the house, simple.' She headed down the path that led around the corner.

Boyle huffed and marched to the front door. There was a glass porch shaped into an arch. He pressed the doorbell and knocked on the door. Evelyn walked around the side of the house, her senses on edge; it didn't feel right. The lawns were manicured, and the borders were planted with colourful shrubs and bushes. She noted the side windows were also closed with the curtains drawn. She couldn't see inside, so she moved on, further round the building. A large conservatory dominated the back of the house; dark blinds covered the windows. A shiver ran down her spine and instinct told her to keep going. Her hand moved to her baton as she skirted the conservatory and approached the back door. She tried the handle: it wouldn't budge. Evelyn eyed a double garage that was detached from the house and noted that both doors were open but there were no vehicles were inside. Would the owner go on holiday and leave the garage doors open? No, she wouldn't.

'There's no one home,' Boyle said, coming around the corner. His voice made her jump. 'Sorry. Did I frighten you?' He laughed. 'Come on. We're wasting our time. Let's get back to the station. I'm starving.'

Evelyn didn't want to pack up and leave. She wanted to see inside the house. The urge to break a window was powerful. She took another look around and saw a double ladder hanging on the wall at the rear of the garage.

'Let's take a look through the upstairs windows,' she said. 'She could be ill in bed or lying on the floor unable to move.'

'Are you mad?' Boyle said. 'I'm not climbing a ladder to look inside. We have procedures to follow. There is nothing criminal going on. The owner is away, that's why she's not answering her landline.'

'It doesn't explain why she isn't answering her mobile.'

'She's probably abroad. Look at the place,' he said. 'She's obviously got money coming out of her arse.'

'Look, Sarge,' Evelyn said. 'I know we don't like each other much, but I have a bad feeling about this. They said this is connected to a double murder in Liverpool, and this woman owns the property where it happened. If we walk away now and someone else comes back to find a crime scene here too, we'll both be disciplined.' She shrugged and pointed at the ladder. 'All it will take is fifteen minutes of our time to take a look inside and we can walk away saying we did our job.' She walked towards the garage. 'What have we got to lose?'

'I suppose so,' Boyle mumbled. She was right: their careers had already been tarnished. If they messed up again, they would be forced out. He followed her to the garage. When he reached the doorway, Evelyn was standing still, looking at the floor. 'What is it?'

'Blood,' she replied. 'Lots of it.'

CHAPTER 4

Laurel sent the images of their male victim to the uniformed officers canvasing the tower block. There were more reports about the disturbance a few nights earlier and the details from each witness seemed to tally. Officers continued knocking on doors and half an hour later one of them called her on her mobile. She met him on the seventh floor.

'What have you got?'

'I've spoken to a resident who has identified the victim as a man living on the eighth floor, Sarge.'

'Brilliant, well done,' Laurel said. 'Do they have a name?'

'Paul,' the officer said. 'She didn't know his surname.'

'When was the last time she saw him?'

'Wednesday.'

'She's sure?'

'Positive. She was on her way to the bingo. She remembers because she won the jackpot.'

'Good. I want every door on the eighth floor knocked on again. Find out where Paul lives and ask his neighbours what his second name was. Well done.'

'Yes, Sarge.' The officer climbed the stairs to the next floor.

Laurel followed him, glancing beneath the stairwell. Something caught her eye. In the corner, hidden in the shadows, was a rolled-up mat and some blankets. Empty tin cans were littered around, most of them had once contained strong lager. She kneeled, peering into the dark, and wondered how many other homeless people were using the tower block to sleep rough at night. There could be dozens, she thought. They would see everything and everyone that moved at night. Braddick had said to tell uniform to interview them without frightening them away, but that would be easier said than done. Sleeping rough wasn't a crime, yet they were treated as lesser citizens by many on the force. They could have seen or heard what had happened in that building and, if they were sober, their testimony was as good as the next person's. Interviewing them could help identify the killers and the victims – if they could be persuaded to talk.

'Excuse me, detective. Have you found them yet?' a voice said from behind her. Laurel turned and faced the speaker. She was clearly a rough sleeper. Her brown hair was matted beneath a black beanie hat and her face was unwashed. She was wearing a dark blue tracksuit and a black bubble jacket that was ripped at the elbows. Her trainers were scuffed and worn.

'I'm sorry,' Laurel said, smiling, 'have we found who?'

'Wanda and Val,' the woman said. She gestured to the top floor. 'You've been searching the top floor. Are they in there?'

'Who are Wanda and Val?' Laurel asked.

'They're my friends.'

'Sorry, what's your name?' Laurel asked.

'People call me Max,' she said. 'It's short for Maxine.'

'Hello, Max,' Laurel said, offering her hand.

Max looked at her, uncertain whether to remove her fingerless mitten or not. After deciding not to, she shook Laurel's hand.

'I'm Laurel. I'm a detective sergeant working on this case.'

'Are they dead?' Max asked.

'Are who dead?' Laurel replied, confused.

'Wanda and Val,' Max said, getting frustrated. 'They're my friends. I saw them go in, but they never came out. Val looked terrified, poor kid. She's been odd lately, hasn't spoken for over a week.'

'Okay. I see. Your friends went to the top floor and you haven't seen them since, right?' Max nodded. 'Are you the lady who called this in, Max?' Laurel asked. Max nodded but she didn't speak. 'Thank you for calling us. It was a very brave thing to do.'

'It wasn't that brave really,' Max said. 'I just called; I didn't give my name.'

'It's surprising how many people don't pick up the phone at all, Max. Tell me about Wanda and Val,' Laurel said.

'Wanda has been around for years. She's streetwise and knows the score, but Val is just a kid,' Max said. 'She's a runaway.'

'Val's a runaway, is she?' Laurel asked.

'Yes. She's a kid.'

'How old is she?'

'Twelve,' Max said. 'I only know that because it was her birthday a few weeks ago. We had a bit of a party for her.'

'Twelve,' Laurel said, nodding. 'Do you know where she's from, Max?'

'St Helens, I think. She has an accent from there or thereabouts. No one asks questions out here. Wanda mentioned she had been in care but didn't like it; she did a bunk and wound up here. Wanda's been looking after her. She's like that, always taking care of people.'

'When did you last see them?' Laurel asked.

'Tuesday,' Max said. 'I told them not to go with that woman, but they wouldn't listen. Val was completely silent, never said a word. She's usually a cocky little so-and-so. She just stood there, next to Wanda, poor little bugger.'

'You said you told them not to go with a woman,' Laurel said. 'What woman?'

'That woman from number ninety. The black one,' Max said, shaking her head. 'She's very pretty, but she's a bad one, I'm telling you.'

'What makes you say that?'

'She has people coming and going all day and night. They take them up in the lifts late at night, when no one is looking, then they leave early in the morning. You can see the fear in their eyes. They're up to no good up there. I've heard from some of the girls on the street that she pays good money for them to do weird stuff.'

'What kind of stuff?' Laurel asked.

'I don't know. I don't want to know either,' Max said. 'Wanda dabbled with that kind of thing when she was broke and needed a drink. She did a turn every now and again for that woman and her men friends.' Max shook her head. 'I told Wanda not to get that poor girl involved, but they went up there anyway.'

'You saw them go there at what time on Tuesday?' Laurel asked, making notes.

'Ten o'clock. I watched and waited but they never came out. There were all kinds of noises coming from there on Wednesday. I got worried about them and called the police.' Max paused and looked at Laurel, waiting for an answer. 'Are they up there, or not?'

'We don't know yet,' Laurel said.

'You pulled some bodies from the bins, though, didn't you?'

'Yes, but we haven't identified them yet.'

'Could it be Val?' Max asked. 'That poor young girl.'

'No, Max,' Laurel said. 'It definitely isn't a twelve-year-old girl. Wherever she is, she isn't in that flat. I can promise you that.'

'Good,' Max said, nodding. She bit her nails as she talked. 'In that case, the woman's body you've found is Wanda. It has to be her.'

'What makes you say that?'

'She hasn't been around since I saw her going in there. That was Tuesday. She never disappears for this long. Overnight, sometimes, but not for this long. We look after each other out here. Everyone does the rounds and talks to each other, letting them know they're okay. Wanda hasn't been around and that's not like her,' Max sighed. 'I warned her not to go near the top floor. All kinds of people come and go from there in a hurry. I watch them. They don't know I watch them,' she whispered. 'But I do. I've got my eyes on them.'

'Good for you, Max,' Laurel said, smiling. 'Can you describe Val for me?'

'She has short brown hair and always wears a baseball cap. You would think she was a little boy, if you saw her. She wears jeans and black trainers and has a black Adidas hoodie. If it's raining, she has a black cagoule.'

'That's very helpful, thanks,' Laurel said. 'I'm going to circulate her description to all our officers. If Val is out there, we'll find her.'

'She's a good kid,' Max said.

'I'm going to give you my number,' Laurel said. 'If you think of anything else, call me.'

'I don't have a phone, luv,' Max said, frowning. 'If you want to talk to me, this is where you can find me.' She pointed to the space beneath the staircase. 'Find that young girl. If she's not in that flat then she's in trouble, find her.'

'I will,' Laurel said. 'You look after yourself.'

'I'm happy to be a witness,' Max said. 'I saw them go into that flat and they never came out. I've been watching them for months. I'll be a witness, no problem.'

'I'll come and find you when I need you,' Laurel said.

Max nodded and walked towards the stairs without looking back. She didn't notice the figure in the doorway behind them. The figure who had captured the entire conversation on camera.

'Sarge,' a uniformed officer called down the stairs. 'We've got a name.'

'On my way,' Laurel said. She took the steps quickly. Her breath was coming in gulps when she reached the next landing; she was still feeling the effects of motherhood. The uniformed officer was waiting there. 'What did you find out?'

'One of his neighbours says his name is Paul Skelton. He lives at number eighty-two. No one has seen him since Wednesday.'

'Let's go and have a look,' Laurel said. They walked along the eighth-floor landing. Laurel leaned over the balcony and looked up at the top floor. 'Skelton's flat is almost directly under number ninety. Do you think someone using a power saw on the floor above would have woken him up?'

'It woke people up on the *second* floor, Sarge,' the officer said. 'There's no doubt about it.'

'I think Paul Skelton was woken by the noise and went to complain about it and got more than he'd bargained for.'

'That makes sense,' the officer agreed. He tried the handle of Paul Skelton's front door and it opened. 'He must have left it on the latch, Sarge.'

'There could be someone hurt in there,' Laurel said, walking in. They didn't have to get a warrant if someone was in danger. The uniformed officer followed her. 'The flat has one bedroom, a bathroom, a kitchen and a living room. You take the doors on the left; I'll take the right.'

They moved quickly down the hallway, checking each room as they went. Laurel was in Skelton's bedroom when the officer caught up. A mobile phone was charging beside a wallet that still had money in it on the bedside cabinet. The flat was well maintained and clean. She was convinced Paul Skelton was an ordinary bachelor who had died in extraordinary circumstances. She looked at the bed.

'He threw the quilt off and went upstairs to complain about the noise. He didn't think it was going to take long.'

'He didn't have a scooby doo what he was walking into,' the officer said.

'Not in his worst nightmares,' Laurel agreed. 'I need you to ask the residents if they have seen a young girl hanging around, goes by the name of Val. She wears jeans, black Adidas hoodie and a baseball cap.'

'Will do, Sarge.'

'I need to get this information to MIT. Can you seal the place up, please? And we'll need uniform to contact his next of kin.'

'Leave it with me, Sarge. You go and catch the bastard that did this.'

CHAPTER 5

Evelyn watched as armed response officers surrounded the house. It had taken less than two hours, from calling in the blood stains, to escalate the situation from a factfinding expedition to a forced entry, which had required a warrant. Apparently, the judge who'd signed the warrant had nearly choked when he'd seen the name on it. Once he'd realised the property didn't belong to the Prime Minister, the order was given, and the armed units breached the front and back doors and the conservatory simultaneously. Evelyn listened as they flowed through each room, combing the house. It was called clear ten minutes later. There was a lot of activity and then the detectives moved in. There were hushed conversations going on near the back door. One of the armed officers ran from the house and vomited on the lawn; a second pushed his way from the conservatory and followed suit on the path. She walked to the back door and approached one of the detectives.

'It must be a bad one if experienced coppers are puking on the lawn.'

'You could say that,' the detective said, unnerved. He didn't give anything away.

'I was first on the scene,' Evelyn persisted.

'Did you call this in?' another of the detectives asked, coming out of the house.

'Yes, sir,' Evelyn said, nodding. 'I had a feeling something was wrong, so we went to the garage to get the ladders. That's when we saw the blood on the floor.'

'Your feeling was right,' the officer said. He looked pale. 'We're going to have to work this one with Liverpool MIT. This is part of their murder investigation.'

'The owner, Victoria May?' Evelyn asked. 'She's dead?'

'Oh, yes, she's dead alright,' the detective said, nodding. 'At least, what's left of her is.'

* * * *

Laurel stepped out of the lift and headed towards MIT. She could hear the chatter of voices drifting down the corridor. It was the sound of the Major Investigation Team in full flow. She picked up her pace as she neared the office, eager to discuss her findings. As she walked in, Braddick was talking to DS Smith. He waved her over as she approached.

'We've got another problem at Stanley House,' she said.

'Like we need another one,' Braddick said. 'What's up?'

'I've been talking to the homeless woman, who called this is in,' she said, taking off her coat. 'Her name is Maxine, and she saw two of her friends going into number ninety at ten o'clock on Tuesday night.'

'Did you get their names?'

'Only their first names – Wanda and Val.'

'And they never came out?' Braddick asked.

'Nope, and Val is only twelve years old.'

'Twelve?' Smith asked. 'What the hell is a twelve-year-old doing there?'

'She's a runaway,' Laurel said. 'Maxine said her accent was from the St Helens area, or thereabouts. No one has seen her or Wanda since. Maxine said Wanda does the rounds every day, checking on everyone. She's never gone missing for long.'

'We have to be thinking Wanda could be our female victim,' Braddick said.

'That's what I think,' Laurel said.

'DS Smith, get on to Children's Services and see if they've got anyone missing who could be Val,' Braddick said.

Smith nodded and went to a nearby desk to make some calls. 'Have you got a description?'

'Yes,' Laurel said. 'Short brown hair, boyish looks, jeans, black Adidas hoodie, and trainers.'

'I saw about a dozen people fitting that description, outside the corner shop last night,' Braddick said, shaking his head.

'It doesn't narrow it down much,' Laurel agreed.

'Guv,' Google said from across the room. He sounded excited and was reading a Word document he had printed off. 'I've got Fabienne Wilder's records; it took a bit of negotiation, but I've got them.'

'Excellent, about time. What do they tell us about her?'

'I've had a good look through them, so I'll summarise.'

'Go on.'

'Fabienne Wilder is a Haitian refugee, adopted by an aid worker after a hurricane trashed her village in ninety-three. She was seven years old when she came to the UK.'

'That makes her thirty-two now,' Braddick said.

'Yes.' Google paused as he read the report. 'All seemed to be well until she was ten and she stabbed her adoptive father to death, claiming he had abused her from day one.'

'Sexual abuse?' Laurel asked.

'Yes.'

'Was it substantiated?'

'It looks like it was, although the adoptive mother said Fabienne was a liar; she disowned her.'

'What did social services think?' Braddick asked.

'They believed Fabienne was telling the truth and removed her from the mother's custody.'

'Mum pretending there were no signs of abuse. Not for the first time,' Braddick said. 'Or the last.'

'Unfortunately, yes,' Google agreed. 'The child protection team put her into care. She didn't settle and was a handful. They moved her around for two years, but she had a history of violent encounters and was eventually put into a secure unit in North Wales when she was twelve.'

'Whereabouts?'

'A place called Corwen,' Google said. 'Do you know it?'

'Yes. It's in the middle of nowhere, not far from Llangollen,' Braddick said. 'She must have been a handful to be sent there. It's an old Victorian asylum – bars on the windows type of place.'

'Maybe she needed to be in a place with bars on the windows, Guv. Everything in her file is disturbing,' Google said.

'Go on,' Braddick said.

'At twelve, her room-mate committed suicide – she hanged herself in their bedroom – and Fabienne claimed she hadn't heard her doing it and that she had slept through it.'

'That's unlikely.'

'There was an accusation made that Fabienne was involved in her death and it may not have been suicide,' Google explained.

'Involved, how?'

'The accusation was that she had encouraged her room-mate to do it,' Google said. 'The report says she had pestered her to kill herself for months. Other residents said they had heard her encouraging her to do it. The girl who killed herself had reported Fabienne to her care worker but, because she had a history of making false accusations against the care staff and other patients, no one listened. There was an investigation, which was left with an open conclusion.'

'No further action?' Braddick asked.

'The case was dropped, and the investigation closed. Things settled down and she started behaving herself, although, there's a note that she was reading unsuitable genres.'

'Such as?' Braddick asked.

'It doesn't specify. They eventually moved Fabienne to a different facility, which was less secure, and she absconded in ninety-nine, aged thirteen.'

'They never recovered her?' Braddick asked.

'Nope,' Google said. 'From her notes, no one seems to have taken responsibility. The authorities in Merseyside put the onus on the Welsh authorities, and they did likewise. Once she turned sixteen, no one was looking for her anyway. Her records were sealed because she was a minor.'

'They must have photographs and prints?'

'I'm having them sent here and to the lab.'

'That's good work, Google,' Braddick said. 'She can't have just dropped off the grid completely. They always leave something behind. Keep on digging.'

'Will do, Guv.'

'That is quite a story,' Laurel said.

'It is. It also puts her at the top of our suspects list,' Braddick said. 'We need to find this young girl, Val, and I reckon Fabienne Wilder knows where she is.'

'Guv,' DS Smith said, covering the phone with his hand. 'I've got a call from Detective Superintendent Casey Prost, from the Cheshire division. She said Victoria May's property has been breached by armed response. There's a likely connection to the Stanley House investigation and she thinks you should see it.'

'Is she dead?' Braddick asked.

'They think so,' Smithy said. 'There's only remnants of the victim.'

'Sounds like our killer,' Laurel said.

'Tell her we'll be there in forty minutes,' Braddick said. 'Laurel, you're with me. Keep on top of everything here, Google.'

CHAPTER 6

Braddick pulled the Evoque into the driveway and stopped next to a row of police vehicles. CSI officers were swarming over a Ford Focus, and a large double garage at the rear of the building. Lines of uniformed officers were trawling an orchard at the back of the plot, conducting a fingertip search. It looked to Braddick that the Cheshire division had the scene locked down and the investigation was going by the book. As he watched them, his leg was shaking with nervous tension – finding another body was never good, but it was an opportunity to find evidence that could identify the killers. There was a dark excitement about it. He focused on a group of detectives who were near the front door, talking and giving directions. They were obviously in charge.

'Let's see what happened to Victoria May,' Braddick said, switching off the engine and climbing out. Laurel opened the passenger door and pulled on her coat. 'Are you cold?'

'Only when I'm around dead people,' Laurel said.

'Fair enough,' Braddick said. 'I know what you mean.'

She was a sensitive soul, but he rated her as a good detective. Her instincts were spot on and her thresholds were similar to his own. She would progress, there was no doubt in his mind. They walked through the cordon and were given forensic suits. As they struggled into them, one of the Cheshire detectives approached.

'Superintendent Braddick,' said a bald man in a badly fitting forensic suit. 'I'm DI Ingleton, Cheshire CID.'

'Thanks for calling us so quickly,' Braddick said, shaking his hand. 'This is Laurel Stewart, my DS.' Laurel shook his hand and they followed him towards the front door. 'What have you got?'

'This is as nasty as it gets,' Ingleton said. 'I believe it was a similar scene in Liverpool?'

'We believe so,' Braddick said, nodding. 'Can you run us through what you have so far?'

'A couple of local plods were sent out here on an errand – to speak to Victoria May for you guys.' As Ingleton spoke, they walked into May's home. They were standing in a wide hallway that was tiled with slate. A sweeping staircase led to the first floor and the walls were adorned with watercolours: mostly impressionist style. Braddick didn't know much about art but he knew they were expensive. Ingleton continued. 'They became suspicious because the curtains were drawn downstairs and the Ford Focus looked out of place – it didn't belong. They looked around the house but couldn't see inside, so they decided to check the upstairs windows and went into the garage to fetch some ladders, that's when they spotted the blood on the floor.'

'In the garage?' Laurel asked. 'At the rear of the house?'

'Yes,' Ingleton explained. 'Both garage doors were open but neither of May's vehicles were there. She has a Porsche 911 and a Range Rover registered to her and her husband.'

'Where's he?' Braddick asked.

'We don't know. We've put out the vehicle details on the PNC – nothing yet. Armed response breached the house and we found a woman's foot nailed to the kitchen table.'

'Just the foot?' Braddick asked, shaking his head.

'Yes. There's some boiled flesh in a pan, but the rest of the body is missing.' He looked from Braddick to Laurel and gestured towards the kitchen door. 'We haven't found anything in the house or garage apart from blood. Forensics are testing it against the foot.' He stopped at the door. 'I've seen it already,' he said, leaning against the wall. 'I've no desire to see it again. The smell knocks me sick.'

'No problem,' Braddick said. The smell of cooked human was strong. It was sickly sweet. Knowing it was a human invoked the gag response. It may have had a different effect had he not known what it was. 'What's wrong with these people,' he muttered.

'Take your time, CSI are finished in there for now. There's forensic evidence all over the place. They're waiting for you before they move the foot.'

'Thanks, it's appreciated.'

Braddick took a breath and stepped into the kitchen. The floor was tiled with stone slabs, slightly uneven and contoured. The walls were covered with mosaic tiles – greys, blues and greens. A huge cooking range filled a stone recess that was decorated with brass pots and pans. The units were fashioned from reclaimed light oak, with stained glass in the doors – everything was expensive and looked antique. In the centre was a large oak dining table. A woman's foot was nailed to one corner; three more nails protruded from the wood in the other corners. Blood and flesh clung to the metal. They walked around the scene in silence for a few minutes, each of them analysing the evidence. Braddick was the first to speak.

'Is this Victoria's foot?' he asked.

'I think we have to assume that for now.'

'So,' Braddick said, turning to Laurel. 'Our killer tidied up at Stanley House, disposed of the bodies, and came to pay Victoria May a visit.' Laurel nodded her agreement. 'We have to assume that Fabienne Wilder was familiar with her landlady and knew where she lived.'

'I would think so,' Laurel agreed. 'It's too much of a coincidence otherwise. Why come straight from Liverpool to here otherwise?'

'Perhaps, something Victoria did or said hastened the need to leave the flat in Liverpool.' Braddick suggested. 'It would answer your question: why they were in such a rush to dispose of the bodies.'

'But what did Victoria do to panic the killer and provoke an attack on herself?' Laurel asked. 'Maybe she threatened eviction, or something?'

'Eviction or sending in the bailiffs?' Braddick suggested. 'If Wilder wasn't on the radar it's unlikely, she paid her bills.' He shrugged. 'Let's presume Victoria May got heavy, making threats to send someone to collect or evict her, and Fabienne panicked because she had a head in a pot on her stove.' Laurel nodded that it was plausible. 'The killer tried to cut up the victim with a power saw, made a racket, and Paul Skelton knocked on the door to complain so they whacked him too.' Braddick paused. 'Then they decided to pay Victoria a visit. Payback time?'

'Why not tell Skelton to get lost and mind his own business?' Laurel asked. 'Why kill him?'

'Maybe he saw or heard something that could implicate the killer.' He looked around again but couldn't find the answers to his questions. 'It is one thing killing her but cooking her is madness. If the flesh in the pot is human, what the hell is going on?' Braddick asked.

'It's deranged at best,' Laurel said, pointing to the foot. 'A revenge kill doesn't explain cooking and eating the victims, and it is way more than killing for the thrill.'

'We're missing something, Laurel,' Braddick said. 'We're missing something at both scenes, but what is it?'

He approached the table and studied the foot. 'There are saw marks in the bone,' he noted. Laurel looked and grimaced. The flesh around the nail wounds were blackened and bruised, suggesting that she had struggled violently against them. 'She put up a fight. They probably removed the foot with the saw,' he said. 'Why take the body and leave the foot? It doesn't make sense.'

'They may have meant to come back for it.'

'Maybe.'

'I hope she was dead when she was separated from it,' Laurel muttered as she inspected the pot. 'They used the same method at Stanley House. It has to be the same killer.' The chopping board was littered with the remnants of their preparation: garlic cloves, onions skins, carrots and stock cubes. Laurel looked around. 'Whoever it is wasn't in a hurry, and they're not bothered about leaving forensic evidence.' She shrugged. 'What are we dealing with here? Are they mad or stupid?'

'Or both?'

'Drug addict in a frenzy? Would drug addicts go to the trouble of eating the victim?' Laurel said, shaking her head. 'This is something else.'

'What is it though?'

'I haven't got a clue,' she said, 'but they don't seem to be ready to stop whatever it is, and they don't seem to be bothered if they get caught. The evidence is stacking up, yet they've made no attempt to cover their tracks.'

'This is personal. They drove a long way to visit Victoria,' Braddick said, looking at the microwave. Victoria's handbag, purse and phone were bagged as evidence. 'They didn't take her things.'

'Did they take the vehicles from the garage to escape, if not, where are they?' Laurel asked.

'Probably.' He walked around the table and wondered how much pain the woman would have endured before the end. There was a tiny butterfly tattooed on the ankle. 'We need to ask Ingleton to let us know about the blood in the garage as soon as the forensics come back. They probably put the body into one of the vehicles to dispose of it.'

His eyes were drawn to an h-shaped wound on the instep. It was very similar to one that he had seen on Paul Skelton's arm. He made a note to see what Graham Libby had to say about it.

'And did they bring Val with them, or is she dead somewhere?'

'I'm hoping she is tucked up in her sleeping bag somewhere or, better still, she has gone home, wherever that is,' Laurel said.

'Superintendent Braddick,' Ingleton called him from the front door. 'We've got a problem.' Braddick walked across the hallway to speak to him.

'What is it?'

'The husband has turned up at the bottom of the drive,' Ingleton said. 'His name is Bruce May.'

'Turned up from where?' Braddick asked. 'Where has he been?'

'He's been to London on a business trip and arrived at Chester station expecting his wife to pick him up. He couldn't reach her on the telephone, so he jumped into a black cab.' He paused. 'He's at the cordon demanding to see his wife.'

'That isn't a good idea at the moment,' Braddick said. 'Has anyone spoken to him yet?'

'We've told him that she's possibly the victim of a crime and I've got a liaison officer on the way. Obviously, he's distressed and wants to know what has happened.'

'Does his wife have a butterfly tattoo on her ankle?' Laurel asked.

'Yes.'

'Someone needs to take him away from here and talk to him,' Braddick said. 'I think it's best if Cheshire deals with it.'

'I agree.'

'I know you have to tread softly, but we need to ask him if he knows anything about her rental business at Stanley House.'

'I'll ask him,' Ingleton said.

'Ask him if he knows Fabienne Wilder, please.'

'Who is she?' Ingleton asked.

'She's the tenant at our crime scene.'

'No problem,' Ingleton said, nodding. He wrote the name down. 'Leave it to me. I'll give him the bad news and let you know if there's anything relevant.'

'Thank you,' Braddick said. 'Do we know who owns the Ford yet?'

'Yes.' Ingleton checked his phone. 'Dennis Hughes, County Road, Everton. Your neck of the woods, I believe. He reported it stolen three days ago.' Ingleton shrugged. 'I'll go and speak to Mr May.' He turned and walked away, thinking about how to tell a distraught husband that his wife had been nailed to a table and eaten. Braddick didn't envy him. He looked at Laurel and shook his head.

'The Ford was stolen. Another dead end.'

'Finding Fabienne Wilder is the priority,' Laurel said. 'She has to be the key to this.'

'Right now, we don't even know what she looks like. I hope the images that the care units are sending over will help. Let's get back to the office. Forensics may have something for us.'

They walked out of the house and climbed into the Evoque. Braddick noticed DI Ingleton ushering Bruce May into the back of an unmarked police car. The husband looked to be hysterical. He glanced at Laurel, but she was looking the other way. Watching a man breaking down wasn't pleasant, no matter how often they saw it. The drive from Cheshire was quiet, and half an hour later they were approaching Frodsham. Braddick kept one eye on the phone, hoping it would ring with more information. His stomach rumbled, reminding him that he hadn't eaten. He couldn't recall the last time he had sat down and eaten a proper meal. Ready meals, sandwiches and soups provided him with the energy to function.

'I'm hungry,' he said. 'Do you want to stop for something to eat?'

'Yes. I could eat,' Laurel said. 'Something vegetarian. I'm off meat today.'

'Soup, maybe?' Braddick said, dryly.

'Funny,' Laurel said. 'Good to see you haven't lost your sense of humour while I've been on maternity.'

'I detect a hint of sarcasm,' he said.

'Perceptive as ever.'

Braddick pulled off the motorway and drove to a Harvester. He was a fan of their all-day breakfast, although it was a while since he had stopped there. The car park was empty, and he drove into a bay close to the door, just as the heavens opened.

'Just in time,' he said, turning the engine off. Laurel smiled but looked distant. 'Are you okay?'

'I'm missing Aimee, that's all,' she said. 'Being around all this death and madness makes me appreciate her innocence. How the hell can I protect her from all the evil in the world?'

'The truth is, you can't,' Braddick said. 'She's lucky to have you looking after her. You'll be a brilliant mum.' He smiled. 'Now, can we eat, please?'

Laurel nodded and opened the door. She climbed out and pulled her hood over her head, running to the diner. Braddick followed her. They stepped inside and waited for a smiley waitress to seat them in a booth next to the window. She looked pleased to have someone to talk to. Braddick ordered a filter coffee and a bottle of fizzy water. Laurel asked for tea. They both ordered the all-day breakfast, although Laurel went for the veggie option. He could see she was reflecting on something.

'What's bothering you? I can hear the cogs grinding in there,' he said, pointing to her head.

'Cooking and eating people then flushing their bodies down the toilet,' she said. 'It's nothing new. Dennis Nilsen did both.'

'He did,' Braddick said. 'I'm surprised you remember him.'

'I was very young when he was convicted. I remember the press calling them the Cranley Gardens murders. I read a few books about him at school. I was fascinated by him.'

'He was big news in the early eighties. The UK's worst serial killer at the time,' Braddick said, nodding. 'He had bodies stashed under the floorboards and in the wardrobe, and a head in the fridge.'

'Not a million miles away from what we've seen,' Laurel said. 'The thing is, Nilsen said he was killing for company – he kept the victims around, dressed them, undressed them, had sex with them, until they started to smell, right?'

'Yes. It was disposing of the bodies that scuppered him. Flushing the victims down the toilets wasn't the best idea. He was only caught because the drains blocked up,' Braddick said, nodding. 'How many did he kill, fifteen?'

'They think so, but who knows how many it *really* was?' she said, shaking her head. 'I grew up reading about these freaks: Albert Fish, Jeffery Dahmer, Andrei Chikatilo, the list goes on and on. They all killed and ate their victims, but they worked alone. This feels like something else.'

'Go on,' Braddick said.

'Are we looking for one killer or two? she asked. 'What are the chances of two people being insane enough to make broth from their victims?'

'Are they insane though?' Braddick said. 'Ian Brady and Myra Hindley weren't raving lunatics, yet they enabled each other to do what they did. What are the odds on that?'

'A million to one.'

'It is very unlikely to find two people so far gone in the head, but we know from the past that it happens,' Braddick said.

'Do you remember that copper in London that was murdered and eaten?' Laurel asked. 'I think the killer was called Brizzi.'

'Stefano Brizzi. Yes, I remember. The copper was Gordon Semple,' Braddick said. 'They met on the net and Brizzi killed him. The neighbours called the police because of the smell coming from the flat.'

'That's the one. He had the head in a bucket, the body in a bath full of acid, and he'd boiled and roasted some of him,' she said, recalling the details. 'He claimed that the devil had told him to do it.'

'What do you think?' Braddick asked. 'Did the devil tell him to do it?'

'They found a downloaded copy of a satanic bible on his laptop,' Laurel said, shrugging. 'But, do I believe he was hearing Satan telling him what to do? No. I don't.' She shook her head as she sat back and tapped her fingers on the table. 'But what I believe isn't the issue, it's what *he* believed. If he believed the devil had told him to do it, how can we argue?'

The waitress brought their breakfasts and they laughed as she placed them on the table.

'What's so funny?' she said, smiling.

'We need to change the subject,' Braddick said, 'or I'll lose my appetite.'

CHAPTER 7

Braddick walked into the office and saw the uniformed figure of the ACC talking to Laurel – she hadn't even had time to take her coat off before he'd pounced. His face was like thunder. It was obvious that the newspapers had got hold of the case. Information has a monetary value and there were plenty of officers looking to boost their income by leaking juicy details to a hungry press. It was simply a matter of time before the grisly murders became public knowledge. The public had an appetite for gore and the press pandered to it. Braddick thought the ACC was being unrealistic about keeping a lid on it, and sometimes sensational headlines prompted witnesses to come forward. Now was a good time to recruit witnesses. Laurel caught his eye and gestured for help. Braddick wasn't in the mood for politics; he steeled himself to approach them.

'Sir.'

'Have you seen the evening edition of the Echo?' the ACC asked, his face reddening. He waved a copy of the local paper.

'Can't say I have,' Braddick said politely. 'I haven't read a newspaper since I bought my first smartphone. I assume the story has broken?'

'*That* is an understatement.' The ACC opened the paper to the front page. The headline was splashed in thick, bold print:

Who ate Victoria Theresa May?

'That will sell a lot of newspapers,' Braddick said. The ACC looked like he was about to cry.

'Yes, it will sell a lot of newspapers, and it will attract scrutiny we don't need right now,' the ACC snapped. 'As if things aren't tough enough – our budgets are already unachievable, without an investigation of this scale. This is a disaster.'

'Too late to stress about it now, sir. The cat is clearly out of the bag.' Braddick shrugged. 'Let's make it a positive and glean some information from it.'

'What?' the ACC snapped. 'Two of the national red-tops are running with this headline tomorrow morning. Look at it, "twelve-year-old runaway missing in cannibal killer investigation". For god's sake! The Westminster press office will be crawling up my backside within the hour, wanting to know what the bloody hell this is about, and you think there is a positive in this, Braddick?'

'Yes, sir, I do,' Braddick said calmly. 'We need to find Fabienne Wilder and we don't even know what she looks like, or who her partner is – if she has one. An appeal for information could give us the break we need.'

'An appeal for information smacks of desperation. It sounds like we don't know what is going on,' the ACC protested.

'That is exactly the point, sir – we *don't* know what is going on,' Braddick said. 'We don't know anything at all, and it is time to appreciate that fact.' The ACC seemed stung by the reality. 'Until we start getting forensic results on the prints we found, we have nothing.'

'Don't we have anything on the Wilder woman at all?' the ACC asked.

'We have her juvenile files, but nothing since she absconded from a care facility when she was thirteen. She's thirty-two now,' Braddick said. 'Her juvenile record is very concerning and she's our number one suspect, but we don't know who she is. We don't even know what she looks like.'

'How concerning is her record?'

'She stabbed her stepfather to death when she was ten and was implicated in the hanging of an inmate at a secure unit in North Wales, aged twelve. Reading between the lines, her childhood has very likely left her with serious mental health issues. She could be a very dangerous woman, but she's been under the radar since she absconded.' He dug his hands deep into his pockets. 'Someone out there knows who she is, someone has a recent picture of her on their phone, and someone knows who her friends are. An appeal could put us ahead of the game, sir.' The ACC still looked disturbed. 'At worst, it might give us somewhere to start.'

The ACC thought about it. He nervously shifted his weight from one foot to the other. As Google approached with Dr Libby, they sensed the atmosphere was tense and kept their distance. Braddick saw them and gestured them over.

'Is there any progress?' Braddick asked.

'I have the initial findings for Paul Skelton and your female victim, and news on the prints that child protection sent over,' Dr Libby said.

'Good,' Braddick said. 'Let's hear them.'

'The prints from Fabienne Wilder are not a match to prints taken from either crime scene.' A ripple of comments ran through the team.

'Not even the flat where she lives?' Braddick asked.

'Nope. Not a single one of her prints have been recovered.'

'We must have this all wrong,' Braddick muttered.

'Her prints should be all over number ninety Stanley House, as you would expect if she lived there, but the bad news is, they are not. It's as if she was never there.' Dr Libby shuffled his files, looking for the results. 'We have matched prints from both scenes to some of the items used. We're still running them through the system.' A murmur spread through the office. 'I can say, the same suspect touched the pans that were used to cook the victims, and the bowl of soup that was carried into the living room. Whoever those prints belong to, they are categorically one of your killers. The other prints at the murder scenes belong to someone else.'

'Okay,' Braddick said, 'we have one suspect yet to be identified.'

'Maybe Fabienne Wilder doesn't live there,' Laurel said, 'but that is not what the neighbours are telling us.'

'What about the May residence?' Braddick asked.

'Plenty of prints but we've not identified them yet,' Dr Libby said.

'And what about the victims?' Braddick asked.

'The female victim at Stanley House is Wanda Richards,' Dr Libby said. Laurel gestured to Google to run a search immediately.

'The woman who called it in said her friend, Wanda, went into number ninety – it fits,' Laurel said.

'Her DNA was in the system. She was thirty-two. Initial findings show she was restrained by the wrists and ankles for an extended period. The scars are deep and vary in age. I can't be certain yet, but there are deep slash wounds to the neck, not connected with the saw marks. I think they cut her throat.'

'Google?' Braddick said. 'See what else is in the system.'

'I'm on it, guv.'

'The male victim, Paul Skelton, has two compressed fractures to the skull, probably caused by the hammer that was recovered from the bin chute.' Dr Libby paused. 'Unfortunately for him, they weren't the cause of death. Exsanguination, I'm afraid. Probably when they removed pieces of the thigh muscles – one of them was in the fridge, the other in the chilli, and there were traces in his stomach.'

'In his stomach?' the ACC asked.

'I'm afraid so,' Dr Libby said, nodding.

'They fed him his own leg?'

Graham Libby nodded.

'This will stay national news until we arrest them.' The ACC waved the newspaper. 'I cannot cope with Hannibal headlines. We need to put a stop to this, Braddick.'

'We do, sir,' Braddick agreed. 'An appeal could speed that up.'

'Tell me exactly what you need.'

'Thank you, sir. Shall we go to my office?'

'Hold on a minute, guv,' Google interrupted. 'I've got the info on Wanda Richards.'

Braddick stopped to listen.

'She was reported missing by her partner, five years ago. Missing persons tracked her down and spoke to her, but she didn't want to be found. She was living rough, in a squat on Breck Road, and refused to contact her family. She was arrested and charged with being drunk and disorderly, back in twenty-twelve, and she has a conviction for soliciting in twenty-sixteen. There were a few admissions to hospital last year, and that is about it. The most recent picture we have is from the custody suite in twenty-twelve.'

'She was homeless and so was Val,' Braddick said, nodding. He looked at Laurel. 'The other homeless people would know them. Are we absolutely sure that Val hasn't been seen by anyone?'

'I've got uniform talking to all the homeless people around the block in case they've seen anything.' She looked at the picture of Wanda. 'She would have been twenty-six when that was taken – you could add on twenty years looking at it.' Laurel looked sad for a moment. 'I'll get this to uniform. It may jog a few memories.'

'I've spoken to child services in St Helens, guv,' DS Smith said from his desk. 'They have a twelve-year-old, named Valerie Sykes, reported missing from a care home in Prescott. She could be our girl.'

'Do they have a photograph?' Braddick asked.

'They're sending me the link to her Facebook page – apparently, she was active on social media. I'll upload her images to the system.'

'Good work, everyone,' Braddick said, entering his office with the ACC. It felt like they were out of the starting blocks at last.

CHAPTER 8

Fabienne let herself into the hotel room. The door to the bathroom was ajar; she stood and watched him vomiting – it made her cringe. He was weak. The sickness had been creeping up on him for months. She had noticed the signs as his brain was disintegrating; it was slow, but obvious to those who were close. Not so obvious to him. He had no idea what was happening to him. His decision making had become flawed, but he didn't realise. Things were being neglected and he wasn't fulfilling his role anymore. As his dementia accelerated, he was becoming more demanding, almost childlike. He couldn't function as an adult anymore. She would have to leave him behind; he was becoming a liability. What he had done to the homeless woman, Wanda, and the neighbour from the floor below, was beyond her comprehension. It heralded the beginning of the end of another chapter. Fabienne existed in the shadows, where normal people didn't venture. That was how they could do what they did without scrutiny. Although she welcomed and absorbed the darkness he had created, she didn't welcome the attention it would bring. Attention was toxic.

She needed to escape but moving would be impossible with him in that state – they couldn't move while he was being sick all the time. The vomiting and diarrhoea were relentless and debilitating. He couldn't move from the bathroom and would slip into unconsciousness for hours at a time. Listening to him retch and defecate was nauseating. She wanted to put him out of his misery but had decided he could be useful alive. He wouldn't understand if she tried to explain it to him – he wasn't long for this world. He was rambling that he thought he had a bad bout of food poisoning, but she knew different – it was the sickness. It was common in some parts of the world, parts of the world she was familiar with. She had seen others succumb to it. It was always the same: their brain turned to sponge while the rest of their body disintegrated inside them. They never recovered and they all suffered a slow and humiliating death. Some might call it karma – for what they had done to other humans – but she knew it was because they were weak. The sickness sorted the chosen from the chaff. Only the strong survived. The weak weren't meant to be here. It was survival of the fittest. The weak would wither and die while the strong moved on. She was moving on – nearly there now. It wouldn't be long before she could take the next step. She was becoming the darkness itself.

He turned his head from the toilet bowl to look at her. His eyes had become dull as he died from the inside, but there was recognition in them, and something else: love. He had loved her, she knew that, but it was never reciprocated. There was no love in her, only darkness and hate. They were acolytes, nothing more. She used them to her own end, all of them. She had been used herself, from an early age, until she was old and wise enough to realise it. Nowadays, she could twist them to her will. Once she had discovered the darkness within her, the tables had turned. She held the power. Then she became stronger, and they could do nothing but desire her, love her. Unreciprocated love was the cruellest kind. She would never love them back and they knew it, but they stayed anyway – just in case she let down her barriers. They held on to the glimmer of hope that one day she would return their love. It was a forlorn hope.

He retched again – blood this time. It was near the end. She closed the bathroom door, so she didn't have to listen to him, and picked up the phone. She called the police and left a message, took the car keys and walked out of the building. As she walked into the night, she felt more powerful than ever. She was transforming into a woman with no empathy, no sympathy and no fear.

* * * *

The television appeal had been authorised and arranged. Braddick was hopeful it would yield new, vital information. He used his phone to order a takeaway and stopped at Tesco for a couple of bottles of Rioja. It was getting on for nine o'clock when he put the key in his front door. As he stepped inside, his food arrived; he paid for it with cash, gave the delivery guy a tip, and headed for the kitchen. The smell of kung po ribs made his mouth water. He kicked off his shoes and dished out his ribs and chilli chips, soaking them with salt and vinegar, before filling a glass with wine and sitting down in front of the television to watch Sky Sports.

He finished half the food, and two glasses of wine, before surrendering and putting the leftovers in the bin. His eyes were tired and itchy, and he rubbed them with the back of his hands. He emptied his glass as his phone rang, disturbing his thoughts.

'DS Braddick.'

His greeting was met with silence.

'Hello?'

A loud burst of static crackled in his ear and the line went dead. He looked at the screen but there was no number listed: it had been withheld. Filling his wine glass, he took it upstairs to the bathroom. He stripped and turned on the shower, waiting for the water to reach the right temperature. A knock on his front door echoed through the house. 'For fuck's sake,' he muttered, wrapping a towel around his waist. He trotted down the stairs to the front door and looked through the glass. There was no one there. Braddick switched on the outside light and peered through the security spyhole: the path was empty. He wondered if it was local kids trying to annoy the policeman from number six. Knock and run was still an annoyingly enjoyable pastime for kids of all ages. Braddick opened the door and stepped out, looking down the path. He couldn't see anyone. Something on the path caught his eye. He squinted to see what it was, but it was too far away for him to focus on clearly. The wind blew, chilling him; goose bumps appeared on his arms. His bare chest shivered against the cold. He tiptoed barefoot down the path to study the item; it looked like two pieces of wooden dowel, about three inches long, tied together in the shape of an X. He picked it up, looked around for whoever had left it there and crept back inside. He closed the door and turned off the outside light, peering through the spyhole again. There was a figure standing inside his gate, staring towards his house.

'Cheeky bugger,' Braddick muttered, snatching open the door. He flicked on the outside light, ready to challenge the intruder, but the figure had gone. He leaned outside and looked up and down the street but there was no one in sight. He closed the door again and studied the wooden item; it looked smooth, the edges sharp and cracked. It wasn't wood at all. He was no doctor, but he recognised bones when he saw them. Someone was playing games. 'Who ate Theresa May?' he said, under his breath. 'This one will attract every nutter in the village.' Braddick put the bones in a freezer bag, planning to give them to Dr Libby the next morning. He checked the spyhole once more then climbed the stairs. Eventually, he stepped into his shower, allowing the hot water to ease his tired muscles. It was going to be a long week; he could sense it.

Outside, hidden in the shadows between the houses across the road, someone watched and waited. Their lips moved constantly as they chanted a silent prayer.

CHAPTER 9

Minutes after the television appeal had finished, twenty-five phones burst into life. Braddick looked out over the river, his mind focused on finding Fabienne Wilder and Valerie Sykes. The next few hours could make or break the case. His angst was through the roof. Television appeals could drive suspects underground, but he didn't think it was the case this time. The killers had made no attempt to conceal their involvement in the murders. He didn't think they would suddenly feel the need to go into hiding. There was something dramatic about the theatrical process they had used; it was as if they were taunting them, leaving forensic evidence for them to find. Why didn't they care? It was a very important question.

'I've got a caller with recent pictures of Wilder, guv,' a detective called out. The detectives' chattering on the phones was reaching fever pitch. 'She's with a male. They were at a party together a few months back.'

'Get them sent to your phone,' Braddick said, walking to his desk. 'Then send them to your laptop and upload them to the system.' A few seconds ticked by. The phones kept ringing. There was an avalanche of information coming in. Sorting out what was relevant was the skill now. It would be easy to miss one tiny gem of evidence in the mountain of misinformation.

'The pictures of Wilder are on the system, guv.'

Braddick leaned over the desk to look at the screen. He was surprised. Fabienne Wilder was stunning. Her dark eyes had a hypnotic quality about them. She wasn't smiling; in fact, she didn't look very happy at all to be in the picture, but she was magnetic, nonetheless. Her beauty was extraordinary. There was a white man standing next to her and he looked out of place. His face was expressionless – a vacant look in his eyes. He was twice her age, at least. There was chemistry between them. Not mutual attraction, but chemistry all the same.

The man was subservient, it was obvious. They appeared to be mutually uncomfortable at having their photograph taken.

'The caller says the guy next to her on the photograph is John Metcalfe,' the detective added. 'The caller lives on the second floor of Stanley House and said the picture was taken at a party at number sixty-four, three months ago. Apparently, Metcalfe was introduced as her associate. She said they were odd – they talked in whispers to each other but didn't touch. She said she saw them together often, going up to the ninth floor, but she didn't have the impression they lived together.'

'They didn't live together?' Braddick mumbled to himself, staring at the image. Fabienne was incredibly attractive. 'If they weren't in a relationship, what was their connection?'

'She said they didn't look like a couple – no kissing or holding hands. She said Metcalfe followed her around like a puppy.'

'Google,' Braddick called. 'Who is John Metcalfe?'

'I'm on it.'

'Good man.' Braddick looked at the image again. 'Get this sent out to uniform – Cheshire, Manchester, North Wales and Cumbria. They're out there somewhere, but I don't think they've gone far. I think they're right under our noses.'

'What makes you think that?' Laurel asked.

'They have made no effort to cover up their trail so far, so why run?'

'Guv,' Miles Smith waved him over.

'What have you got, Miles?'

'This guy works for the social security on County Road,' Miles said. 'He says he dealt with a housing benefit claim for number ninety Stanley House, late last year. It sticks out because the woman was good-looking, but he said she'd smelled like something had died in her pocket. He said she was rank, so bad he remembers her.'

'Send him the recent photograph,' Braddick said.

'Yes. He says that's her.'

'Was her name Fabienne?'

'He says not but he can't remember the name she used. I've asked him to call back when he gets into work and finds the claim.'

'If she's been using an alias it would explain how she has stayed hidden all these years.'

'John Metcalfe, guv,' Google shouted. 'He's on the system.'

Braddick and Laurel walked over and looked at his screen. The image of Metcalfe was from the custody suite. He had a cut above his left eye and a split lip. His hair was greasy, and he had a week's stubble.

'John Metcalfe, aged fifty-seven, arrested on a sexual assault charge two years ago,' Google stopped to read on. 'He was attempting to assault a prostitute in his car when a passer-by intervened. There was an altercation. Metcalfe was dragged from the car and injured, and the woman pressed charges. He served eight months. He's got previous too: fraud, GBH, assault and, surprise-surprise, rape.'

'Get his prints to forensics. He might be in the queue – if they haven't come up in their searches already. Dr Libby is trying to rush through the results. This will speed things up.'

'Yes, guv.'

'We need copies of the statements from that assault case. Let's see what he had to say for himself. It might shine some light on what he is doing following Fabienne Wilder around. He's old enough to be her father.' Braddick read the charge sheet again. 'Who is he, Google?' Braddick asked. 'What does he do?'

'It says he's a self-employed builder, runs a limited company, Metcalfe Brothers Limited, registered in Allerton, and he owns a house in Southport, which he rents out. There have been no tax returns filed for the last two years.'

'Laurel,' Braddick said. 'Get his photograph to uniform at Stanley House, ask the neighbours if they've seen him with Wilder. We need a warrant for the property in Southport and his business address in Allerton. Organise uniform and armed response to attend both. If he's seen the appeal, he might be on the run already. Let's hope they weren't watching.'

'Yes, guv,' Laurel said as she answered a phone. She listened to the caller and gestured for Braddick to pick up the nearest handset. 'Dr Libby is on the phone for you. He says he knows you're busy with the appeal, but you'll want to hear this.'

'Dr Libby,' Braddick said. 'How can I help?'

'Sorry to disturb you, but this is important,' Dr Libby said. He sounded excited. 'The bones you found in your garden last night were chicken bones. They had been fastened together with horsehair.'

'What does that mean?' Braddick asked.

'I have absolutely no idea,' Dr Libby replied.

'Probably someone following the story in the press, taking the piss out of us,' Braddick said, dismissing it. 'This case is likely to attract the ghouls and crazies out there. People who howl at the moon in their underwear will be having wet dreams about this.'

'I don't doubt it, but I don't think you should be opening your front door in a towel for a while. You need to be careful.'

'I appreciate your concern,' Braddick said.

'The main reason for my call is far more serious.'

'What is it?' Braddick asked.

'We ran a camera survey of the drains under Stanley House, as you requested, and it revealed a large blockage of fat beneath the tower block. At first, we thought it was a fatberg, but it isn't.'

'Don't keep me in suspense,' Braddick said.

'It's human fat,' Dr Libby explained. 'And skin and bones.'

'Another body?'

'Bodies, I'm afraid,' Dr Libby said. 'My initial tests from the blockage are showing multiple DNA strands. The tissue is degraded but we can split one from the other. There are multiple victims down there.'

'Jesus Christ,' Braddick said.

'Oh, I don't think he's been anywhere near here for a long time,' Dr Libby said. 'His opposite number seems to be a frequent visitor.'

'Doesn't he just,' Braddick said. 'From the remains you've found, are we assuming they flushed parts of their victims down the toilet?'

'It looks that way.'

'Any idea how long it has been going on?'

'I can't tell for sure.'

'Is there anything else?' Braddick asked. 'Give me some good news.'

'Depends how you look at it, but there's another finding that will interest you.'

'What?' Braddick asked. The case was snowballing. It was already national news. The fact there were multiple victims, who had been dismembered and flushed away, would play to the media's bloodlust. 'I don't need any more victims.'

'No more victims just yet. I've found another suspect.'

'What?'

'I've cross-checked the prints from the Victoria May scene with the Stanley House scene, and there's a match I didn't expect,' Dr Libby explained. 'Two of the prints in the bedroom at Stanley House match a multiple hit at the May home.'

'A multiple hit from where?' Braddick asked. His heart was beating quicker.

'All over the house,' Dr Libby said. 'The owner of those prints must have lived in the May home.'

'The husband?' Braddick said, slapping the desk.

'That was my first instinct, although, without his prints, I can't be one hundred per cent sure they're his,' Dr Libby said.

'I'll have his prints sent to you,' Braddick said. 'Thanks, doctor.' He ended the call and looked at the screen again. Nothing added up. He frowned, confused by the information.

'What are you thinking?' Laurel asked.

'Okay, listen to this.' He turned to update Laurel and the rest of the team nearby. 'Forensics have found body parts in the drains beneath Stanley House.'

'Were they flushed down the toilet?' Google asked.

'It looks like it. We have multiple victims down there.'

'Can we access the drains directly?' Laurel asked.

'We need to find that out,' Braddick said. 'Get an engineering team over there and see if they can be opened up.'

'Will do.'

'Dr Libby said they have found prints in the bedroom of number ninety that match a set of prints taken from the May residence,' Braddick said. 'It's likely that the prints belong to someone who lived there. That changes the dynamic of the investigation.'

'Bruce May?' Laurel asked. 'Chester CID would have printed him, right?'

'I don't know,' Braddick said. 'I spoke to DI Ingleton about Bruce May, and he said May was distraught when he'd interviewed him; so much so, they'd had to put him up in a hotel and call an end to the questioning. He said he'd arranged for May to be re-interviewed properly in the morning. Can you check with him, please?'

'Guv,' Google said. 'This is interesting.'

'What is it?'

'Scottish Power have replied to our enquiries. For the last two years, the electric and gas bills for number ninety have been paid from a bank account belonging to a Mr Bruce May.'

'Are you kidding me?' Braddick said.

'Nope.'

'Laurel,' Braddick shouted. She looked up from her screen. 'Put in a call to DI Ingleton and find out where Bruce May is staying. Tell him to bring him in – voluntarily if possible, if not, arrest him.'

Laurel nodded and picked up the phone.

'When?' she asked.

'Right now,' Braddick said, grabbing his jacket. 'Follow me down to the car,' he added. 'We're going to Chester. Google, I need you to coordinate the information coming in, keep me up to speed.'

'I'm on it, guv.'

CHAPTER 10

George Hodge sipped his tea, holding the cup with both hands. His fingerless gloves offered little protection at night against the cold, especially in the winter. He listened to the police sergeant, who was asking questions of his friend, Ellis, and shook his head. Ellis was too drunk to know his name was Ellis, but the sergeant persisted; he looked tired and stressed as he shrugged his shoulders and looked at George.

'Your friend isn't being much help,' he said. 'Too many ciders. I think.'

'Too many? That depends on where you are standing,' George said. The sergeant frowned. 'Ellis needs that stuff. He struggles with life. Too much is never enough.'

'It won't do him any good,' the sergeant said.

'Look around you, can it do him any more harm? He can't fall any further,' George said. 'You're asking questions of us homeless people – looking for witnesses?'

'We're talking to everyone,' the sergeant said.

'Normally, you wouldn't give us the time of day, but today, we're human again.'

'I didn't mean any offence to you or your friend.'

'Unfortunately, Ellis has been self-medicating with alcohol, so, from your standpoint, he has had too many ciders.' George continued to sip his tea; it was hot and sweet. 'In his defence, Ellis is a war hero,' he said, ruffling Ellis's hair. Ellis tried a smile, but it turned into a grimace. 'He was a sergeant – like you – did two tours of Iraq and two in Afghanistan.'

'Really?' the sergeant said.

'Yes. He was part of a unit that rescued some Afghan regulars who had been captured and tortured. It wasn't a pretty sight and it fucked his head up.' He slurped his tea. 'He can't sleep, without having nightmares, and he suffers from claustrophobia to the point that he can't live in a house. Not even the house where his wife and kids live.' The policeman looked embarrassed. 'Ellis needs his medicine to sleep, so, from his standpoint, he hasn't had enough cider yet.'

'I didn't mean to sound ignorant,' the sergeant said.

'We're used to it,' George said. 'I might be able to help. Let me see your photographs.' The sergeant showed him the images of Fabienne Wilder and John Metcalfe.

'They're the people Wanda hung around with sometimes.'

'Who's Wanda?' the sergeant asked.

'She's one of us,' George said, nodding. 'The black woman lives on the ninth floor and the man is a frequent visitor. They're bad news, mark my words.'

'What makes you say that?'

'I watch and I listen,' George said, lowering his voice. 'Wanda told me that they have parties. Weird parties, if you know what I mean. She went to one and she wasn't the same after that. I asked her about it, but she wouldn't talk to me, said she was frightened to say anything. She hadn't wanted to go but they'd paid her well.' He looked along the landing to make sure no one was in earshot. 'I have seen people coming and going from those flats at all hours. Off their heads, most of them.'

'Flats?' the sergeant asked. 'Flats, plural?'

'Yes. All the top floor flats. There's all kinds of shenanigans going on up there.'

'Tell me what you've seen.'

'People. Some of them go there through choice, and some of the women go because they're being paid,' he explained. 'You understand what I mean, don't you?'

The sergeant nodded that he did. 'How do you know they're being paid?'

'I live on the streets, sergeant,' George said. 'When you live on the streets, you get to know who works on the streets.'

'I understand,' the sergeant said.

'I've seen some people leave there looking very distressed, and I've seen people leave in a hurry, too.'

'In a hurry?'

'Yes,' George said. 'Running down the stairs like a scalded cat. Frightened to death, some of them.'

'How do you know they were frightened?'

'Two tours of Helmand.' The sergeant looked at the floor as George continued. 'I've seen enough frightened people to know one when I see one. They take people up in the lifts, late at night.' He lowered his voice. 'Black women, mostly. Frightened, like rabbits. You can see it in their eyes.'

'Do you ever see the same people coming and going?'

'Yes. I never forget a face.'

'Would you be willing to look at some pictures for us?'

'Yes. No problem. I can tell you you're not the only ones interested in that place either.' George leaned closer to the sergeant. 'There are a couple of vehicles that turn up and stay a few hours. They always park in the rear car park, at the back of the building, so they can see if the lights are on or off.'

'Do you know what make of vehicles they are?' the sergeant asked.

'Of course, I do. I'm homeless, not stupid,' George said. 'One of them is a Range Rover and the other is a Porsche 911. You don't see many of them around here.'

The sergeant smiled and nodded his head. 'I don't suppose you do,' he said, writing it all down. 'Would you be able to identify the drivers?'

'No problem,' George said. 'It's always the same bloke. I never forget a face.'

'I know where to find you if I need to talk to you again,' the sergeant said. 'You have been a great help.' He slipped a twenty-pound note into George's gloved hand.

'There's no need for that,' George said.

'Buy Ellis some medicine.'

'You're a gentleman.'

'You take care of him,' the sergeant said. 'And yourself.'

The sergeant walked away and took out his mobile to call Laurel. A figure stood in the shadows of the stairwell, watching and listening, their camera phone capturing images of the conversation. The images were saved to the device and uploaded to the internet. As the sergeant talked to Laurel, the figure sank back into the darkness and merged with the night.

CHAPTER 11

Braddick and Laurel sat opposite DI Ingleton and his superintendent, Casey Prost. Casey was annoyed by the intrusion and the implication they had somehow mishandled a suspect in a major murder investigation. She was indignant when Braddick had asked them questions about what Bruce May had said. Braddick wasn't impressed with her attitude, and he was even less impressed that Bruce May hadn't been printed the day before.

'The man was hysterical. We actually called a doctor to sedate him,' Casey argued. 'Anyway, what's the big deal, he's hardly your main suspect, is he?' She shrugged. 'He wasn't even there when the murder took place. The man was in London when she died!'

'I'm not here to pick holes in your procedures, Casey,' Braddick said. 'And I don't want an argument. I need to interview Bruce May and I need his prints sent to Dr Libby, that's all.'

'And we've arranged that for you,' Casey said. She shifted her substantial bulk in her chair. Braddick thought she was the spitting image of Oliver Hardy, without the moustache. 'I'm being about as courteous and cooperative as it gets. Once his solicitor is here, you can speak to him.'

Braddick smiled and shook his head. He thought Casey Prost was a patronising bitch, but he kept it to himself. There was nothing to gain from antagonising her.

'Run it by me again,' he said, turning to Ingleton.

'Again?' Ingleton complained. 'Are you joking?'

'Do I look like I'm laughing?' Braddick asked. 'Where had Bruce May been?'

'He said he'd had a series of business meetings in London,' Ingleton said. 'He has the receipts for a first-class return ticket from Chester to Euston, and an internet invoice for a hotel called the Kennedy, which is next to the station. He was there for three days.' He shrugged. 'When he arrived back, his wife wasn't there to meet him as they had arranged, and he couldn't reach her on the phone. I've seen the missed calls on his phone – he called her fourteen times with no reply, so he decided to take a taxi and he paid for the cab from Chester station to his home with a debit card, and I've seen the receipt. I've spoken to the cab firm, and the cabbie who drove him, and they've both confirmed he was picked up at the station from the London train.' He paused to think. 'How much more information did I need? The man was distraught to the point that we called a doctor. He'd just found out his wife had been murdered – he'd produced evidence for his whereabouts when the murder had taken place – so printing him wasn't my priority. What more could I do?'

'Follow procedure,' Laurel said. Casey turned purple with anger. Laurel looked at her, unnerved.

'Bruce May isn't a criminal mastermind,' Ingleton snapped. 'The man is in an interview room down the corridor. Go and take a look. You can't miss him; he's the one crying into his coffee. What is your problem?'

'Slapdash procedures,' Laurel said.

'Fuck you,' Ingleton said.

'Not without a few pints of Rohypnol inside me, thanks,' Laurel replied. 'Printing the spouse should be routine, upset or not,' she added. Casey glared at her. Laurel didn't back down. 'Everyone is a suspect until they're not a suspect. When did that change?'

'I would tell your pit bull to bite her tongue before she pisses me off,' Casey said.

'Tell her yourself. She doesn't need me to help her. She can handle herself,' Braddick said.

'I'm warning you, Braddick,' Casey said, standing up. 'You're here because we're cooperating with you on this joint investigation. Let's not get into a slanging match about procedure.'

'All things considered, I have to agree,' Braddick said.

'That's good to hear.' Casey nodded and relaxed a little.

'Not with you,' Braddick said. 'I mean that I agree with my DS – everyone is a suspect until they're not.' He shrugged. 'He should have been printed.'

'Well, in this instance, he wasn't,' Casey said. 'And do you know what?'

'What?'

'He didn't run around Chester murdering people,' she said, sarcastically. 'He stayed in his hotel room all night. Do you know how we know that? Because I had uniform posted outside his room. I didn't win this job in a raffle, Braddick. I know how to handle a murder case.'

'I don't doubt it.'

'Good. Then wind your neck in.'

'Consider it wound in. Not to worry,' Braddick said, smiling. 'We'll get there one way or the other. I do appreciate you cooperating, Casey, but that doesn't mean I won't tell you when I think someone hasn't done their job.'

'Has he been printed yet?' Laurel asked.

'Yes,' Casey said. Her face flushed with anger again. A knock on the door interrupted them and Casey opened it.

'Mr May's solicitor has arrived,' a uniformed officer said. 'He's in the reception area interview room I'm afraid. There's no room at the inn. The custody suite is crammed full of pissheads.'

'Superintendent Braddick will be with him shortly, thank you,' she said, turning to him. 'I'll leave you to it. It's race day. We'll be snowed under all day.'

'There's nothing like drunken racegoers to keep you on your toes,' Braddick said. 'It goes with the territory, I suppose.'

'It does,' Casey said, stepping aside; there still wasn't much room to pass by. 'After you. I'll be in my office if you need anything.'

'Thanks,' Braddick said.

Laurel squeezed past without looking at her. She was neither impressed nor phased by her rank. Laurel rated other officers on their merits, not their stripes. She had been warned by Braddick that her attitude might cause her problems, but it had gone in one ear and out the other. They walked down the corridor, side by side.

'I don't think she likes me,' Laurel said. Braddick glanced at her and smiled.

'What makes you think that?'

'Just a feeling I get when she looks me up and down, as if I'm something she's stood in.'

'I think you're being oversensitive,' Braddick said.

'Bollocks.'

'There's no need for that.' Braddick smiled.

'Anyway, what are you smiling at? She doesn't like you, either.'

'You think so?'

'One hundred per cent. She hates you.'

'That hurts.'

'Suck it up.'

Braddick sucked in his cheeks and shook his head. The interview room was down the stairs, near the reception area. It was a busy police station. All the seats were full, and a revolving door turned constantly as people entered and exited. A woman in a sparkly gown teetered near the reception desk, shouting that her car had been stolen. Braddick doubted she could remember her name, let alone where she'd parked her car. He also wondered who was supposed to be driving it. They crossed reception and walked into the interview room and introduced themselves.

'I'm Detective Superintendent Braddick, and this is Detective Sergeant Stewart, Liverpool Major Investigation Team.' Braddick sat down.

'I'm Alan Williams from Williams and Godwin. Is my client under caution?'

'No, not at the moment, although that might change,' Braddick said. 'We need to ask him questions about his wife's business.' Williams scribbled something on his notes. Braddick couldn't care less what it was.

'Your wife owns the apartments on the ninth floor of Stanley House in Liverpool,' Braddick said.

Bruce May looked blankly at him. His dark hair was obviously dyed and made his skin look pale and pasty. The grey suit he was wearing looked dishevelled and was creased at the knees.

'Is that a question?' Williams asked.

'No, it's a fact,' Braddick said without looking at him. 'Have you ever been to Stanley House, Bruce?'

'Yes, but not for a while. I went there a lot when she was thinking about buying the flats.'

'When was that?' Braddick asked.

'About fifteen years ago. It was a nice place then. That was before the social started paying the rent direct to the tenants.'

'We're interested in the tenant at number ninety,' Braddick said.

'I'm not sure I can help,' Bruce said.

'Why were the other flats on that floor empty?' Braddick asked.

'There was a fire in one and the others were rundown. Victoria was in the process of renovating them. She was so proud of her properties – never let a place unless she would live there herself.' A tear ran from his eye. Braddick watched him wipe it away, trying to measure the man. He appeared to be distraught. 'She was too proud. It cost her thousands when other landlords didn't care.'

'Who has access to the empty flats?' Braddick asked.

'Victoria, obviously, and the builder who's renovating them, probably,' Bruce said. His hands were shaking. Braddick couldn't tell if it was distress or nervousness.

'Do you know who the builder is?' Braddick asked.

'She uses a guy called John Metcalfe. Has done for years. He renovated the flats when she first bought them.'

Braddick glanced at Laurel. The man photographed with Fabienne.

'Do you know him?'

'Who?'

'The builder, John Metcalfe,' Braddick said.

'I know of him, that's all.' Bruce looked away and shook his head. 'Only because Victoria mentioned his name every now and again. He does all the work on her properties – has done for years.'

'Yes, you said. Have you ever met him?' Braddick asked.

'No. Not that I can remember.'

'How many years has he worked for her?'

'I'm not sure exactly, to be honest,' Bruce said. His face reddened.

'That's odd,' Braddick said.

'What is?'

'You said fifteen years,' Braddick said.

'It's about that.'

'The fact you haven't met him, if he worked for your wife for a long time, is odd,' Braddick pushed.

'Why is it odd? I had nothing to do with her business and she had nothing to do with mine.'

'What do you do?' Braddick asked.

'What?'

'What do you do?' he repeated. 'As a business.'

'I'm in haulage,' Bruce replied. He looked confused by the change of tack. 'Shipping and logistics.'

'So, you haven't been there recently?'

'Where?'

'To Stanley House, to the apartments,' Braddick pushed. Bruce's eyes darted from his solicitor back to Braddick. 'Have you been to Stanley House recently? It's a straightforward question.'

'No.'

'Are you sure?'

'Yes.'

'Do you know this woman?' Braddick placed an image of Fabienne Wilder on the table. He could see from Bruce's reaction that he did. His eyes twitched and he quickly looked away. There was something else there too: affection.

'Do you know her?'

'No.'

'You sure?'

'Yes.'

'Look again. Her name is Fabienne Wilder, and she lived at number ninety, Stanley House,' Braddick said. Bruce shifted uncomfortably in his seat and shook his head. 'She's one of your wife's tenants, are you sure you don't know her?'

'Yes.'

'My client has answered the question several times. Please move on, Superintendent Braddick,' Alan Williams said.

'Do you recognise this man?' Braddick asked, placing another image on the table. Bruce May shifted uneasily, undoing the top button of his shirt. Sweat formed on his forehead. He swallowed hard and took a sip of water.

'No. I've never seen him before.'

'He's John Metcalfe – your wife's builder. He was often seen at number ninety with this woman.' Braddick tapped the image again. 'John Metcalfe and Fabienne Wilder.'

'Obviously I know his name, but I wouldn't have recognised him. I don't know him.'

'Are you sure you haven't met him?'

'I told you. I haven't been there for years.'

'Did you ever meet any of your wife's tenants?'

'I never had anything to do with my wife's business.'

'You never went there with your wife to visit the flats, and stayed in your car while she went inside to talk to her builder or her tenant?' Braddick asked.

'No. I've never been there for years.'

'You've never been there in your Porsche 911 and waited in the car park at the rear?' Braddick asked.

'Why do you ask that?' Bruce asked nervously, fidgeting with his hands.

'It's not a trick question. Have you been there in your Porsche?' Braddick pushed the question.

'No.'

'I'll ask you again. Have you been there and parked at the back of the flats?'

'No.'

'You look like you're lying,' Braddick said. 'Why would you lie to me?'

'My client has answered your question, several times,' Williams said. 'He doesn't know this woman and he hasn't been there recently.'

'I heard what he said, but your client is lying,' Braddick said. He glanced at Williams.

'Do you have evidence to back that up?' Williams said.

'Yes.' The solicitor decided to back down and Braddick continued. 'You're lying to me. Why are you lying to me, Bruce?'

'I'm not lying.'

'We've lifted prints from Fabienne's apartment, and they match prints taken from your home,' Braddick said. 'Prints that are all over your home, the kitchen, the bathrooms, the bedrooms, the bannisters, the door handles – everywhere. They were left by someone who lives in your house, Bruce. Why would that be?'

Bruce looked down at the table. 'I don't know.'

'You said you haven't been to Stanley House recently, but we have witnesses who put you sitting in a black Porsche in the rear car park.' Braddick stood up and leaned against the wall. 'You *have* been there, so why are you lying to me?'

'I haven't been inside,' Bruce muttered.

'So, you have been to Stanley House?' Braddick asked.

'Yes.'

'Why lie to me?'

'I don't know.'

'Are your prints in Fabienne's apartment?'

'No.'

'Are you sure you don't know her?'

'Yes.'

'If you don't know her, why have you been paying her utility bills?' Braddick asked. The solicitor looked shocked.

'What bills?' Bruce asked. His voice wavered. He looked shaken.

'Her electric and gas bills.' Braddick said.

'I don't know what you're talking about.'

'Here, look,' Braddick said, placing the information on the table. 'The money comes from this bank account to Scottish Power. Mr B May, that's you.'

'It wasn't me,' he said, shaking his head. 'I haven't used that account for years. I haven't done that.'

'A man fitting your description has been seen in a Porsche, which you drive, parked behind the flats, and someone is using a bank account in your name to pay bills for a woman you've never met?' Braddick said. 'Come on, Bruce. Do you know how ridiculous that sounds?'

'I want to speak to my client alone,' Williams said. Braddick glared at him. 'I want to speak to him alone, right now, Superintendent Braddick.'

'Okay,' Braddick said. 'You need to spell out to him where this investigation is going. When we resume, we're going to read him his rights, and if he lies to me once more, we'll charge him and take our chances.'

'Charge me with what?' Bruce asked. He looked frightened.

'Murdering your wife for a start, and then we'll see what else we can find.'

CHAPTER 12

John Metcalfe woke up on the bathroom floor covered in vomit. He was cold and naked. The smell was nauseating, which told him he had defecated too. His memory was fuzzy, but he knew he had food poisoning. It had to be something he had eaten that had made him so ill. He looked at the door and wondered where Fabienne was. She wouldn't leave him like this, surely not. For years he had done everything she had asked of him and more. She had asked him to do some bad things for her and he had done them without question. He had been loyal. There had been a lot to put up with. Her other friends had driven him to distraction. They became addicted to her, needing to do bad things for her with each other. He had watched – hating it but loving it too. They wouldn't leave her alone and she wouldn't tell them to go. She welcomed their affections but never returned them. They worshipped her just as he did. It was impossible not to. Sometimes he wished he had never met her; life would have been easier if he hadn't – easier and mundane. That was what she called the others in society – nonbelievers. The mundane. Fabienne had shown him what living was about. Good and evil, love and hate, sex and power, life and death. He had never really felt those things before, not so intensely. The intensity of taking life and absorbing it into your body was the greatest high he had ever felt, and he couldn't get enough. Fabienne gave him that. She showed him glimpses of hell and he embraced it with a passion. It was Fabienne he desired, but he couldn't have her. No one could. She promised, one day, he could join with her in body and soul, but it wasn't time yet. It was never time. The years had ticked by and he was no closer to having her. He had given her his last penny, his life and his soul and he had risked everything, yet still she took from him. She sucked the life force from everyone she met. To love Fabienne was to throw your life into the darkest reaches of hell, but that was where the pleasure and the pain were at their most intense. So intense it couldn't be tolerated for more than a few stolen moments. She could take him there and let him wallow in the ecstasy and the agony just long enough to make him want more. A wave of nausea hit him, and he vomited blood onto the tiles. His stomach cramped painfully. *Where's Fabienne?* Didn't she know how he was suffering?

The sound of the hotel door being opened disturbed his thoughts. He looked up as the bathroom door was slammed open. Armed police pointed their weapons at him. He could hear them shouting but their words meant nothing to him. He couldn't understand them. They cuffed him and dragged him off the tiles; he wondered where Fabienne had gone before he drifted into the darkness. He knew evil things would be waiting for him, and this time she wouldn't be there to bring him back. Terror gripped his soul.

CHAPTER 13

When Braddick and Laurel returned to the interview room Bruce May was visibly upset. His eyes were red and teary; he couldn't make eye contact with the detectives. Alan Williams was scribbling profusely in his notebook and he had opened his top button and loosened his tie. His demeanour had changed from arrogant to uncomfortable. There was a tense atmosphere in the room.

'Have you finished talking to your client?' Braddick asked.

'Yes, thank you, Superintendent Braddick,' Williams said, without looking up; he continued to scribble. It was obvious that he no longer wanted to be there. Braddick could spot a solicitor who didn't want to represent their client a mile away. It usually spoke volumes about their innocence.

'Interview resumed,' Braddick said. He looked Bruce May in the eyes. 'Read him his rights.' Laurel read them but Bruce didn't appear to be bothered. 'Are you ready to talk to us, Bruce?'

'Yes.'

'Are you ready to tell me the truth?'

'Yes.' He closed his eyes and rocked back on his chair. 'I've never been in that apartment,' he said.

'We have prints from your house that match prints from the bedroom in Fabienne Wilder's apartment; the apartment your wife rents to her,' Braddick said, sighing. He was losing patience. 'You have been seen in the car park and you pay her bills. There's no point lying when the evidence is clear.'

'It isn't clear,' Bruce said.

'It is pretty clear to me,' Braddick said.

'The prints you found will be Victoria's,' Bruce said.

'Victoria's?' Braddick repeated. *We haven't recovered her body yet.*

'Yes,' Bruce said, nodding. He looked at the table and wiped another tear from his eye. 'She was having a relationship with that evil bitch.' Braddick sat back and absorbed the information. He looked at Laurel, who looked as shocked as he was.

'Your wife was having a relationship with Fabienne Wilder?' Laurel said.

'Yes.'

'How can you be sure?'

'I used to follow her there sometimes, and sit outside like the spineless bastard I am.' He paused to wipe his nose. 'I would sit in the car park and watch the windows because I didn't have the nerve to confront them. How sad is that?'

'Why didn't you tell us this from the start?' Braddick asked. 'I don't understand.'

'I was ashamed.' He shrugged. 'My wife loved another woman more than she loved me. It has been very difficult for me to deal with, so I just block it out most of the time.'

'Did you meet Fabienne?' Laurel asked.

'Once,' Bruce said. He looked up. 'I felt brave one night when Victoria had gone there.' He stopped and shook his head. 'Brave might not be the word. I was incensed. I was parked at the back, watching the windows, when the lights went off. I decided to go up there and knock on the door. About halfway up the stairwell, she was there – on the steps, just standing there.'

'Who was?' Braddick asked.

'That bitch,' Bruce said, gesturing to the image of Fabienne. 'She was standing there in the dark as if she was waiting for me. I nearly had a heart attack.'

'What happened?' Laurel asked, frowning.

'I told her to leave my wife alone,' Bruce said, looking from Laurel to Braddick. 'She said, "you tell her to stay away from me and see what she says". She was smiling, the bitch. I said she would be sorry if she didn't stay away from Victoria and she laughed at me.' Bruce looked broken. 'I was angry; I threatened her, and she pulled out a knife – the type with a blade on one side and teeth on the other, like a hunting knife but bigger.' He paused as he pictured the memories. 'I could tell by her eyes that she would have used it. She stood there, smiling at me. Then Victoria appeared, on the stairs behind her. They held hands. She said, if I didn't go home, I would never see her again. I didn't know what to say, so I went home.'

'When was this?' Braddick asked.

'Two years ago.'

'And you stayed with her?' Laurel asked.

'I loved Victoria,' Bruce said, choking back a sob, 'but she was obsessed with that *bitch*. I mean, she was absolutely obsessed with her. It was unnatural. She spent thousands on her. She thought I didn't know. Every time my back was turned, she was there, like a rat up a drainpipe. Whenever I challenged her about it, she told me to live with it or leave.' He shook his head. 'All those other flats are empty because that bitch told Victoria to keep them empty.'

'Why did she want them empty?' Braddick asked.

'So, she could do whatever it was they did in there without disturbing the neighbours.'

'What was it they did?'

'God only knows. She wouldn't talk to me about it,' Bruce sobbed. 'I couldn't leave her. I thought it was a phase, you know, going with another woman. When I asked her if they were having sex, she would get angry and say I wouldn't understand, and she had never touched Fabienne like that.' He sniffled; his shoulders shook. 'I knew she was evil, but I didn't know she was capable of what she did to Victoria.'

'What makes you say she was evil?' Braddick asked.

'Things Victoria talked about, and she began to read books about the occult, witchcraft, devil worship – all kinds of rubbish. It was unnatural. God knows what garbage she put into her head. Victoria changed.'

'Changed how?'

'She became distracted and she wasn't getting any rent for those apartments. Her business began to struggle.' He paused to blow his nose. 'All I know is she was obsessed with her.'

'Did Victoria tell you what they did there?'

'No. She said I wouldn't understand.'

'But she was reading books about the occult?' Braddick asked.

'She was reading all kinds of stuff, mostly books by Anton LaVey. He founded the church of Satan,' Bruce said. Braddick looked at Laurel and she shrugged; the name meant nothing to them. 'Look, I'm being honest with you; they won't tell me anything here, did she suffer when she died?'

'Yes. She suffered terribly,' Laurel said, nodding. Braddick looked at her and shook his head. 'She was nailed to a table. It couldn't be much worse.' Bruce began to shake again. She waited until he had settled. 'You need to tell us what you know about Fabienne Wilder.'

'I don't know anything about her, but I should have seen this coming,' Bruce sobbed. 'I knew it was taking a turn for the worse.'

'What do you mean?' Braddick asked.

'Not long ago, I heard Victoria arguing with her on the telephone,' Bruce said. 'She said that she was sick of being strung along and she had waited long enough. I didn't know what she was sick of waiting for, but she said she wasn't going to wait any longer and she threatened to evict her from the flat.' He wiped his mouth on his sleeve. 'Of course, I was delighted. I thought I would get my wife back. I didn't think this would happen…'

'You couldn't have seen this coming,' Braddick said. 'No one could have predicted this.' Bruce May broke down, saliva dribbled from his chin. His sobs came from deep inside his chest. Braddick thought he might choke to death. It was a sad sight to witness.

'I think my client has been through enough for one day,' Williams said. 'He is clearly devastated. I suggest we call a halt to this for today?'

'No problem,' Braddick said. 'My DS will verify the prints with forensics. As long as they don't match your client's, he's free to go.' He turned to Laurel. 'Can you speak to Dr Libby about the prints, please.'

'That's fine,' Laurel said.

Braddick left the room. He felt sorry for Bruce May but couldn't help wondering how a man could stay with his partner in that situation. Whatever his thought process had been, he didn't deserve what had happened to his wife. He wondered how he would have coped, had the boot been on the other foot. It was a test he wouldn't ever need to take. His mobile vibrated in his pocket. It was Google.

'Google?' Braddick crossed the reception area and stepped into the lift, pressing the fourth-floor button; a group of uniformed officers got in, filling it. They were talking about how much they hated working when the races were on. One of them had a tip for the last race, but his colleagues were berating him about the last tip he'd given them; apparently, the horse was still running.

'They've found John Metcalfe in a hotel in Chester, guv,' Google said.

'No one gets found in a hotel,' Braddick said, smiling. 'They didn't just stumble across him. How did that happen?'

'They received a tip-off from a female, saying he was staying there.'

'A female, surprise-surprise,' Braddick said. 'I'll bet that female was Fabienne Wilder.'

'My thoughts exactly.'

'Has he said anything?'

'No, guv. He's in a bad way,' Google said. 'He lost consciousness in the ambulance on the way to hospital.'

'What is wrong with him?' Braddick asked, shocked.

'It looks like a drug overdose. He was found unconscious in the bathroom, lying in his own blood and shit, guv. Apparently, he had been there a while. He was completely incoherent. His heart stopped en route to the Countess Hospital and they had to defibrillate him.'

'We need to talk to him as soon as he regains consciousness.'

'I've spoken to Cheshire,' Google said. 'They'll contact us as soon as he opens his eyes.'

'Did he book in with Fabienne Wilder?' Braddick asked.

'No. The hotel says he checked in alone.'

'We need the CCTV from that hotel. Find out what vehicle he arrived in,' Braddick said.

'I've already asked for it. They're sending it over.'

'Good, thanks,' Braddick said. 'A drug overdose doesn't sit right with me.'

'There were mushrooms at Stanley Court, guv,' Google reminded him.

'True.' Braddick wasn't convinced. The nagging doubt that they were missing something was like a barking dog in his head.

'We'll know when the toxicology reports come back,' Google said.

'Is there anything else back from the lab?' Braddick asked.

'Nothing yet.' Google sighed. 'Hold the line and I'll call Dr Libby.'

'I've asked Laurel to call him, no worries.'

'Hold on, guv. Miles has just handed me a note. Dr Libby called a few minutes ago. The prints from the bedroom at number ninety are Bruce May's. They're a perfect match.'

'Shit!' The uniformed officers turned to look at Braddick. He showed them his identity card, quickly.

'What is it, guv?'

'I've just been mugged,' Braddick said. 'I'll call you back.'

The lift doors opened on the second floor and Braddick squeezed out. He ran to the stairs and took them two at a time. When he reached reception, he sprinted to the interview room. Laurel was running down the corridor towards him. They burst into the interview room, startling Alan Williams.

'Where is he?' Braddick asked, panting.

'He went to the toilet,' Williams said, looking confused.

'I've been in there,' Laurel said, 'he's not there. The window is open.' She looked at Braddick and shook her head. 'He's gone.'

'What's the problem?' Williams asked.

'Your client deserves an Oscar, that's what,' Laurel said. 'The prints are his.'

'We need to ask Casey Prost to distribute May's picture.' Braddick sighed. 'It's race day. There are thousands of people out there on the streets. The chances of finding him are zero.'

'She'll be smiling from ear to ear after the grief we gave her earlier,' Laurel said. 'Losing a suspect in a police station is right up there with the biggest fuck-ups ever made.'

CHAPTER 14

Fabienne drove through Wrexham and joined the A5 at Llangollen, then headed north towards Betys-y-Coed. She slowed down briefly as she passed through Corwen, to look at the building where they had caged her when she was younger. The urge to stop and burn the place down was difficult to ignore. She would do it one day; it was a promise to herself. It hadn't been an asylum for years, but it still needed to be burned down. She had read about it closing, amidst allegations of abuse and maltreatment of the inmates going back decades. The allegations were all true – she knew from her own experiences there. It was ironic that they sent children damaged by abuse into a system riddled with it. The more damaged they were, the more vulnerable they became.

That vulnerability was attractive to predators, but Fabienne wasn't weak like the others. She'd often wondered what attracted the abusers – if it was her fault, they'd zoned in on her. Maybe they could sense the darkness within her, smell the rottenness of her soul. They would have been well advised to have targeted someone else. Every one of her abusers had died. Her adopted father had been first, the roommate who hung herself was second. Her death had been particularly rewarding. A teacher at the Corwen institution had been third, although no one but Fabienne knew what happened to him. He had helped her escape and run away and had agreed to arrange somewhere for her to stay on the promise that she would have regular sex with him. He was besotted with her. She was beginning to learn how powerful her sexual attraction was, and she used it to manipulate people. He had smuggled her through the security system and taken her to a remote cottage on the Denbigh Moors, which he had rented under an alias. The plan was for Fabienne to live there, with him supporting her financially, and she would repay him sexually. That way, he could go home to his wife and children every night with no questions asked. Of course, she had no intention of letting him touch her, but she needed him to get her through the locked doors and out of the asylum. The escape went well, and no one knew she had gone until the following day. They'd reached the cottage without any drama and she was surprised how peaceful it was. He had tried it on within fifteen minutes of arriving at the cottage. She had stuck a carving knife into his guts and dragged him into the bath to bleed out. It had taken longer than she'd thought, and he begged for his life until his last breath. She'd disposed of the body, bit by bit, across the moors and in the nearby lakes and rivers. She'd thought about eating the tastiest parts of him but had resisted the temptation. His meat could make her strong, but it could also make her sick. She had eaten humans in the weeks following the hurricane. Her village was so remote that they'd had no food for weeks; they'd had no choice but to eat the dead. She had enjoyed it. Even at that young age, she'd felt the connection between her and evil. Human flesh had brought them closer to one another.

No one ever came looking for her and she'd stayed there and healed herself for a while. There was an affinity with the mountains and forests that she couldn't explain. Maybe the remoteness reminded her of her homeland. It all felt like a lifetime ago, yet, here she was, a fugitive once again. She thought about her past and her future. The drive through Snowdonia would give her time to relax and work out her next move. Although she knew what needed to be done, she had to be meticulous in her planning.

The roads were quiet as she climbed the Llugwy Valley towards the mountains. There were only a few tourists at that time of year, and she hadn't seen a police car since crossing the border into North Wales. Bruce May had changed the plates on the 911 the day before so she wouldn't trigger any VRN cameras. The light was fading, and she was relieved when she saw the signpost directing her to the smallholding in the Ogwen Valley, where Bruce and his wife, Victoria, had retreated to in happier times. They hadn't used it for years. Not since Victoria had first become entwined in Fabienne's web. Victoria had been mildly interested in the same sex when she was younger, dabbling with a schoolmate for a while, and it had stayed with her as an adult, although she hadn't acted on the impulse for years. When she met Fabienne, the desire she'd felt was incredible; the sexual attraction had been immense. It wasn't long before she was staring at Fabienne like a love-struck teenager. Her need to please Fabienne and do her bidding had been insatiable, seeking favour at every opportunity. Victoria was easy to manipulate and Fabienne had introduced her to her dark side. She'd taken to the ceremonies like a duck to water and had done as instructed with whoever Fabienne told her to. Her desire to please Fabienne meant she'd progressed quickly through the layers. Victoria had requested every step she had taken down the left-hand path, and Fabienne had encouraged her every step of the way, into the darkness. She had written her final chapter herself. Victoria hadn't enjoyed it, but she wasn't supposed to. Her agony at the end was intense, yet she'd never asked for it to stop. The next part of Victoria's journey was a solitary step into the unknown. It always was. No one came back to explain what it was like, although Fabienne had a good idea that her pain would linger for eternity – she hoped it would.

The mobile rang again. It was Bruce May. He was desperately trying to reach her. It was pitiful how he was behaving. The Mays had known what they were doing and what the implications would be. The fact that Bruce May had panicked and let Victoria go into the night alone was not her concern. He had stayed, in the vain hope it would endear him to Fabienne. It was a selfish act. He was a coward, and cowards deserved everything that happened to them. The drops running from his eyes were crocodile tears. The death of one of their own was supposed to make them stronger, but he was a jabbering wreck after the event. It was sickening. Fabienne loathed him and his type. They pretended to belong to her for the physical experiences it would bring – for them it was about sex, but when it came down to the real evil, they didn't want to know. Belonging was total. There were no half measures.

She had made him turn off the GPS tracker on the 911 before she'd taken it, and she'd promised to let him know where she would be hiding. Of course, she had no intention of making contact until she was ready. He was on his own until then. Victoria had told her about the farmhouse in the mountains and had asked her to go there with her, just the two of them. Fabienne had known that Victoria desired her; they all did, but none of them got close. That was part of the power she wielded over them: desire, lust, love and fear. There was always the fear. Whatever they felt, it had the same effect. She could persuade them to try things they would normally never consider, but not with her. Never with her. Only with the other minions. She knew how to make them lose all their inhibitions and let the darkness in. Their sessions were a toxic mixture of hallucinogenic fuelled sex and violence. It was a hugely addictive state of mind to be in. Once they were hooked, it was too late for them. She milked them for whatever she needed, and they couldn't say no. They craved the darkness so much they could no longer see the light. John Metcalfe, Victoria May and her husband, had all been the architects of their own demise. Metcalfe had lost his mind; he'd taken things too far and Fabienne had let him. There were lines that society wouldn't accept them crossing, and he had crossed them. The trick was not to let society know; as long as they didn't find out, it didn't matter. But the group had become sloppy in a frenzy of self-indulgence – Fabienne couldn't care less what they did to each other, they were sheep. Gullible idiots. She had to take back control of the business side of things before it all unravelled.

Fabienne indicated left and turned up a farm track that weaved up the steep gradient to the base of Mount Tryfan. The farmhouse was hidden from the road by a rocky outcrop, covered with evergreens, and she parked the Porsche at the rear. She didn't want it to be seen on approach. The building was in darkness, as she'd expected, which was a relief. She had half expected Bruce May to be there, waiting for her. In truth, he would never guess that she had stolen the keys to the farm from Victoria's keyring months before she died. She had taken the bunch and had copies made as a precaution. Victoria owned a lot of properties and Fabienne had known she would need somewhere to hide. She had spent too long in one place and too long in the company of fools. It was time to trim the flock.

The deterioration of John Metcalfe had led him to make mistakes. It was simply a matter of time before the police became aware of them. Taking people from the streets was never advisable, and they never had. It was a golden rule. A rule *he* had broken. Missing people attracted attention sooner or later, even if some of them wanted to be missing. Everything came to an end, eventually. The infection in John Metcalfe's brain had accelerated the process. His lack of judgement had turned the simplest session into a frenzy. The clean-ups had become more and more complicated. She had seen the writing on the wall months before. It was time for her to blend into the mundane, for a while at least. Her transition into the darkness was almost complete. She could feel it. Until then, she had to protect her liberty and stop the wheels from falling off.

She stepped out of the vehicle and grabbed her bag before taking off her gloves. Her hands were stiff and hot. It started to rain, and dark clouds sped across the sky. Fabienne tipped back her head and let the raindrops splash on her face. It was invigorating. She felt strong. A flash of lightning streaked above the black mountain, followed by a deafening thunderclap. It was as if Mother Nature herself was protesting at her presence. Fabienne looked up at the mountain and smiled. The ancient rocks, as old as time, loomed above her, threatening to collapse and smother her, but she didn't fear them. She didn't fear anything, not anymore. The rain became a downpour and she ran to the door, sheltering beneath a slate porch while she fumbled the key into the lock. It turned with a click and the door opened. She paused and looked down the valley. In the near distance, Lake Ogwen was almost black, its waters rippled beneath the wind. The valley looked foreboding as the shadows deepened. A cold wind sliced through her clothes making her shudder. The smell of coal dust and damp drifted to her from inside. She shivered and stepped in, closing the door behind her. The thick stone walls muffled any noise from outside; it was silent apart from the ticking of a grandfather clock. She could see it in the hallway, which ran from the living room into the kitchen. Putting her bag down on the stone floor, she switched on the lights.

The room had an open fireplace with logs stacked either side of it and a slate chimney breast that reached up to the ceiling; oak beams striped the walls. She walked to the fireplace and knelt next to the hearth. There were knots of rolled newspaper in the grate and a large box of matches on the hearth. She put on her gloves, lit a match and set fire to the paper. The flames flickered and spread from front to back. Fabienne stacked some logs on top and listened to the wood crackle as it burned. Blue flames danced and leaped and died as the resin seeped from the wood and sizzled. It wasn't long before the fire was roaring, and she tipped coal onto it from a scuttle. She crouched and let the flames warm her bones; the fire was mesmerising. Her mobile rang again, and she looked at the screen: Bruce May. Again. This time, she answered it.

'Fabienne?' he said, his voice panicked. 'What have you done?'

'Bruce,' she answered.

'Oh my God,' he said, almost in a whisper, 'what did you do to her?'

'I did nothing to her.'

'Who did it?'

'John.'

'John Metcalfe is out of control,' Bruce said, angrily. 'I can't believe what he's done. He's a mad man.'

'Why can't you believe it?' Fabienne asked. 'It was what she wanted.'

'Nobody wants that,' Bruce said. 'I know that much.'

'You know nothing, Bruce,' she said. 'Absolutely nothing. That's your problem.'

'I know how much I've risked for you,' he snapped. 'I've lost everything.'

'It will be worth it, eventually,' she said. 'I promise.'

'You promise?'

'Yes. I promise I'll look after you,' Fabienne said. There was a pause.

'Where are you?'

'At your cottage in the Ogwen Valley,' she said.

'What? How—'

'Don't worry about that now,' she said. 'Hurry up and get here. I'll wait for you.'

'How did you know about that place?' Bruce asked, confused.

'Victoria told me about it.'

'I haven't been there for years.'

'I know you haven't,' she said.

'The police are after me. I can't hire a car.'

'What did you expect?'

'I don't know,' he muttered. 'Not this.'

'We'll leave this place together,' Fabienne said. 'There will be nothing to fear. I'll fix everything.'

'Will we …' his voice trailed off. He couldn't ask her because he didn't want to hear the answer. 'You know what I mean.'

'We'll see. The future is unclear. Just hurry,' she said.

'I'll get there somehow. Give me a couple of hours.'

'Okay. See you soon.'

'I love you, Fabienne,' Bruce said, his voice breaking.

She hung up and stared into the flames. He was weak, not worthy of her company, let alone her affections. It would take him at least three hours to get there. She checked her watch. There was plenty of time to do what needed to be done. She scrolled through her mobile and found the numbers she wanted. There were some very important calls she needed to make.

CHAPTER 15

Valerie Sykes was swimming in and out of a dreamlike state. She felt like her body was immersed in water. The pain in her hands and feet was terrible. They were tingling and throbbing, white hot inside. Fear gripped her. She was scared. The man she had met, John Metcalfe, was an evil pervert. It was the week before Wanda had gone there and never come out. There were other women there too: they were black and didn't speak much English. He had asked them to do things they didn't want to do. When they said no, he'd become violent. There were blank spaces in her memory. She remembered being with Wanda, talking about making some easy cash, and Wanda had told her what went on up on the top landing, warned her not to go there, but she was desperate for money. She had gone to the top floor and knocked on the door of number ninety. The lady who'd opened the door was black, and she was beautiful and charming. Valerie remembered her eyes. They chatted and then the woman had left, giving Valerie a hug. John Metcalfe had come, given them some money, and they'd drunk the mushroom tea. Valerie had never taken mushrooms before. She had seen older kids snorting coke and, once, she'd shared a few puffs on a spliff. It had made her feel sick. This was another league. The tea had hit her like a steam train. She remembered Metcalfe taking them to the flat next door. The black woman was there already, lighting candles and humming a strange tune. That was the extent of her clarity. The rest was dreamlike; it was dark, and it was frightening. The man had taken one of the other women into another room. She'd heard arguing, shouting, and then screaming. She remembered blood on her skin, then nothing but nausea and numbness, especially in her lips and face. Her face was still numb. It was dark where she was. Dark and cold. No light penetrated her space. She was hungry and thirsty, and she'd wet her pants. Her jeans clung to her, making her cold and uncomfortable. She wanted to shout for help. She knew she had to shout for help, but she couldn't. The desire to stay in the dream was powerful. It was safer than going back to reality. She wanted to stay asleep where he couldn't reach her, where *she* couldn't come near her. The charming woman, Fabienne, had changed during the evening. She had started out beautiful but had eventually become evil itself.

* * * *

John Metcalfe was semiconscious when the neurologist examined him. His mind was tortured with dark dreams; images of dead people drifted through his brain, screaming at him. They wanted him to let go and join them, but he didn't want to. It was frightening where they were. He tried to cling to the light, but his grip was slipping. Fabienne's voice echoed around his mind. She was talking to him, soothing him, telling him to let go, into the darkness. He was obsessed with her, worshipped her, but he didn't want to go into the dark, not without her. He held on tightly. She began to grow angry, her voice hardening. He couldn't stop her voice growing louder and louder. Then he heard the doctors talking and his mind became still, the images vanished and Fabienne was gone. Reality dragged him back.

'I've never seen a case as bad as this before,' the doctor said. 'It is like variant CJD, but more aggressive. This is Prion's disease.'

'Variant CJD?' Google asked. 'Mad cow disease, but in the human form?'

'Yes, basically,' the doctor said. 'We've scanned him, and his brain is like a sponge. I've given him something to settle him down, but I'll be surprised if he lasts the night to be honest. He shouldn't be alive.'

'Variant CJD is caused by infected cattle being put back in the food chain by being fed to other cattle, right?' Google asked.

'Yes. The cattle were effectively cannibalising other cattle, eating infected brain and bone matter. Prions are a protein found in the brain. They should be straight. The infection is caused by folded prions. It only takes one folded prion in the brain to infect the healthy tissue and it becomes catastrophic quickly. Once the infection takes hold, the brain disintegrates rapidly. Holes appear in the brain matter, hence the reference to spongiform.'

'I understand, thanks,' Google said.

The doctor removed his glasses and cleaned them. 'This man is connected to the murders in the press, isn't he?'

Google nodded.

'"The Hannibal killers", I read in one of them.'

'Yes. He's connected,' Google said.

'They mentioned a young girl,' the doctor said. 'Has she been found?'

'Not yet. We're looking for her.'

'So, he's been eating humans?'

Google nodded again.

'Their brains?'

'In soup,' Google said.

'He ate the wrong one,' the doctor said. 'One of his victims was infected. It is very rare in Europe. Prion's disease used to be common in countries where tribes ate their enemies as a matter of course. It is human CJD; if you eat an infected human, you will develop this very quickly. I think it's nature's way of eliminating humans who eat other humans.' He paused. 'My point is, I think the victim who infected him was probably from the southern hemisphere.'

'Really?' Google said. 'That's very useful, thank you, doctor.' John Metcalfe had eaten an infected human and become infected himself; it had spread through his brain. *Tough titty*, Google thought. *Karma at its finest*. 'Thanks again, doctor.' Google turned to leave, he paused at the door. 'Has he said anything at all?'

'No. Nothing. He isn't likely to – his brain is mush.'

Google closed the door behind him. A uniformed officer was sitting opposite, reading a newspaper; he didn't look up as Google left.

Inside the room, John Metcalfe was trying to decipher what he had heard. It wasn't food poisoning, he was dying. The screaming began again, beneath it Fabienne was encouraging him to let go. He felt the doctor injecting something into his foot. The needle went between his toes. *That's an odd place to inject a patient*. He felt the doctor approaching him. His breath tickled his ear as he spoke.

'Fabienne says to keep you alive as long as possible, John,' the doctor whispered. 'Enjoy your stay. I'll make it as painful as I can.'

CHAPTER 16

Braddick and Laurel climbed the steps to the ninth floor of Stanley House. It was a hive of activity: CSI officers were busily processing the top floor apartments, brick by brick. The sound of JCBs digging up the drains drifted to them from below. Braddick looked over the balcony at the action in the courtyard and immediately wished he hadn't. A wave of nausea hit him, and he held the wall to quell the fear of falling. On the ground, uniformed officers had sectioned off a large part of the courtyard with tape. Canvas hides had been erected to stop the public taking pictures of what they were doing. The landings were busy with onlookers, despite the efforts of the police. Every move was being filmed. It was obvious that human remains had been uncovered in the sewers, but the police had to stop images of their recovery being splashed all over the internet. Braddick watched CSI officers carrying plastic sacks from the tent that covered the open sewer to a fleet of vans. The tower block had become a giant crime scene and a magnet for ghouls. Braddick moved away from the balcony and they both approached Fabienne's flat. Dr Libby met them at the door.

'How's it going?' Braddick asked. They walked slowly down the landing as they talked.

'I feel like we've entered the twilight zone,' Dr Libby sighed.

'We have on this one,' Braddick said.

'Oh, yes. This is not one to share with the grandkids,' Dr Libby agreed.

'Take us through what you have,' Braddick said.

'We're beginning to put the pieces together. John Metcalfe left prints at both crime scenes. Lots of them. We pulled his prints from the kitchen – here, and at the May home,' Dr Libby said. 'His dabs are all over three other flats on this landing, and in the kitchen, bathroom and bedroom at the May home. He's one of your killers.'

'Okay,' Braddick said. 'So far so good.'

'Obviously you know Bruce May left prints in the bedroom at number ninety, so he could be an accomplice.'

'He certainly knows more than he admitted to us,' Laurel said. 'He denied being in that flat or knowing John Metcalfe at all.'

'That is unlikely.'

'Why?' Braddick asked.

'Metcalfe and May left DNA on the mattresses in number eighty-nine and number ninety – blood and semen,' Dr Libby said. 'We haven't got the results for the other flats yet, but I'm guessing we'll find their DNA there, too.'

'May left blood and semen?' Laurel asked, astounded.

'Yes.'

'He's a better liar than I thought.'

'He had you fooled,' Braddick said, 'I was on to him.' She glared at him for a second before realising it was a poke at her. He winked. 'Bruce May is a pathological liar. He's involved in this, without a doubt.'

'Without a doubt,' Dr Libby agreed.

'Okay,' Braddick said. 'We've identified two of the killers, even if one of them is a cabbage. The ACC will be pleased.' He paused. 'Apparently, Metcalfe is a mess.'

'Yes. I've no doubt he is. His brain is infected and from what I've heard, the infection is advanced,' Dr Libby said. 'Prion's.'

'Have you ever seen anyone with prion's disease?' Laurel asked.

'I can't say I have. But I know the only way for a human to contract any kind of spongiform encephalopathies, which is what prion diseases are, is by ingesting meat from an infected mammal. Be that cattle or human.'

'He got what he deserved in my mind,' Braddick said.

'Yes. I agree. It isn't very pleasant. I've seen plenty of people with brain wasting conditions. None of them experience any type of remission. Metcalfe is merely a shell.'

'Good. Let's hope it's painful,' Braddick said. 'Karma working her spell.'

'Perhaps,' Dr Libby said.

'Talk us through what else you've found,' Braddick said.

'Okay. We entered the other apartments. Starting at the far end of the landing, things became increasingly more disturbing as we progressed towards number ninety.'

'Disturbing is not a good word,' Braddick said. They reached the end of the landing and watched as CSI officers entered and exited the flats, carrying equipment in and evidence out.

'Disturbing is the only word I can think of that fits,' Dr Libby said. 'Follow me and see for yourself. I've been trying to find the words to describe this but it's beyond me. We're going to need help understanding it. I don't even know what to write in my notes.'

'Okay,' Braddick said. He sighed and looked at Laurel. 'I'm not sure what to expect any more.'

'Not on this case,' Laurel agreed.

They followed the doctor to the flat next door to Fabienne's; he gestured for them to follow him in. Braddick stepped inside and walked down the hallway. It was the same layout as the other flats. The rooms were empty and the floors bare. It looked like it had been stripped, ready to be decorated.

'It all looks quite normal until you turn the lights out,' Dr Libby said. He turned off the lights and used an ultraviolet torch to illuminate the walls. They were covered in an unrecognisable script that glowed. It ran the length of the room, floor to ceiling. 'I'm no expert on these matters, but this is some form of occult script.'

'Any idea what it means?' Braddick asked.

'Not a clue, I'm afraid. It's gobbledegook to me.'

'And this is in the other apartments too?'

'Yes, but this one seems to be the epicentre. Come and look at this.' He turned on the light and blinked. 'The floor and ceiling in the bedroom are particularly impressive.' They followed him into the main bedroom. He repeated the process. A large circle had been painted on the concrete floor; a nine-angled star had been drawn inside it and occult symbols were scrawled around the circumference. The mirror image of it was daubed on the ceiling. 'I think this place has been used for some kind of ritual.'

'I agree,' Braddick said. 'This explains some of what we've seen. They're a cult?'

'It looks that way,' Dr Libby said. 'There are similar markings in the other flats. Some are less detailed than this. The other bedrooms all have mattresses on the floor that are heavily stained with blood and semen. There are plenty of other samples; I would guess we'll have the results in the next forty-eight hours. Lots of both to match to any suspects.'

'Which plays along with the ritual theory, right?' Laurel asked. 'Did you confirm the identity of the mushrooms you found next door?'

'Psilocybin mushrooms; compressed and concentrated. I would be surprised if anyone ingesting the stuff would remember their name,' Dr Libby said. 'It's very powerful. I'm speculating but, if someone ingested some of it, they would be very susceptible to suggestion. It would certainly lower any inhibitions.'

'Like having group sex with strangers?' Braddick asked.

'Yes, exactly.'

'Somewhere in the melee, it turns to violence,' Laurel said.

'Probably. Come and look at this.' The doctor pointed to the bathroom. 'All the white furniture in the bathrooms have tested positive for blood: the baths, showers and sinks, but especially the toilets. It backs up our theory they were used to dispose of parts of their victims.'

'Incredible,' Braddick said beneath his breath. He shook his head and took a deep breath. 'Any prints in here?'

'Dozens,' the doctor said. 'We'll cross reference them at the lab. I need to farm out some of the testing to another lab, we can't do it all.'

'Okay. I'll get the authorisation.'

'I know you need the results yesterday, but what we have pulled from the drains is going to take us six months to sift through,' Dr Libby said. 'We simply can't keep up.'

'Do what you need to, Dr Libby,' Braddick said, studying the walls. It reminded him of a horror film he'd watched on Netflix. That was fiction, created to frighten and entertain; this was reality, and it had no place in reality. 'Do you know anyone who can decipher this script to give us an idea of what we're dealing with?'

'I am one step ahead of you there,' Dr Libby said. 'I have called an author colleague of mine to come and have a look. He will be able to help.'

'An author?' Braddick wasn't sure who would be an expert on such matters, probably someone at Netflix.

'Yes. He's written a few books on the occult.'

'Do you think he's ever come across anything like this?' Braddick asked.

'I don't know. I've never read his books,' Dr Libby said. 'He knows a lot more than I do on the subject.'

'Great. I'm willing to give anything a go. When will he be here?' Braddick asked, checking his watch.

'He's on his way,' Dr Libby said. 'He lives in the city so he shouldn't be long.'

'This artwork is incredibly detailed. It would have taken a long time to paint all this. Victoria May must have known what was going on here,' Braddick said.

'It can't be seen with the naked eye in daylight,' Dr Libby said. 'She may not have seen it.'

'What did they use to do this?' Laurel asked.

'A type of luminous paint. If it is exposed to light it will glow in the dark for a while. It is readily available, but we should be able to identify what type it is once we've analysed it.' Dr Libby waved his hand over the circle. 'We'll be able to narrow down where it was purchased. It might help.'

'Probably from the internet,' Laurel said. 'If it is, there'll be a paper trail.'

'I'm guessing the Mays paid for it,' Braddick said.

'Definitely,' Laurel agreed. 'Victoria didn't just know what was going on here, she was involved. How else would they have access to all the flats on this landing?'

'Is there any sign of forced entry?' Braddick asked.

'No,' Dr Libby said.

'We need to compile a list of her properties and search them all,' Braddick said. 'If she let this go on here, she may have let it happen elsewhere.'

'I'll give Google a call,' Laurel said. 'Do you want warrants for them all?'

'Yes. We need to search everywhere she owned but start with the empty ones.'

Braddick looked around and shook his head. The image of a group of people, high on hallucinogenic mushrooms, sitting in the dark chanting and fornicating with each other, drifted through his mind. That was strange enough, but at what point had it turned to murder? How did it reach the point where someone was killed, dismembered, eaten, their bodies disposed of down a toilet? What kind of twisted mind enjoyed such an act and how difficult must it be to find like-minded people to enjoy it with?

'Dr Libby,' a uniformed officer called from the front door. 'There's a Malcolm Baines asking for you at the cordon. He says you're expecting him.'

'Yes. Let him through, please,' Dr Libby said. 'You might get some insight from him into what this is all about. He knows what he's talking about.'

'I hope so,' Braddick said. He studied the nine-angled star and frowned. It made no sense to him. 'This is what we were missing, Laurel. Magic mushrooms and a pile of mumbo-jumbo.'

'They're ritual killings. It explains the theatre.'

'It fits,' Braddick said. The doctor approached with a shaven-headed man who looked uncomfortable in his forensic suit. 'You must be Mr Baines. Thank you for coming so quickly.'

'Please, call me Malcolm,' he said, shaking Braddick's hand. 'I'm happy to help. What is it you want me to look at?'

'We are investigating a series of murders,' Braddick said, purposely vague. 'During the search of these flats we've uncovered this script.'

'I'll turn off the lights so you can see what we're looking at,' Dr Libby said. He switched on the ultraviolet torch and switched off the lights. The walls glowed with the luminous script. There was silence while Malcolm walked around the room. He studied it, concentration on his face. There was an eerie glow to the script. He spent a few minutes reading the symbols, nodding, frowning and shaking his head. After a while, the doctor spoke. 'Does it mean anything to you?'

'Yes,' Malcolm said, nodding. 'This is script taken from the writings of a cult known as the Order of Nine Angels – the circular emblem on the floor is their mark.'

'Nine Angels?' Braddick said, none the wiser.

'Yes,' Malcolm said. 'That wall is predominantly covered with their writings, but these marks over here are something completely different.'

'Different how?' Dr Libby asked.

'These are symbols used in voodoo ceremonies, but they're not African,' Malcolm said. 'I think they're from the Caribbean – I've seen this type of script in books written in Haiti.'

'Haiti? Are you sure?' Braddick asked. Laurel looked at him, surprised.

'As sure as I can be. Does that fit with what you know already?' Malcolm asked.

'The tenant of the flat next door, Fabienne Wilder, was a Haitian orphan,' Braddick said.

'Fabienne is a very popular name there. That can't be a coincidence,' Malcolm said.

'No, it can't,' Braddick agreed. 'Tell me more about voodoo. What does the script say?'

'Voodoo is revered there and in Africa,' Malcolm said. 'The practitioners are feared, not respected,' he emphasised. 'Feared. They can terrorise entire communities with threats and curses.'

'Show Malcolm the bones you found,' Dr Libby said.

Braddick took his phone from his pocket and opened a photograph. 'Look at this. Can you tell me what it is?'

Malcolm looked at the image and glanced at Dr Libby.

'They're chicken bones fastened together with horsehair,' Dr Libby said.

'Where did you find this?' Malcolm asked, concerned.

'Someone left it on my path,' Braddick said. 'They knocked on the door and ran away.'

'It's a hex,' Malcolm said. Braddick frowned.

'Someone is wishing you bad luck,' Laurel said.

'Oh, no,' Malcolm said. 'It's much more than that.'

'What do you mean?' Braddick asked.

'This type of hex is a mark,' Malcolm explained. 'It's like a wanted poster from the Wild West. Someone has marked you.'

'For what?' Braddick asked.

'They want you dead, I'm afraid.'

'They'll have to get in the queue,' Braddick said, smiling. 'There's a few in front of them.'

'I told you it was bad luck,' Laurel said. She smiled but there was concern in her eyes.

'They're too late,' Braddick said, sarcastically. 'If I didn't have bad luck, I would have no luck at all.'

'Adds up with the voodoo mumbo-jumbo,' Laurel said. Malcolm smiled uncomfortably. 'Sorry. No offence meant, Malcolm.'

'None taken. I study them and others like them. That doesn't mean I believe in it.' Malcolm pointed to the wall. 'This "mumbo-jumbo", as you put it, is a very powerful way of controlling those who believe in its power. It instils fear in its followers.' Malcolm shrugged. 'Like most religions, it's about controlling the masses.' He crossed the room. 'Some of the writings on the other wall are from other tranches of satanism,' Malcom explained. 'I can recognise work from at least three other sects on there, but the main thrust of the message is from the Niners. Sorry, that's what people in my business call the Nine Angels.'

'No problem. Tell me about them,' Braddick said.

'Okay. They began as the Temple of Set in the sixties, and faded away into obscurity, returning in the eighties as the Nine Angles.'

'Angles?' Braddick said. 'Not Angels?'

'Yes, they started as the Nine Angles. You see the nine-angled star, in the circle?'

'Yes. What does it mean?'

'That's where their name comes from. They began as the Nine Angles, like the star, you see?'

'Yes,' Braddick said.

'It comes from the Baha'i faith and represents the manipulation of the human mind. They call it mankind's last chance.'

'Last chance at what?'

'Surviving as a species.'

'Baha'i, what is that?' Laurel asked.

'It is the name of the beast: Satan,' Malcolm said. Braddick and Laurel stayed quiet, their scepticism clear. They looked at each other. 'The symbol has been taken by the darker faiths as an emblem of power and control.'

'Controlling what?' Braddick asked.

'Their followers, their associates, and each other,' Malcolm said. 'Initiations and certain rituals would be carried out around the circle. Their teaching would be recited here. Probably chanted repetitively until they'd memorised it. Usually, hallucinogenic drugs are used, and the congregation are encouraged to copulate.'

'Congregation?' Braddick said. 'You make it sound like a church.'

'That is what this is,' Malcolm said. 'This is a place of worship. The readings on the walls would be recited and memorised as if it were the Bible.'

'Like brainwashing?' Laurel asked.

'Exactly like that,' Malcom said. 'The Nine Angles began as a right-wing political group, who had a penchant for ritual sex. It was hijacked by members with a darker agenda. There was a split in the late nineties and the Angel sect was formed.'

'Then what?' Braddick said. 'What exactly are they?'

'They are a very powerful, dangerous sect,' Malcolm replied. 'Much more extreme than they were before the split.'

'You said there was a split in the group, a split over what?' Braddick asked.

'The original followers were less fanatical about true satanism and were overwhelmed by a more violent wing of the group. The founder members left or were forced out. Some of them died in mysterious circumstances and several vanished. No one took their deaths and disappearances seriously,' Malcolm explained. 'Satanism wasn't taken seriously at all back then.'

'I can understand that it had followers in the seventies,' Dr Libby said. 'It was almost trendy to be linked to satanic groups back then. No one took them seriously.'

'The idea of satanic cults is *still* not taken seriously,' Malcolm said. 'I can tell by the expression on your face that you think this is hocus-pocus.' Braddick shrugged and smiled, embarrassed. 'They are very real. Look around you. You said people have died here?'

'Yes. They have.' Braddick rubbed the stubble on his face, feeling awkward.

'What more evidence do you need?' Malcolm asked. 'They're as serious about this as you are. I know you're taking the murders seriously. So are they.'

'Okay, I understand what you're saying. So, we know who they are. What else can you tell us about them?' Braddick asked.

'I have studied them for decades, but I'm not sure how much would be relevant to your investigation,' Malcolm said. 'I've written two books about them. How long have you got?'

'As long as it takes,' Braddick said. 'We need some insight into how they operate and what this is all about.'

'I'm not sure where to begin. We could be here for weeks,' Malcolm said.

'Give us an abridged version,' Braddick said.

'Okay. I'll do my best. Obviously, they're a satanic cult. There are lots of fake Satanists out there, but the Niners are the real thing. They've dozens of websites run by their followers and they're very intense.'

'They have websites?' Braddick was astounded.

'Yes. Dozens of them.'

'I don't know why I'm surprised,' Braddick said. 'I bet they have a Facebook page?' he added sarcastically.

'There are dozens of them too,' Malcolm said.

'Twitter?' Laurel asked.

'Yes. Their social media footprint is comprehensive, although the Niners are not a centralised group with a structure. It's more of a collection of smaller groups with a similar interest in the darker side of religion.'

'Religion,' Braddick repeated. 'I'm struggling to call it that.'

'That is exactly what it is,' Malcolm explained. 'There's no other name to describe them. Cult, sect, faction, group – none of them apply to the Niners. They're a religion like any other, except theirs is to worship evil, not good.'

'Okay, I get the point. Get the team to go through the information available on them on the internet, please,' Braddick said to Laurel.

'Tell them to google, O9A,' Malcolm said. 'You will be amazed at what comes up.'

'O9A?'

'Yes… but tell them not to search it from their personal devices. They monitor who looks at their sites, especially if the portals are opened.'

Braddick frowned.

'They have hidden doors in their websites. When they're opened, they get a notification and they can see the IP address of the device searching their material. They're very paranoid about people searching their information and they're very advanced at using software.'

'Okay,' she said, 'I'll warn them.' Laurel moved away to make the call.

'Please, go on,' Braddick said.

'I'm not sure what to tell you that is relevant,' Malcolm said.

'Forget the history for now,' Braddick said, 'what are they doing here, in this building?'

'I'll tell you what I can see on the walls. Stop me if there's anything you don't understand.'

'Okay.'

'The markings in this room are essentially a calendar,' Malcolm said. 'Starting with January here, going all the way to December over there. This section at the bottom marks the days of ritual for each month. This is January, for instance, January the seventh is St Winebald's day, which should be celebrated with the sacrifice of a male.'

'Sacrifice? And they specify what sex the victim should be?'

'Yes. Many of their calendars even specify what age group the sacrifice should be. You'll see them if you look online. They're very detailed.'

'This is difficult to fathom.'

'Each religious day has its own intricacies, it's as complicated as any biblical celebration and just as difficult to believe,' Malcolm said. 'Walking on water, parting the Red Sea with a staff, Noah's Ark, Jesus rising from the dead?'

'What's your point?'

'Do you believe they happened?' Malcolm asked, eyebrows raised.

'Not personally,' Braddick said.

'Are they easy to *fathom*, as you put it?'

'Not if you put it like that,' Braddick said. 'If they're out there following these calendars, how are they getting away with killing people?'

'During some research, I found that they target people no one will miss. Also, their members are encouraged to offer themselves up for sacrifice. If they allow the group to sacrifice them, they carry power and kudos into the next life,' Malcom explained.

'Like a suicide bomber,' Braddick muttered.

'Exactly the same. Brainwashing desperate or vulnerable people has been happening since the dawn of time, although, I have my own opinion on why the Niners actually encourage their members to do that.'

'Which is?'

'Convincing a volunteer to be murdered gives them time to manage their disappearance from society, so no one makes too much noise when they're gone,' Malcolm said. 'Snatching people from the streets attracts attention, so if they promise their followers a reward in the afterlife, they have a never-ending queue of martyrs for their rituals.'

'How convenient,' Laurel said.

'These are clever people who manipulate weaker members to do their bidding,' Malcolm explained.

'What else is written there?' Braddick asked, shaking his head.

'January twentieth to the twenty-seventh is the time to select a victim for sacrifice on February second, which is Candlemas.' Malcolm looked at the detectives, who appeared too stunned to speak. 'Candlemas is a blood and sexual ritual. Some rituals are just blood, some sexual, some both.'

'For fuck's sake,' Braddick said. 'Do these nutcases actually believe in this?'

'Oh, yes, very much,' Malcolm replied. 'It would be a mistake to think they're nutcases. They absolutely believe in the dark side of religion and you would be amazed at how many followers they have.'

'Do any of these rituals involve eating their victims?' Laurel asked.

'Yes, it says here,' Malcolm said, pointing to the script on the wall. 'March the first, the festival of St Eichatadt, should be marked by drinking the blood and eating the flesh of a sacrifice to honour the demons.' Braddick and Laurel listened intently.

'They're honouring demons,' Braddick said, rolling his eyes.

'I know it sounds unbelievable, but their calendar is important to them.'

'How many dates are there like that?' Braddick asked.

'Blood rituals?'

'Yes.'

'There are approximately thirty-eight blood sacrifice dates in the satanic calendar that would entail eating the victim,' Malcolm explained. 'I have to stress that most satanic groups are all about sex. They use animals instead of humans for blood rituals – sheep, goats, pigs and the like.' He paused. 'Only the real hardcore groups, like the Niners, go to the extent of what you're dealing with here.'

'Satanic-light,' Laurel said, sarcastically.

'I can understand your scepticism,' Malcolm said. 'Every religion has its extremists – Muslims, Catholics, Protestants, Jews all have their militants, that's simple to understand, isn't it?' Laurel nodded. 'The same rules apply on the opposition bench.'

'This is madness. There are thirty-eight blood rituals?' Braddick asked.

'Approximately.'

'Why approximately?'

'Some nexions take it more literally than others,' Malcolm said. He saw the detectives frowning. 'Sorry. A nexion is what they call their groups. Each one is independent and, while there's no central hierarchy, kudos is given to those who live their way.'

'Which is?'

'What you're looking at, right now. Their websites are very graphic. They're essentially guides about how they should live – satanic worship for dummies, if you like.' Malcolm studied the script around the calendar. 'This particular group are far from dummies. They appear to take this very seriously. They take it very seriously indeed.'

'Who is at the centre of this group?' Braddick asked.

'There is nothing here to identify her.'

'Her?' Laurel asked.

'Yes. The dominant character will be a woman.'

'Why are you so sure it's a woman?'

'Without sounding completely mad,' Malcolm said, 'their focus is a female goddess called Baphomet. Each nexion has a female at its centre who is trying to become her; the more evil acts they witness, the closer to her they become.'

'I don't get it,' Laurel said.

'There are levels within the religion,' Malcolm said. 'Like Scientology. The Scientologists' ultimate goal is to reach a level called The Clear. Each level achieved takes them closer to The Clear.'

'Okay. I can follow that,' Laurel said.

'The Niners have levels too, like the layers in an onion. Newer members are the outer layers and will not be allowed to attend the blood sacrifices until they can be trusted. Only the core layers are completely trustworthy.' He shrugged. 'They have to progress one level at a time. I know it sounds like madness, but that's their aim. Their websites will tell you the same thing.'

'We're not dealing with sane people here, are we?' Braddick asked, shaking his head. 'They can't be sane to believe this.'

'Plenty of people believe that Jesus turned water into wine, that his mother was a virgin, and that God made the universe in seven days,' Malcolm said. 'They're not all insane, are they?'

'No,' Braddick said.

'But you don't believe any of those things happened, do you?' Malcolm asked.

'No, of course not. This is different. They're killing people,' Braddick said, pointing to the circle.

'The mainstream religions on the planet kill hundreds of people every day,' Malcolm said. 'Especially people who disagree with them or worship something else.'

'I'm struggling with this,' Braddick said.

'During the course of my research, I have met judges, senior police officers, teachers, lawyers, bankers and sportsmen who are followers of the left-hand path. Some believe more than others, obviously, but be in no doubt that they do believe. It would be a mistake to think you are looking for a bunch of lunatics dancing under a full moon dressed in bedsheets.'

'Can I ask you to take a look at what has been written in the other apartments and see if there is anything you can give me that may help to identify who is involved, or where they might be now?' Braddick said.

'Of course,' Malcolm said. 'I'll write down anything I think is useful to your investigation. On one condition.' Braddick looked surprised, his eyebrows raised as Malcom continued. 'These groups are very dangerous, and they communicate with each other on the dark web, or in chatrooms on their websites. I've been keeping a low profile since my first book on the subject. I don't want my name mentioned or written down on anything. The Niners hate journalists, writers or anyone who tries to expose them. They post the identity of anyone who talks about them on their websites and make them targets. Like your hex,' He shrugged. 'I don't want to be more of a target than I am already.'

'Okay,' Braddick said. 'I understand. Everything about this case is being kept under wraps, don't worry.'

'Under wraps? I think it is far from under wraps. Not from the headlines I've read,' Malcolm said, smiling. 'I'll take a look at the other rooms in this flat and then move along the landing. I'll let you know what I find.'

'Thank you. You've been a great help,' Dr Libby said.

'I'm sorry if we seem reluctant to accept what you're telling us,' Braddick said. 'It is difficult to take in.'

'I understand,' Malcolm said, leaving the room. They were quiet for a moment when he'd left.

'Was that helpful or not?' Dr Libby asked.

'Very,' Braddick said. 'At least we have a motive, it answers a lot of questions but not all of them.'

'What are you thinking?' Laurel asked.

'I'm not buying into this,' Braddick said, gesturing to the script. 'There's something missing. I can't put my finger on it, but something is bugging me.'

'At least we have something solid to go on,' Laurel said. 'Although I don't think the ACC will want to hear that we're hunting a cult.'

'That isn't going to go down well,' Dr Libby said, looking at the script again.

'These people are dangerous, aren't they?' Laurel said. Braddick and Dr Libby remained quiet. 'Mumbo-jumbo or not, I feel a little bit scared now.'

'It changes the perspective of the investigation,' Braddick said.

'It has certainly made me look at things differently,' Laurel said.

'What do you mean?' Braddick asked.

'We're not just looking for two people anymore, are we?' she said.

* * * *

On the seventh floor, beneath the stairwell, Maxine was trying to sleep. The unwholesome odour of the excavations below drifted up, making her feel queasy. Rotting flesh and excrement, not a pleasant mixture; there would never be a fragrance called Decomposition. The sound of chatter echoed from the walls, making it difficult to settle. Policemen, technicians, neighbours, journalists and ghouls had infested the tower block and their voices had become a monotonous drone, climbing the stairwells, reverberating from the concrete. Resting had become impossible since the murders had been uncovered.

Maxine tried to sleep during daylight hours, when it was safe to drift off without the fear of being attacked, robbed or raped. Sexual assault was on the increase amongst the homeless. The darkness of night brought fear and uncertainty with it. It was better to be awake and aware of what was going on when night came. Those who sleep on the streets always sleep with one eye open – that's what she told any newbies she met. People came and went on the streets. For most, it was a temporary state. They had hit rock bottom for whatever reason. Their lives had spiralled out of control and they dropped out of society for a while. For others, it was a permanent lifestyle. There was no way back for them. They would see out their days on the streets, until they became too old and sick to function anymore or died underneath their cardboard shelter where no one knew their name. Each day was an age. Hunger and thirst were constant companions. Fear and exhaustion weighed them down. The uncertainty was relentless. There was no peace of mind. That was why so many self-medicated with alcohol and drugs. Finding somewhere safe and dry to sleep was the key to survival and the tower block had been kind to her, until now. She had always felt secure under the stairs but not anymore. The murders had changed the dynamic of the building and tiredness was seeping into her bones. Desperation saturated her soul. She needed to sleep.

Maxine turned to face the wall and closed her eyes. She pulled her sleeping bag over her head to muffle the noise and keep out the cold air. An ice-cold draft touched her skin, making her shiver. It spread through her like a virus through a crowd. She felt a terrible sadness touch her inside, so deep and dark that a tear ran from the corner of her eye. A sense of dread made her curl up inside her sleeping bag and she hugged her knees. Maxine began to sob like a baby, crying so hard she could hardly draw breath, but she had no idea what was making her so sad. The faces of all the people she had loved and lost visited her waking thoughts: her parents, grandparents, cousins, aunties, uncles, siblings; and then her husband was there, smiling at her. His face was healthy and fresh, a sparkle in his eyes, belying the cancer that raged inside him. The expression on his face changed. He looked frightened, terrified. Then he was dying, gaunt, yellow-skinned; thinning lips, agony in his eyes. He opened his mouth and black slurry ran from the corners down his chin, just as it had done at the moment of his death. All the pain of his death returned to her tenfold. The grief she felt was debilitating. Desperation gripped her thoughts.

From the corner of the stairwell, dark eyes watched Maxine as her shivering became worse. Her teeth were chattering, and her fingers trembled. She felt bitterly cold, colder than she had ever been, yet it was daytime. Maxine rolled away from the wall and clambered out of her bedding. She shuffled towards the landing wall and looked over the edge. The air was warmer there, comforting and bright. She moved closer, leaning into the void, soaking up the warmth. The darkness in her mind began to shift. She looked around for someone to talk to. The urge to converse with another human was overwhelming. She felt alone and frightened. It was unexplainable yet terrifyingly real. Maxine closed her eyes and tilted her face skyward, searching for the warmth of the sun. It felt good, drove the fear away a little. She opened her eyes and saw young Val on the landing opposite. Val was waving, pointing to something behind Maxine.

Strong hands gripped her ankles and lifted her from the landing. She felt herself being thrown into the void. Her scream was blood-curdling, high-pitched and desperate. Her arms and legs flailed frantically in the air. The fall from the eighth floor to the concrete seemed to take an age. She hit the ground with catastrophic force. The tower block fell silent for a few moments, until a woman who had seen her fall started screaming. Within seconds, several others had joined her. Their voices echoed across the block.

CHAPTER 17

Laurel reached the courtyard and pushed her way through a throng of onlookers. Uniformed officers were holding back the crowd. She showed her warrant card and ducked beneath their arms. The mangled body of the jumper was surrounded by CSI officers and uniformed policemen. Laurel jogged across the yard towards them.

'Let me through,' Laurel said, gasping for breath. The officers stepped back to let her see the body. Maxine was twisted and broken, her eyes staring accusingly at a point somewhere above her. 'Did anyone see what happened?'

'That lady over there, sarge,' a uniformed officer said. 'She said she saw her leaning over the balcony wall and then she fell.'

'People don't just fall from a building.' Laurel looked up and shook her head. She wondered how frightened she must have been. 'They either jump, or they're pushed.'

'Do you know her?'

'She's a witness,' Laurel said. 'Her name is Maxine. She's the one who called this in.' She looked along the landings above but there was no one there. 'Send a couple of officers up both stairwells. Tell them to question anyone who looks like they're in a hurry. Someone else must have seen what happened.'

'Yes, sarge,' the officer said, moving away. He summoned three other constables and they split into two and headed for the stairwells. From the corner of her eye, Laurel thought she'd seen someone on the ninth floor, wearing a baseball cap, but when she focused on the balcony it was empty. She put it down to a trick of the light.

CHAPTER 18

Bruce May got off a train at Betws-y-coed station. It was cold and wet, and the taxi rank was deserted. The cobbled street looked like the skin of a giant black reptile: wet and slithery. Yellow light reflected in it and leaves tumbled in the wind. He walked towards the streetlights in the distance, passing climbing gear and souvenir shops that were closed and in darkness. Some of them looked closed for the winter, their window displays gone. He could hear the waterfalls roaring in the distance. It was a calming sound in a chaotic world.

Fifteen minutes later he reached the centre of the village and headed to a big hotel, The Royal Oak. It was a three-storey Victorian building with a grand facade to the front. A conservatory, which housed a busy bar-restaurant, had been attached to the rear. The lights drew him like a moth to a flame. As he approached, he could hear the buzz of people talking, laughing and joking and music playing. The conservatory windows were steamed up – the bar was packed with climbers and outdoor types. He picked up the pace, eager to be inside, craving the light and warmth and the sound of people enjoying life. He'd been in the dark too long. The door opened as he approached and a group of men dressed in fleeces and Gortex walked out, laughing raucously. Bruce stepped inside and headed for the bar; he ordered a double Grouse, which he gulped down in one before he'd paid for it. He wiped his lips and ordered another. The burning liquid warmed the cockles and settled his troubled mind a little. He asked the barman for a cab and tucked away four more double whiskies while he waited. It took forty-five minutes for it to arrive and he was feeling tipsy, his nerves jangling as he climbed inside. Victoria's death hadn't caught up with him yet. He was pretending it hadn't happened. His desire to be with Fabienne dwarfed everything, including his grief. He would feel better when he saw her. Everything he had done for the last two years had been to endear himself to her. He had never wanted anyone so much in his life. Neither had Victoria, and that had driven the wedge between them. In the end, Victoria resented him. She became reckless in her attempts to impress Fabienne. He wondered if her ultimate sacrifice was worth it. Only Victoria would know.

The taxi driver was sullen and spent most of the journey talking on hands-free in Welsh. Bruce wasn't bothered; he wasn't in the mood to have a conversation. When they reached the Ogwyn Valley, the taxi turned off the main road and drove up the track to the cottage. Potholes made the ride bumpy and uncomfortable. The car's headlights illuminated the way, making the driving rain look like icicles spearing towards the windscreen. The silhouette of a rocky outcrop appeared in the distance and the bare branches of straggly trees waved in the wind like bony fingers. Mount Tryfan loomed above him, its colossal mass black against the dark sky. Bruce told the driver to drop him off, telling him he would walk the rest of the way. He climbed out of the cab and fastened his coat against the howling wind. The taxi turned around and headed back to the main road. Bruce watched it weave down the valley towards Betws-y-coed. Something niggled in his mind. Something told him to run. His knees began to tremble. He couldn't decide if it was fear or the cold, or something much worse.

Bruce fastened his coat and trudged along the track, thinking of days gone by when Victoria was still in love with him. The days before Fabienne. They were good days and he yearned for them, despite his desire for Fabienne. His desire for her was like heroin to an addict. It was in his mind every waking second, demanding to be satiated. The craving never waned. He missed the comfortable life they had shared before the burning passion devoured everything they had.

As he turned the corner into the yard, the cottage came into view. There was a flickering light downstairs. His heart beat faster. Fabienne had lit the fire. It would be nice and warm by now. She had been there a few hours at least. He spotted the Porsche and walked towards it. The driver's door had been left ajar and the interior light was on. He cursed beneath his breath. He loved that car; the rain would have soaked the carpets. Fabienne must have rushed inside out of the rainstorm and forgotten to close the door properly, the wind had probably blown it open again. He peered through the rain at the cottage but couldn't see any sign of Fabienne. In his heart, he wished he could see her face, smiling through the window, blowing kisses and waving, pleased to see him arrive. The flames danced and flickered, casting an orange glow on the yard, but Fabienne didn't appear. He began to feel uneasy about the situation. Something felt wrong. Very wrong.

Bruce ran to the Porsche and looked inside. There was a puddle of rainwater in the footwell. He noticed the keys were still in the ignition and he swore as he took them out, locking the car before putting them in his pocket. The boot was half open, too. He pressed it closed with both hands, pulled his coat over his head and ran to the cottage. The door was unlocked. He stepped inside, excited to see Fabienne's face. He was desperate to hear her voice, calming him, reassuring him that everything would be alright. No matter how dark things were, she made him feel safe. She was part of the darkness. It feared her.

The smell of burning flesh hit him like a sledgehammer. His senses were suddenly ultra-aware. The air was thick with the sickly-sweet odour. He was confused at first, but his confusion quickly turned to fear.

'Fabienne,' he called. 'What the hell are you doing?'

The fire was burning fiercely, stacked with logs and coal it crackled and snapped. A noise from the kitchen grabbed his attention so he walked down the narrow corridor to the rear of the cottage and switched on the light. The kitchen was empty. A saucepan was bubbling on a small gas cooker, the blue flame hissed beneath it. The scent of garlic and meat drifted to him. He frowned, angry and scared.

'Fabienne,' he called as he approached the stove. His hands were shaking. There was no reply. A gloopy liquid simmered in the pan; the powerful smell that exuded from it made him gag. 'Fabienne!' he called, louder this time. 'What the hell are you doing?'

He turned off the gas and removed the pan from the heat, turning his head away from the smell. His stomach was performing somersaults. He had an idea what was in the pan, but he didn't want to think about it. Surely Fabienne wouldn't have gone that far in his house, he thought. He had heard whispers from others on the periphery of the group about what went on at some of the rituals, where only the members of the inner circle were invited. The blood rituals were only for the hardcore, handpicked by Fabienne. He had heard the rumours and dismissed them as exaggeration. Victoria wouldn't talk to him about them. She'd shut him out as if he couldn't be trusted. He was her husband, yet she wouldn't betray Fabienne to him. Some of the associates were desperate to be invited to the blood rituals but he had no interest in their madness. He had enjoyed the sexual rituals but had no desire to progress. The truth was, he didn't believe; he desired, but he didn't truly believe. Victoria had transgressed through the levels and look what they had done to her. Her fascination with Fabienne and the occult had been their ruin. They had lost everything, including her soul.

'Fabienne!' he shouted, louder this time. He felt confused and alone, like an abandoned child. 'Fabienne! Where are you?'

There was no reply.

'What the hell is going on, Fabienne?' he shouted. 'Answer me!'

There was nothing but the ticking of the clock and the crackle of the fire. He walked from the kitchen into the living room and looked at the flames. The smell of burning flesh was intense. He looked into the flickering fire – logs and coal were fused together around something that didn't belong there. A large bone, with charred flesh attached, sizzled amongst the coals. He noticed a bin bag on the hearth and lifted the flap to peer inside. The bag tumbled forward, spilling the contents. Four fingers and a thumb protruded from inside. He recognised the rings on the fingers. It was Victoria's hand. He staggered backwards in shock. The whisky was coursing through his veins. Bile rose in his gullet and he tripped over a low coffee table, cracking his head on the stone wall. He felt blood running from his scalp as unconsciousness swept over him.

CHAPTER 19

The Major Investigation Team was gathering for an update. Half the desks were occupied, half were empty; the empty desks were piled high with files. A lot of the detectives were out following leads. Braddick was tired and he rubbed his eyes, they felt gritty. He slurped from a cup of strong coffee and checked his notes. It was getting late; the city's streetlights glinted on the dark surface of the river, making it impossible to see where land ended, and the water began. The ACC had been in his office for the entire day, besieged by the press, which was so far the only blessing in the case; the story was huge, nationally and internationally. Their investigation had snowballed, from the grisly discovery of a head in a pan, to the hunt for multiple accessories to murder and the almost impossible task of identifying the victims. The information gleaned from studying the online footprint of the Niners motivated his team further. The groups were highly intelligent, highly focused individuals, who had the ability to attract and manipulate weaker-minded people. Braddick had initially pigeonholed them as lunatics, but he realised they were anything but. Their research had also proved they were well established and not a new phenomenon. Society didn't understand them, or acknowledge them, therefore, they didn't exist.

'I can't find anything about Maxine,' Laurel said, looking at her laptop. 'I don't even know if that's her real name. There were over one hundred women called Maxine reported missing in the last ten years.'

'How do you lose a hundred people with the name Maxine?' Braddick said. 'Don't get involved, Laurel. It will bend your brain. The answers are not online.'

'I know,' Laurel said. 'I just think it's really sad.'

'It is really sad, but you can't change what she did. She made a choice to end her life, there and then.'

'It's hard to imagine being in such a dark place.'

'It can't be fun living in a stairwell,' Braddick said. 'There's a reason she was there in the first place, remember that. You can't shoulder the blame because you spoke to her. She could have jumped at any time.'

'I know,' Laurel said, despite her gut-feeling that Maxine wasn't the jumping type. 'I just felt like I'd connected. Trying to find her family feels like right thing to do.'

'What makes you think there is a family, or that they will want to know?' Braddick asked. Laurel frowned at him. 'All I'm saying is there's a reason she chose not to be with them. If there is anyone, Maxine decided not to be with them. She chose solitude for a reason.'

'Maybe, maybe not,' Laurel said. 'No harm in looking.'

'She might be in the system,' Braddick said. 'Wait for forensics.' Laurel nodded her head and carried on her search. Braddick wondered if she had heard a word he'd said. If she had, she'd chosen not to listen. Becoming a mother had made her a more caring individual, he thought, nothing wrong with that.

'Ready when you are, guv,' Google said, interrupting his thoughts.

'Carry on,' Braddick said, sipping his coffee. He watched the screens as Google prepared to start the briefing.

Google brought up a map of the north-west and north Wales, which showed the position of thirteen properties owned by Victoria May. They were in geographical clusters of two or three, close together.

'These are the properties owned by the Mays,' Google said, changing the image. Immediately, ten locations were removed from the list. 'Three of them are empty, so we've started with them. Two of the empty properties are in the city and have already been checked over by uniform, which leaves this one here, in Snowdonia. We have a warrant and North Wales Police are dispatching units as we speak.'

'Do we have a timescale for NWP arriving there?' Braddick asked.

'They'll be there within the hour,' Google said, glancing at his watch.

'Good.'

'We're also going to search John Metcalfe's business property tonight. There may be something there to help us identify other members of this group.'

'Are we hoping to catch a break and find someone holing up in one of them?' a young detective asked.

'We don't know until we get there. We do know that John Metcalfe and Bruce May were involved at both crime scenes. Finding out exactly what their roles are is paramount, but, Malcolm Baines, an expert on the occult, thinks everything they have done was orchestrated by a woman,' Google said. The images of Fabienne Wilder and Victoria May appeared on the screens. 'What was May's involvement? We don't think she was just an innocent victim. We have to assume Fabienne is the leader. She is the key.' Whispers of opinion spread through the gathering. Google continued. 'Witnesses and neighbours at Stanley House all put Wilder living at number ninety, yet we have found no forensics to support that. We need to locate her.' The image changed again to a social security application. It was a screenshot of an online questionnaire. 'Information from the appeal told us that Wilder applied for benefits last year using the name Fiona Oruche. It might not be the only alias she has used, but let's focus our efforts on this name for now.'

The photograph of a young black male appeared, next to him was Fabienne Wilder. Braddick was drawn to her eyes. They were almost hypnotic. The man next to her looked mesmerised by her.

'Fiona Oruche is the name she used seven years ago when this man, Simon Hall, befriended her. He contracted a brain virus and died. His mother says Oruche had encouraged him to kill and eat a woman the year before in Manchester.' Google looked at Miles and gestured for him to add some details.

'When I pressed Simon Hall's mother, she came up short of details, so we can't check if there actually was a female victim or not,' Miles said. 'She admits her son was losing his grip on reality at the time, but she is convinced he was telling the truth.'

'Hall's medical records show the neurologists didn't test for prion's disease, but Dr Libby thinks, in all probability, it's what killed him; the same disease that infected John Metcalfe.' Google pointed to the image of Fabienne. 'We need to get GMP to help us search for anything linked to Fiona Oruche, Simon Hall or Fabienne Wilder in Manchester. Miles, can you put your team on the Manchester connection?'

'Yes, sarge,' Miles said.

Braddick stood up and the screen changed. The images of three arrest records appeared. The women in the photographs looked downtrodden and despondent. Their eyes belonged to women who had struggled every day to survive. They were clearly images from the custody suite.

'Forensics have matched prints taken from number eighty-nine, Stanley House, to these three women: Sara Larkin, Melissa Walker and Maggie Bennet. They all have form for soliciting, drugs, assault and shoplifting. We need to trace them.' Braddick paused. 'Speak to vice and find them. We need to talk to them to find out what went on in those flats.'

'Do you think they'll talk, guv?' Miles asked.

'The chances are they were paid to take part in ritual sex acts with whoever attended. If we handle them with care, they may be inclined to tell us something about the people that attended. If they witnessed anything more than just sex for cash, we need to know about it. They could be witnesses. Ian, put your team on finding them, please.'

'Yes, guv.'

'Make sure they know we're not interested in them or they'll go underground.'

'Guv.'

'We'll recap at eight o'clock tomorrow morning,' Braddick said, clapping his hands together. 'Those of you who aren't involved in the Metcalfe search, get yourselves home and get some rest. See you bright and early tomorrow.' He looked at Laurel. 'That includes you, sergeant. Go home and see Aimee before she forgets who her mother is.'

'Thanks, guv,' she said, scrabbling into her coat. 'You're a good one. Let me know if you find anything juicy.'

'Juicy?' Braddick said. 'I'm not sure I want to find anything juicy. This case is weird enough.'

'Funny man,' she said, walking away. 'You know what I mean.'

'See you in the morning,' Braddick said. He had no intention of disturbing her at home, juicy evidence or not.

* * * *

Braddick parked the Evoque across the road from Metcalfe Brothers Limited. It was a two-storey building with a corrugated roof, and car parks to the front and rear. The plot was surrounded by a high security wall. The top of the wall was encrusted with broken glass, jagged shards stood sharp and threatening, glinting in the streetlight. The lampposts were wrapped with barbed wire to discourage people climbing them. Rusted metal gates hung awkwardly in the entrance, the hinges rotten and detached from the concrete posts. At first glance it looked like they hadn't been maintained for years and would collapse with a good shove. He could see a concrete mixer and a transit van rotting in the yard, engulfed in brambles. John Metcalfe hadn't looked after his business for a long time.

Braddick looked at the gates through binoculars. Closer inspection showed the security chain was in good condition. The keyhole was bright and shiny. It was used regularly.

'What do you think?' Braddick asked Miles.

'Not much going on in there, guv,' Miles said, opening the door. He climbed out and zipped up his coat against the wind. 'I'll give armed response the green light.'

'Not yet,' Braddick said. 'I want to talk to the surveillance team first.'

'Okay, guv,' Miles said. 'Has something got you spooked, what's wrong?'

'Everything about this case is wrong, Miles,' Braddick said. 'We're missing something. It's staring us in the face, but I can't see it. Let's have a chat with surveillance before we go rushing in.'

'They've had eyes on the place for twenty-four hours, guv,' Miles said. 'Nothing has moved in or out.'

Braddick climbed out of the Evoque and jogged over to a white panel van. He knocked on the door. It slid open and he climbed in.

'Superintendent Braddick,' a sergeant said. He was wearing overalls and a baseball cap. 'It's all quiet in there. No sign of movement, no lights and no vehicles.'

'Good. At least I think it's good,' Braddick said. Something didn't sit right in his mind. 'Let's get this over and done with.'

'Yes, guv,' the sergeant said. He spoke into the radio. 'Green light. Go, go, go.'

The entry team cut the chains on the gates and they clattered to the ground. The armed response officers moved across the car park in a well-practiced formation. A second team covered the windows and the rear. There was a slight pause before they battered down the front door; there were tense minutes as they combed the building. They switched on the lights, illuminating the interior, but the yard was still cast in shadows. The building was quickly called clear. Braddick crossed the car park and looked around. There were several vehicles parked at the side of the building and Braddick saw two shipping containers at the rear. He walked around the building and noticed the locks on the containers were new. The metal glinted in the torchlight.

'What is it, guv?' Miles asked.

'The place looks unused, but look at this,' Braddick said, pointing to the padlock. 'Let's get some lights set up out here,' he ordered. 'Ask uniform to search the containers first.'

'Guv,' Miles said. He spoke to a group of uniformed officers and they began to organise searching the outside.

'You're clear to go inside, sir,' an ARU officer shouted. Braddick walked towards the main door. 'Upstairs is a storage area for materials, wood panels and plasterboard. Downstairs there's an office and a large workshop.'

'Okay, thanks. You're with me, Miles,' Braddick said.

'It stinks in there, guv,' the officer warned. 'It smells like something has died.'

'Let's hope it's something and not someone,' Braddick replied. They walked to the front of the building and stepped inside to a small reception area. A narrow doorway led into a much bigger office beyond it. Braddick was surprised how organised it was, despite being covered in a thick layer of dust. Lever arch files lined the shelves in organised rows and a large wooden desk was stocked with pens and pencils, a stapler and a hole punch, all lined up neatly. Cobwebs were hanging from the ceilings like gossamer bunting and there was a noxious odour in the air. A staircase behind the desk climbed to the first floor. 'Ask uniform to give upstairs a once-over when they've finished outside,' Braddick said. Miles nodded.

They walked into the workshop; bright strip lights buzzed and flickered, the starters struggling to warm up. A flatbed truck was parked at the far side. The Metcalfe Brothers' logo was painted on the doors. A pair of double ladders was stored above the driver's cab and a concrete mixer was strapped to the flatbed. The walls were covered with pegboards that were loaded with tools of all descriptions. Each tool had its shape outlined in marker pen, so it was obvious when one was missing. Everything had a place and there was a place for everything; it showed signs of an obsessively tidy mind, just like Stanley House. Apart from the dust and cobwebs, it was the hub of a well-organised construction company, except time had stood still inside. Braddick walked to the truck and looked into the cab. There was nothing amiss, yet the stench of decay was stronger. The stink was stronger near the truck. He put his hand over his nose and mouth and moved towards the back of the building. The cloying smell became overwhelming. He walked towards the rear wall and studied the floor.

'What are you doing, guv?'

'Following my nose,' Braddick said.

'Of course, you are,' Miles said. 'I should have known.'

'Call the ARU back in,' Braddick said, stopping next to the truck.

'What is it?' Miles asked. He followed Braddick's gaze.

'We need to move this truck and look underneath it,' Braddick said, staring at some tyre tracks in the dust. 'It has been moved regularly and it has been moved recently.' He kneeled. Beneath the truck was a rectangular hatch. It was fastened with heavy bolts and padlocks. 'There's a cellar underneath here. That's where the smell is coming from.'

'I think you're right. Wait two minutes, guv,' Miles said, 'I'll get the men with the bolt cutters and machine guns to open that.'

CHAPTER 20

Bruce May felt like there was a marching band in his head. His mind was spinning. Bright lights shot through his brain. When he tried to open his eyes, the pain increased. Nothing was in focus. The taste of whisky stuck in his throat. Blue lights strobed the cottage, raised voices pierced the silence, and the stench of burning flesh filled the air. The atmosphere was tense. He could hear men shouting and his eyes flickered open again. This time, his vision was clearer. Rough hands grabbed him and turned him over, pushing his face into the floorboards. His arms were pulled behind his back, painfully, and his wrists were cuffed. He could hear the ticking of the clock over all the noise. That felt bizarre; tick-tock, tick-tock. It was a surreal moment. The entire scene was bathed in blue light. He tried to get to his feet, the weight on him was crushing his chest.

'Keep still,' a voice shouted at him. He felt a knee in his back, pressing the breath from his lungs.

'What the hell is going on?' Bruce moaned. 'Get off me!'

'Shut up,' a voice said, angrily.

'I won't shut up,' Bruce mumbled. 'This is my house. Tell me what is going on.'

'You're under arrest, fucking sicko,' the policeman snarled.

'I haven't done anything!' Bruce protested. 'Where is Fabienne?'

'You tell us where she is,' the policeman said.

'I don't know. I haven't done anything.'

'You haven't done anything?' another officer said, sarcastically. 'Where shall we start? There are parts of a woman, in a binbag, in your living room, you freak.'

'I didn't do that,' Bruce protested.

'Of course, you didn't. I suppose you didn't put some of her on the fire, either, did you?'

'No, I didn't!'

'The rest of the body is in the boot of the Porsche, sarge,' another officer said. 'There are two more bin bags in there.'

'I think some of her is in a pan on the stove, guv,' a third voice added. 'It stinks in there.'

'Merseyside did say it was linked to the Hannibal murders,' a sergeant said.

'Hannibal murders?' Bruce said, confused.

'Get him out of here,' the officer in charge said. 'There are some people from Liverpool who are very keen to talk to you, Mr May. I hope you have a toothbrush with you, because I can't see you getting out this century.'

'I haven't done anything,' Bruce said, meekly. 'Honestly.' He could see the hatred in their eyes. If they could have bludgeoned him to death and got away with it, they wouldn't have hesitated.

'Get forensics in here and let's get a truck to remove the Porsche,' the officer said. 'Put a cover over it for now to keep the rain off it.'

Bruce was dragged off the floor and bundled out of the cottage. His mind was in a whirl; the smell of his burning wife filled his nostrils. The harsh reality of his position was becoming clear; he wretched and vomited on his shoes. Fabienne Wilder had taken his wife, his freedom and his soul. His love for her turned to hate and started to fester inside him. He felt despair rushing through his veins. The rain soaked him as they dragged him across the farmyard. An icy gust of wind cut through his clothes, making him shiver. He was crying like a child, but it didn't matter anymore – nothing did. The rear doors of a white van were opened, and he felt his weight being lifted from the ground. The officers thrust him into a seat and fastened him to the bulkhead, banging his head against the metal. He knew it was no accident. His brain rattled around inside his skull, making him dizzy.

'I haven't done anything,' Bruce mumbled again. He looked at the angry faces around him. No one was listening to what he said. No one cared. 'I didn't kill my wife. I loved her.'

'Shut up, you freak,' one of the officers said.

'Sick bastard,' another added, slamming the doors.

Bruce was left alone in the darkness. He heard the keys locking the custody van. *Fabienne.* He wondered where she was and what she was doing – had she plotted this all along, or had he been unlucky? Was she out there in the mountains somewhere, watching him being dragged away by the police, or was she long gone? Victoria was dismembered. Parts of her were in the back of his Porsche, his living room, and on his fire. Other parts of her had been cooked on his stove. Who would believe him if he tried to protest his innocence? He looked around in the pitch black. The engine started and he felt the van moving. This would be one of the longest journeys he had endured, and he had no idea where it would take him.

CHAPTER 21

Malcolm Baines closed the curtains before he turned on the lights – he didn't want anyone outside being able to see in. They were watching him again; he could sense it. There was no evidence to prove it, but he knew: a car in his rear-view mirror for too long; the stranger across the road reading a newspaper, glancing in his direction; a woman in the supermarket walking down the same aisles. Everyone was a suspect. His paranoia was reaching epic proportions; he hadn't felt so frightened since the months following the release of his first book. That was a very uncomfortable time. Threats had been made online and through the post, and images of him were posted on the dark web. The police weren't interested in his accusations that he was being followed, and harassed online. It wasn't a priority for them. Unless a crime was committed, or he could identify an individual making threats, there was nothing they could do. This time felt different, there was substance to his claims, real people were involved. There were faces and names behind the shadowy crimes. People had been murdered. It was all over the television, newspapers and the internet; the discovery of bodies in the drains was of interest worldwide. It gave credence to what he'd been saying for years – no one would admit he was right, of course, but they couldn't deny there was something behind his exposé. Not this time. What had happened at Stanley House was horrific, but not surprising to him. He knew they were there, lurking in the darkness, blending in with the mundane during daylight hours, only revealing their true selves behind closed doors, after the witching hour. They had finally exposed themselves and Malcolm embraced it. He remembered picking up a rock when he was a boy, watching the woodlice and earwigs scurrying for cover, seeking a dark place to hide. This was what he'd been waiting for. They were scurrying for cover, but they had left irrefutable evidence behind and it was beyond anything he could have imagined. The aftermath would echo through the years. People are fascinated by monsters, especially human monsters. Films would be made, documentaries commissioned, and books written. Malcolm needed to ride the crest of the wave; his books were already out there. It would make him unpopular, but it wouldn't be the first time. This could be his ticket out of the UK, a chance to live in the sunshine and write – somewhere he didn't need to look over his shoulder.

He poured himself a brandy and sat down at his computer. His inbox was crammed with requests to be interviewed about the murders and the occult connection. His agent had called with multiple requests to take quotes from his books. Malcolm had agreed – the more exposure, the better, and he could use the money. He was barely keeping his head above water. He'd been trying to gain publicity for his works for over a decade and no one had wanted to know. Even the local bookstores had blanked him: they said his books were too niche and didn't appeal to their core customers – that might change now. He'd sought publicity through the local papers and radio stations, but no one returned his calls. Most of the press had labelled him as a crank, trying to sell a book that no one wanted to read. Things *had* changed.

Suddenly, people wanted to listen. He opened his inbox and glanced through the messages. The BBC, ITV, Sky and Fox had all contacted him. Keeping his involvement out of the news hadn't worked. There were so many pictures of the tower block online, it was obvious the news channels would be scanning the faces, trying to identify the people in forensic suits. It hadn't taken them long to find him. He needed time to think about what he was doing. The window of opportunity wouldn't be open for long. If he was going to sell his soul to the press, he had to do it right.

Malcolm decided to leave his messages for another time and scrolled through his browsing history to an active Niners' site he'd been investigating. There were plenty of them, but this one was the real deal. He'd found the entrance to the back door of the site, the portal, the week before. It was well hidden but there were clues in the text to guide interested parties to the inner circles. He clicked on an icon shaped as a nine-angled star. The search icon appeared as the portal opened and he was allowed access onto the dark web. He typed into the search bar: Stanley House cannibal murders. The screen was filled with links to conversations about the subject. Twitter, Instagram and Facebook were alive with photographs and chatter, but it was mostly gossip; the dark websites were far more detailed. Malcolm skipped through the legitimate links and opened one titled The Watchers. Images from the tower block appeared. The removal of body parts from the drains had been photographed extensively from the landings. There were dozens of images of people in forensic suits carrying evidence bags. Malcolm scrolled through them, following the chatter attached to each one. Most of it was unpleasant nonsense, posted by individuals who had probably never been a member of anything remotely linked to the Niners. They were threatening posts, bragging about what they would do if they lived closer to the site. Their lack of understanding was staggering: wannabies dabbling in a dangerous world. Some of them would eventually be sucked into the periphery of a group, used for either money or sex, or become a victim – probably all three. He didn't have much sympathy for them. They were idiots. It wasn't a game that could be played when the mood took them: once they were in, they were in. No one walked away from the *real* believers. Meddle with fire, expect to get burned – in more ways than one. They had no idea what they were messing with.

Malcolm opened a dozen links before he found one that actually looked interesting. There was a video of the detective sergeant he had met the day before, Laurel something or other. He couldn't remember her name. Not that it mattered. In the video she was talking to a homeless woman, with the caption: Witness. Malcolm scrolled past it until another image appeared. The homeless woman was dead, broken on the courtyard. It was obvious she'd fallen from a great height. A teenager wearing a baseball cap was standing over her, crying. The caption beneath the image read: Dead Witness. He sat back and sipped his brandy. This was exactly what he was warning people about – people who followed an ideology online but remained anonymous – they were invisible. Claiming that a potential witness had been eliminated, brutally, under the noses of the detectives investigating the case, was powerful stuff. Very powerful indeed. It said, *Look at what we do to informers*. It hinted that they were everywhere and nowhere. Phantoms. Watching and waiting, ready to dole out their punishment when necessary.

The person who had posted the link wasn't taking the credit for killing the homeless woman, but they were praising whoever had. They made a joke that the police were treating it as a suicide, which was true – they were. The image of Sergeant Laurel next to the body was underneath it. The picture had been taken from the top floor. Only policemen and CSI officers were allowed up there. He could see from Laurel's expression that she was upset. It was yet another threat to those who felt inclined to meddle in their affairs. Malcolm felt his guts twist, he felt sick. As he scrolled down, the images became more recent, some from earlier in the day. He knew what was coming before it happened. He scrolled through a few more and there it was.

An image of him donning a forensic suit had been posted above a rant about him being a mundane insect, who needed to be squashed beneath the heels of the Niners. It described him as a worthless writer of untruths. Links to his books had been posted, along with other images of him walking from flat to flat on the top floor of Stanley House. Some of the contributors said he should be culled, and others had offered to carry it out. He had heard it all before but that didn't make it any easier to hear it again. Most of it was bluster by keyboard warriors, but some of them were seriously dangerous. The dangerous assassins wouldn't comment on a thread like that, they would read it and react without anyone knowing. The real Niners sat quietly, watching, reading, and researching their targets. They would make it look like an accident, just like the homeless woman, or they would be sure the body was never discovered. The idiots on the periphery, the wannabies, would never know who had acted on their behalf. No one would. No one needed to. The Niner would know the evil he had committed and that was enough. That was everything. Committing evil was reward enough for this world. What would happen in the next was anyone's guess.

Malcolm wondered how many of the real Niners were reading the same pages he was; he wondered how many had already downloaded his image to their phones. It was exactly what he'd been trying to avoid for years. He'd been on their radar for a while, but not recently. This would return their original, vitriolic threats to the forefront. He'd asked Braddick to keep him out of the limelight when, really, he had no control over it. The case was huge. What did he expect? He should never have become involved, but he hadn't been able to say no. When

Dr Libby had phoned, and mentioned murders linked to the occult, Malcolm couldn't get in his car quick enough. He had brought this on himself. It was too late to complain. The damage was done. He would have to be careful, and that was that.

Malcolm took a glug of his brandy, swallowed it and took another. He scrolled on. There were dozens of images from the tower. Two homeless men were pictured talking to a uniformed officer. The comments below identified them as possible witnesses. There were more images of Superintendent Braddick and his sidekick, Laurel, and other detectives. He reached another set of images, which concerned him greatly. The first was of Braddick, standing on his path wearing only a towel. His home address had been posted beneath it. The conversation linked to it was threatening and graphic. The threats ranged from smashing his windows to slashing his tyres. Several people were threatening to firebomb his home.

Alongside it was an image of his sergeant, Laurel. She had a baby carrier fastened to her chest; her husband next to her. They were outside their home taking some shopping from their car. Beneath the image was their address. Malcolm read the comments beneath it and shook his head. He took out his mobile and dialled Dr Libby. Braddick and his sergeant were in grave danger and he had to let them know.

CHAPTER 22

Valerie Sykes felt sad. Her friends, Wanda and Maxine, were dead, and it was Fabienne Wilder who was responsible. Val hated her. Despised her. But more than anything else, she feared her. She was evil and Val knew she had to avoid her. Fabienne didn't know she had stayed around – yet. She would soon, though, and she would be furious. She would come looking for her, no doubt about it. Val had to make sure Fabienne didn't find her, by hiding in the dark places and skulking in the shadows. The tower block had become her home and she knew it like the back of her hand. She had used all the rat-runs, service tunnels, alleyways and snickets to move unseen through the building. Max had showed her the best places to sleep, the warmer spots, the dry spots and the quiet places, and she moved between them, searching for sanctuary. Val missed Max. She'd tried to warn her, and she sensed there were more evil acts to come. Anyone who had seen people come and go from the top floor was in danger. Val wanted to hang around and help if she could. She couldn't help Wanda and Max, but she might be able to help others.

* * * *

George put another blanket over Ellis; the cold was biting. Ellis was too drunk to feel it and that was dangerous, especially when the sub-zero nights were approaching. If left unattended, he would wake up with frostbite – or not wake up at all. George would look after him through the winter. He had every chance of making it to next summer if his liver held out. Ellis was spending more and more time wasted. His tolerance for alcohol was dwindling as his liver became weaker. He seemed to be in a constant cycle of drinking and topping up the next day. It was unsustainable. Getting him to eat something, or drink anything but cider, was a relentless task. He would die of malnutrition if left to his own devices. Looking after Ellis gave George a focus, something to get out of his sleeping bag for. The days could be long when there was nothing to do. That's why so many who live on the streets seek an escape. Ellis used alcohol; watching him deteriorate gave George a reason to stay sober. He'd been sober for three years, the decade before that was a blur. Every day was a battle. Drinking from dawn till dusk was easy, choosing not to was hard.

George shuffled into his sleeping bag and settled down next to Ellis. Their proximity would help to keep them warm. He pulled two sheets of cardboard over them – it would keep the heat in and the frost from their skin. They had taken advantage of the police cordons and sneaked into the bin room. The residents had been told not to use the rubbish chutes until further notice, and George grasped the opportunity to sleep in the enclosed space. It had doors, which they'd closed to keep the wind off them. He closed his eyes and yawned. It wasn't often that they got to sleep in an enclosed space. They would sleep well tonight.

Outside the bin room someone was listening, waiting for the two men's breathing to change, making sure they were asleep. Talking to the police was punishable: burning was reasonable retribution. They took the top from a bottle containing petrol and poured the contents under the door. Val watched them from the stairs, knowing what they planned to do. She had to find a way to warn the men.

CHAPTER 23

Braddick answered his phone and was asked to hold while he was connected to the North Wales Police detective who had supervised the raid on the May property. He was awaiting the results of the search in the Ogwen Valley.

'Superintendent Braddick,' the detective said. 'Daffyd Griffith here. Sorry to keep you waiting.'

'No problem, Daffyd,' Braddick said. 'I appreciate the call.'

'We've arrested the owner of the property, Bruce May,' Daffyd said. 'He was trying to dispose of a woman's body on his coal fire. He was rambling that it was his wife, Victoria.'

'Did he admit killing her?'

'Nope,' Daffyd said. 'He denied killing her or moving her body. She's in a number of bin bags in the property and his Porsche 911.'

'How is he claiming she got there?'

'He said a woman called Fabienne Wilder drove the Porsche there with the body in it, and that he arrived there later by train.'

'Is there any sign of Wilder being there?' Braddick asked.

'No. There's no sign that anyone else has been there. He has the keys to the Porsche in his pocket and he doesn't have the train ticket, says he threw it away.' Daffyd paused. 'We can't be sure, but we think he cooked some of her on the stove.'

'Where is he now?' Braddick asked.

'We'd normally process him at St Asaph, but the chief has agreed to bring him straight to you. He doesn't mind where,' Daffyd said. 'Do you have a preference?'

'The new Matrix headquarters at Speke,' Braddick said. 'I'll arrange for our forensic team to move the victim.'

'Consider it done,' Daffyd said. 'How's the rest of the investigation going?'

'It's going to be challenging to say the least,' Braddick said.

'I don't envy you on this one,' Daffyd said. 'It's certainly under the spotlight. Let me know if there's anything else I can do to help.'

'Thanks again,' Braddick said, ending the call.

Braddick clenched his jaw; partly angry, partly glad, he wasn't really sure how he felt. It was a huge relief – Bruce May had been caught red-handed. After their last encounter, Braddick was itching to sit down opposite him. It would be a different result this time.

He put his phone away and waited as uniformed officers pushed the truck out of the way to expose a wooden hatch that was at least six feet wide. Bolt cutters were applied to the lock and the chains were pulled away. The metal clasp rattled loudly. The ARU positioned themselves around the opening and two men lifted the hatch. Torches and machineguns were aimed into the cellar. There was a tense moment of silence as the scene below was analysed. The sound of female voices filled the air, muffled and distorted. An ARU officer summoned Braddick to take a look. The stench of human waste was overpowering. He stepped forward and peered into the cellar. The smell of stale sweat was so bad it made his eyes water. Eight sets of terrified brown eyes looked back at him.

'What the hell is going on here?' an officer asked.

'My guess would be people trafficking,' the ARU officer said.

'I would say so,' Braddick agreed. 'It smells like they've been down there a while.'

'What do you want us to do, guv?' a uniformed sergeant asked.

'Let's get them out of there, and get the paramedics in here,' he shouted, covering his nose. The black women huddled together, frightened and dazzled by the torchlight. They were bound hand and foot with zip ties and had been gagged. They looked weak and malnourished. 'This is what we've been looking for.'

'Guv?'

'This is what ties Fabienne Wilder, the Metcalfe brothers and the Mays together,' Braddick said. 'She had to be more than just a tenant. Have the shipping containers in the yard been searched?'

'I'll take a look,' Miles said. 'What are you thinking, guv?'

'I think we've just found the real reason we're here,' Braddick said. 'Find out where they're from.' Officers climbed down the stairs to rescue the women. 'I'm guessing Africa,' Braddick said to himself.

The officers removed their gags; foreign voices drifted up to him, none of them familiar. One officer moved from woman to woman, asking them questions. He looked up at Braddick.

'They were offered passage across the channel from Calais, guv,' he said. 'They paid five thousand euros each and were promised work and accommodation when they got here.'

'Thanks,' Braddick said, nodding. 'This is not quite the accommodation they envisaged. Let's make sure they're allowed to use the toilet and given water before they're moved. Processing them could take hours and they must be starving. Get on to headquarters and tell them to organise a bus and some food.'

'Will do, guv. There's a supermarket down the road. Shall I send someone out for water?'

'They shouldn't be fed until they've been checked over,' a paramedic said.

'Okay,' Braddick said. 'Are you about to check them over?'

'Yes,' the paramedic said.

'Then what's the problem?'

'Do you want me to get water, or not, guv?'

'Yes. Keep the receipts,' Braddick said, dryly. 'I can see the ACC checking my expenses with a magnifying glass. They are starving, poor buggers. A couple of sandwiches won't hurt.'

The paramedic nodded that he'd understood and went to work as the women were brought up. Braddick followed Miles outside and walked towards the containers. Uniformed officers were cutting the locks when he arrived. They opened the door to the first one. There were mattresses on the floor and a pile of soiled blankets in the corner. Empty water bottles were filled with yellow liquid, but there were no humans inside. He surmised that the women in the cellar had been brought there in that container. It would have been a cramped journey for them. He looked down at the identification codes on the door.

'These markings are individual to each container, like a registration plate; find out who owns these containers,' he said. Miles nodded and took out his phone to call the office. 'Although, I think I know already,' Braddick said to himself.

'Superintendent Braddick,' a uniformed officer called from the other container. Braddick walked over to him and looked inside. There were bodies everywhere. Black bodies. All female. The scent of unwashed humans and excrement drifted from inside. 'Some of them are still alive, guv.'

'Get some more ambulances here,' Braddick ordered. 'Let's do what we can for these people. Get some water over here.' Officers moved quickly and began removing the living, one by one. They were covered with foil blankets and given a sip of water. The dead were left inside to be dealt with later. It started to rain. 'Can we move them inside with the others, please. They must be freezing.' Ambulance men and uniformed officers set up a line to move the women one at a time; they worked as a unit, the wellbeing of the trafficked women their priority. Braddick wondered where they had come from, and what they had endured to make it across Africa and the Mediterranean to end up in a shipping container in Liverpool. They were human beings with families somewhere, desperate and vulnerable. Prime pickings for the likes of John Metcalfe to exploit.

'I've got the name of the owner, guv,' Miles said. 'A company called May's Logistics.'

'Bruce May is the owner?' Braddick said.

'Yes, guv.'

'How long has his company been going?' Braddick asked. Miles asked the detective he'd called.

'Twenty years or so, under different names,' Miles said.

'Ask him how long containers have been delivered to this site,' Braddick said. Miles repeated the question. 'I want to know how long they've been playing this game.'

'Fifteen years, on and off,' Miles said.

'Which is about the length of time May said Metcalfe had been working for his wife. They were at this a long time before they met Fabienne Wilder.'

Braddick tried to slot things into place. 'She's a new addition to their group. They were bad before she came along, but she fitted right in there.'

'Bruce May is on the list of directors for Metcalfe Bros, guv,' Miles added.

'I'm looking forward to speaking to that man,' Braddick said. 'I'm going to nail the bastard to the wall.' His phone vibrated. It was Dr Libby. Braddick checked his watch, it was getting late. Too late for a social call. 'Dr Libby?'

'Braddick,' Dr Libby said. 'Where are you?'

'I'm at Metcalfe's builders yard,' Braddick said. 'I think we've found out what links them.'

'Oh, good. Listen, Malcolm Baines has been on the phone,' Dr Libby said, hurriedly. 'He's very concerned indeed.'

'Okay, what's the problem?' Braddick said, surprised that Dr Libby hadn't asked what they had found. He could hear the panic in his voice.

'He's been searching the dark web, looking for chatter about Stanley House. There are photographs of you and Laurel on there.'

'Taken at the crime scene?'

'Yes—'

'That was bound to happen,' Braddick said, watching the women being cared for. 'Every man and his dog have been taking pictures.'

'You don't understand; some of the images have been taken at your home address and at Laurel's house. There's a photo of her with her husband and Aimee.'

'What?' Braddick hissed.

'They have posted pictures of her and her family outside their home. Someone is following her,' Dr Libby said. 'They're following you too. There are pictures of you wearing just a towel on your doorstep.'

'I see,' Braddick said. 'That's not good.'

'They've posted your addresses online.' Dr Libby sounded concerned. Braddick had never heard him frightened before. 'You're big and ugly enough to look after yourself, but I'm worried about Laurel, Braddick.'

'Okay, okay, I appreciate that. Thanks for your concern,' Braddick said, trying to calm him. 'I'll send a car over there now. Don't worry. I'll make sure she's not in danger. Let me make a call and I'll call you back.'

'Okay, Braddick,' the doctor said. 'Hurry.'

CHAPTER 24

Sara Larkin was trying to get to sleep in her cell. She was two weeks into an eight-week prison sentence, and she was climbing the walls. Her craving for nicotine was off the scale but the screws wouldn't give her any replacement therapy until she'd seen the prison psychologist, who didn't have an appointment free for a week. Some days were worse than others: she could go a whole day without craving a cigarette, yet the next she could be a wreck. Another con had offered to sell her a home-made cigarette and a lighter for ten pounds. That was extortionate, but if she'd had the money, she would have paid it. Luckily, she was broke. It was a no-smoking prison and there were detectors everywhere. Making tobacco illegal had created a new way of making ridiculous amounts of money by smuggling it in. They weren't illegal on the outside, so the risks were minimal, and the profits were high. The penalty for smoking a contraband cigarette was loss of privileges for two weeks. It made no sense to get caught smoking, but addiction makes no sense at all. It's the nature of the beast.

Prison wasn't all bad. At least it was warm and dry, and she wasn't hungry. There were no bills to worry about. She could relax and not have to think about being used and abused for fifty quid a trick. It was a massive weight off her shoulders. There were more upsides than downsides to being inside. It was relatively easy to do the time. Walking the streets in the wind and rain was difficult. Kneeling in front of an unwashed stranger was difficult. Climbing into the back of a van, with no idea who the man is, that was difficult. Getting knocked about and throttled by the men who liked it rough was difficult. Serving eight weeks in a warm, dry cell, with three hot meals a day and a clean bed, was simple in comparison. Not being able to smoke was the biggest drawback. The patches made it bearable and they would prescribe her some, eventually. She would have to grin and bear it until then.

The newspaper and television headlines were leading with the Hannibal murders at Stanley House. The story had made her a bit of a celebrity on her wing. When it was aired on the evening news, she'd told everyone that she'd worked in the flats and attended some of the sessions. Her fellow inmates and some of the screws had quizzed her for information about what had gone on there. She couldn't tell them what she'd really seen: it still didn't feel real. She'd had nightmares for months – still had them, although less frequently. Sara had made up a few ritual-based stories and spiced them up with 'sex on an altar' and other nonsense. The truth was too frightening to tell. No one would believe her anyway. The first time she'd gone there, she'd been tripping so hard on the mushroom tea that she couldn't remember everything. She remembered feeling very sore for a week and struggling to sit down for any length of time. They had cut people and let the blood run into a chalice. She remembered being made to drink from an ornate cup, and the coppery taste of blood. It made her gag. The entire experience had left her frightened and ashamed. She'd vowed never to do a gig like that again, but the money was too good to turn down. The second time, the men had been like animals, on her like a pack of dogs, and the women weren't much better. One woman, who was there voluntarily, went bat-shit crazy, screaming and demanding to leave, but no one was allowed to leave and she was dragged into another room, bound and gagged; Sara had seen her through the crack between the doorframe and the door. She had no idea what had happened in that room, but in the morning, when the sun came up and it was all over, Sara had seen the woman running down the stairs like the devil himself was chasing her. She lost her shoe, but she didn't stop to pick it up; she just kept on running. Sara never saw her again.

It begged the question as to why she was there in the first place. Someone must have lured her there and played down what would happen. The ceremony she had witnessed and participated in was obviously not what she'd expected. Some of the attendees crossed the line, and things became too weird for most people. Normally, Sara wouldn't have entertained what went on, but the money was *ridiculously* good – it was like, a-week's-wages-in-one-night, good. She could act weird for that kind of money. It was a case of retreating into her mind while they did what they wanted to her body. Disassociation was an essential skill in her profession. She'd been grateful for the mushrooms – at least she could drift away from reality for parts of it. Some of it she would rather forget completely but couldn't.

She remembered the black woman: the woman with the eyes that held you. Fabienne, something or other. She was in charge, making suggestions. Disgusting suggestions. They had done whatever she'd said, yet no one dared touch her. She'd been the worst of them all. Her mind was sick and twisted. Things had escalated each time she went there, until it culminated in pure horror on their last gig. Sara had tried to block out the events of that last night, but they kept returning. She couldn't forget it. It was like something from a horror movie. They'd made them watch what they did to her. When they were done with them, the mood changed again. She didn't think they would have been allowed to walk out of there, having witnessed what they had. Sara had feared for her life and the lives of the other two working girls. She'd remembered an old trick she was taught by an older woman, who'd been on the streets for decades. 'If you need to get away in a hurry, mess yourself,' she'd said, and Sara had done just that: she'd started to urinate and then ran to the bathroom, taking a candle from the hallway. No one had wanted to be peed on, so they'd let her go. Sara set fire to the toilet roll and the shower curtain, and mayhem had followed. The flames had spread quickly, and smoke filled the flat in minutes. Everyone ran for the door. Sara grabbed her clothes and the other two girls, and they ran down nine flights of stairs, struggling into their clothes as they went. Their feet didn't touch the ground and they didn't stop running until they thought their lungs would burst.

Fabienne and her cronies kept her number and had tried to call her again, but Sara threw the phone away and changed her number. She wouldn't go back there if it was the last job on the planet. She had thought about going to the police many times but didn't think they would believe her. Not until now. The headlines had set a dog barking in her head, one that was difficult to ignore. She could get the truth off her chest, and make some money from the press, if she sold her story. It could be the opportunity she needed to get out of this life; she could set herself up with a little cake-making business and leave the vile punters behind. It was a dream, but some dreams come true. Some people made it off the streets. Maybe her story was worth that. Maybe.

She was half sleeping, half dozing when she heard footsteps on the landing outside. Not the solid sound of the screw's boots on metal, this was more of a muffled noise. As if someone was trying to be quiet but failing badly. Sara turned onto her back and stared at the door. The footsteps stopped directly outside her cell. Her heart pumped madly for a moment as she listened. She wasn't going to approach the viewing hatch. That would be stupid. She had heard stories of inmates being drawn to the hatch and then sprayed in the face with bleach or mace; she wasn't falling for that one. No one had any reason to attack her. Not that she could think of. Most of the cons liked her. Sara was popular. She was convicted on a soliciting charge, nothing heavy. There were plenty of nonces to assault if anyone had the urge. Some of the women were in for abusing their own children. They needed to be straightened out, sick bastards; attacking them was justified. She wondered if anyone might have heard she was at Stanley House and thought she was actually involved in the Hannibal murders, that she was actually a killer. It was a possibility, she thought. Maybe that was reason enough to attack her; surely no one thought she was involved? They couldn't think that. Not for a moment. Another shuffle outside her door snapped her back to reality.

She listened; her breath stuck in her lungs. There was a scratching sound. She thought she heard a gurgling noise. A throaty cough, maybe. The type of noise a heavy smoker with a chest infection would make. As if their lungs were flooded with phlegm.

Tap, tap, tap, on the door.

She froze, gripping the sheets to her chest. The sickening gurgling sound again.

Tap, tap, tap.

'Sara,' a voice whispered. Sara listened but didn't dare move. The voice was female and very old. It was the voice of a woman too old to be a screw. 'Sara. Can you hear me?' She couldn't think of any inmates who sounded like that.

'Sara.'

Tap, tap, tap.

'Sara,' the voice whispered again.

Tap, tap, tap.

'Sara, I know you're not sleeping. You can't sleep.'

Tap, tap, tap.

'Sara!' Louder this time, but she still didn't move, she didn't flinch.

Silence.

The hatch snapped open and a beam of light pierced the darkness of the cell. She heard something clatter on the floor and the hatch closed. Footsteps moved from her door, drifting away down the landing. Sara grabbed her penlight and shone it on the floor. She frowned. There was an X-shaped cross on the floor. It looked like it was made from wood, or bone, fastened together at the centre with black cotton. Although, it may have been hair. She had no idea what it meant or who had pushed it into her cell, but she knew instantly that it was connected to Stanley House and Fabienne Wilder. It was a warning to keep her mouth shut. A chill spread from her head to her toes. Sara was terrified.

CHAPTER 25

Melissa Walker and Maggie Bennet were sitting on Maggie's settee, drinking Chardonnay and smoking cigarettes. They were quiet while they watched a piece about the Hannibal murders on Sky news. The story was huge, and it appeared to be gathering pace. The reporter was outside the tower block, speculating about the suicide earlier that week. Some articles on the internet intimated that the woman may have been thrown over the balcony as part of some wider conspiracy to silence witnesses. Some of the residents were refusing to comment for fear of reprisals, and some had left completely, staying with friends or family. Rumours of a link to the occult were creeping into the articles, further fuelling the flames. It was attracting attention from all over the world. The article mentioned satanic script daubed on the walls, something the police had tried to keep quiet. Sources in the police force and the forensic companies were being exploited by the press, their secrets sold for cash.

'I'm frightened, Maggie,' Melissa said, slurping her wine. She inhaled deeply on her cigarette. 'I knew this would happen, eventually. It was always going to happen.' She inhaled again. 'What are we going to do?' She stood up and reached for the wine, filling up both glasses. Her long, dark hair hung loosely at her shoulders. Despite looking every day of her forty-three years, she was still slim and attractive – too skinny for some punters, not quite skinny enough for others. 'You can't please them all,' she used to say.

'They've had CSI units all over the place looking for DNA and, from what I'm hearing, they've found more evidence than they can test.'

'Who told you that?' Maggie asked. Her frown made deep wrinkles at the corners of her eyes. It aged her ten years.

'One of the coppers I "do", told me,' Melissa said. 'He's a regular. He reckons that the forensic unit can't cope with what they've recovered, and they've had to sub out to other companies.'

'When did he tell you that?' Maggie asked.

'Yesterday.'

'You haven't told him that we've been there, have you?'

'Of course not. I'm not stupid,' Melissa protested. 'But what if they find out we've been there, with those weirdos?'

'You're overthinking it, Mel,' Maggie said. She pushed her blond hair behind her ears. It was streaked and permed and afro-like at times; the roots were silver grey. Maggie was the right side of forty but looked older. Her curves were her assets. The only thing she wasn't addicted to was exercise, she would brag.

'I don't think I'm overreacting,' Melissa insisted. 'If they find out we were there, they might think we're involved.'

'Don't be silly, Mel. We're hookers. People pay us to go to their homes and have sex. The police know we're hookers, we know we're hookers, everyone we had sex with at those parties knows we're hookers. If they ask us why we were there, we say, "because we're hookers". We're not telling lies, are we?'

'I suppose not.'

'We'll be fine.'

'I'm worried about it.'

'Don't worry about it,' Maggie said. 'They're not interested in a couple of old tarts like us.'

'They will be if they find evidence that we were in there. We've left DNA in those flats,' Melissa said. 'That copper said nowadays, if you've been somewhere, they can tell. Everyone leaves DNA, he said.'

'You can't be sure. How do you know?'

'We must have left something behind.'

'You don't know that for certain.'

'I know we were careful most of the time, but that place was like a zoo. Once that mushroom tea was down me, I didn't know what I was doing – if I'm honest. Our fingerprints will be everywhere.' Melissa lit another cigarette. She inhaled deeply and exhaled through her nostrils.

'Like where?' Maggie asked, frowning.

'Everywhere,' Melissa said. 'I went to the kitchen for a drink of water; I went to the toilet a few times. We weren't wearing gloves, Maggie.'

'So, what if we did?' Maggie argued. 'We had a legitimate reason to be there. We were working. We're hookers. That's what we do.'

'I'm telling you, it's only a matter of time before the coppers pull us in for questioning. People have died up there, and they'll want to talk to anyone who's been anywhere near.'

'If they do, we stick to our story,' Maggie said. 'We're hookers. We were paid to go there on an overnight rate. There were no names given. We didn't ask any questions and they didn't tell us anything. If they show us photographs, we don't recognise anyone. They paid us cash. We made our own way in and our own way home. The police can't implicate us in anything. We'll be fine.'

'What if one of the others says something?' Melissa asked. 'We can lie for England, but if the coppers start putting pressure on people to name names and tell tales, people will crack. They'll start pointing fingers to save their own necks. That Sara, for a start, she's a gob on legs that one. I know she's in the clink but what if she grasses?'

'Don't call her names, Mel. If it wasn't for her, we might not have got out of there that night,' Maggie said. 'I'm not her biggest fan but she was a bloody superstar that night – starting that fire saved our bacon. I don't think we were supposed to leave there that night. We owe her one, Mel.'

'I know we do. I haven't seen her since,' Melissa said. 'I never had the chance to say thanks. But she's a weak link. If the police put pressure on her, she'll spill the beans. She's got form for talking to the police, Maggie. She can't hold her own water.'

'She did us a solid favour, but it doesn't change the fact that she's a really unreliable witness. The police will take whatever she says with a pinch of salt. Anyway, it's her word against ours: two against one. We'll be fine. If we stick to the plan, we'll be fine,' Maggie emphasised. 'We didn't see anything, we don't know any names, and that's that.'

'Okay, Maggie,' Melissa said. 'I suppose you're right. They're not mind readers. If we stick to our story, no one can prove otherwise.'

'That's right.'

'I wonder how many they did?' Melissa said, Maggie looked confused. 'How many they murdered up there, I mean.'

'I don't know, and I don't want to know, either,' Maggie said. 'The less I know, the better.'

'The newspapers said there are multiple victims in the drains,' Melissa said. 'That's awful. Imagine ending up being cut up and flushed down the bog. I wonder how many poor women died up there, Maggie.'

'We'll never know,' Maggie said, topping up their wine again. 'Best not to think about it too much.'

'I know some of the girls who went there before us,' Melissa said. She emptied her glass in one gulp. 'Sue and Ellen; they're not around now.' Maggie passed her a cigarette and she lit it, sucking deeply. 'The rumours are, they went there and were never seen again. That's what June Fish Face said.'

'June Fish Face doesn't know her arse from her elbow. I've heard those rumours too, Mel,' Maggie said, 'and I've heard they're both back down south, working in Brighton.'

'Really?' Melissa asked.

'Yes. They reckoned they could get more money working down there.'

'Were they from there?'

'Yes,' Maggie said. 'Didn't you notice their accents?'

'Not really,' Melissa said. 'I don't notice stuff like that. I'm away with the fairies most of the time, aren't I?'

'You can't listen to what anyone says about that place at the moment. This story has grabbed the imagination of every empty-head in the city.' Maggie pointed to the windows. 'Everyone out there is claiming to know someone who lives in the tower, or used to live in the tower, or once knew someone who lived in the tower, or went past the tower on the bus one day, blah, blah, blah. They all want to claim some kind of celebrity from it; they just want attention, whereas we know exactly what went on there and don't want any.'

'I don't think we have any choice, Maggie,' Melissa said, shaking her head. 'If we get pulled, how many times shall we say we went there?'

'Twice.'

'Only twice?'

'Yes.'

'Do you ever think about her?' Melissa asked, almost in a whisper.

'No. And neither should you.'

'What they did to her was vile. I have nightmares about her.'

'Shut up,' Maggie said. 'Enough of that. We can't help her now; we couldn't help her then. It's best forgotten.'

'But what they did …'

'I'm not going to tell you again.' Maggie shook her head and wagged a finger. 'We said we wouldn't talk about it ever again. I intend to stick to that promise. I suggest you do, too. We have no idea who is listening.'

'Listening?'

'Yes, listening. People do it all the time when there's been a big crime.'

'What people?'

'The police, or the suspects.'

'What do you mean, Maggie?'

'The police listen to people to gather evidence, and suspects listen to find out what the witnesses are going to say,' Maggie explained. 'We don't want either side knowing what we know, do we?'

'No,' Melissa whispered. 'Of course, we don't.'

'Then don't talk about her again – just in case someone is listening.'

'What, through the walls?' Melissa was still whispering; the colour had drained from her face. She was frightened.

'They can listen from anywhere nowadays, Mel,' Maggie said. She put her finger to her lips. 'Promise you won't mention what happened to us in there, ever again.'

'I do,' Melissa said.

'Promise.'

'I promise.'

A knock on the door made them jump.

'Who is that?'

'I can't see through walls, Mel,' Maggie said. She stood up and pretended to be unruffled, straightening her hair in the mirror. 'I'll go and answer it. Stop being so bloody nervy, will you? You'll have me on edge all night.'

Maggie walked into the hallway and switched on the light. A small object on the floor beneath the letterbox caught her eye. It was an x-shaped cross. She picked it up and stuffed it into the back pocket of her jeans, deciding not to tell Melissa – she was jittery enough. Maggie walked to the door and opened it. There was no one there. She closed the door and leaned against it. It was no coincidence that it had been put through her door. She had no idea what it meant, but she knew who it was from.

CHAPTER 26

Laurel was feeding Aimee while Rob made them a late supper: chicken fajitas. She could hear the meat sizzling in the pan and tried not to think about the crime scenes she'd worked on the last few days. The whiff of garlic took her back there for a second. It was difficult to erase the stench of death from her memory; it was clinging to her on an industrial scale. She felt like she needed steam cleaned; her shower hadn't washed away the feeling that filth was clogging every pore. Explaining it to Rob was impossible: she didn't want to contaminate his mind with the dross from her own. He worried about her working at the MIT anyway. They had spent many an evening discussing her return to work. He'd wanted her to ask for a less dangerous role. Laurel had argued that there were no such things as less dangerous roles in the police force; they were all equally hazardous. Rob disagreed, but he knew how proud his wife was of her position as a detective in MIT. There was no way she would step down – backwards or sideways – and he knew it. He was fighting a losing battle.

Aimee chugged her milk and managed a smile. She reached out a tiny hand to touch her mother's face and became fascinated by a ginger curl. Her eyes widened as she tried to focus.

'I hope you like that colour,' Laurel said, 'because you've got the same, darling. You've got your daddy's blue eyes and mummy's red hair.'

'Are you ready to eat?' Rob called from the kitchen. 'This is nearly ready.'

'I'm ready when you are, Aimee has guzzled her milk. She'll be asleep in a minute. Yes, you will,' she said to Aimee, kissing her forehead, 'you'll be asleep in a minute.' Aimee gurgled and smiled. Laurel's mobile began to vibrate. She'd left it in the kitchen. 'Can you see who is ringing, please?' she called to Rob.

'Have a guess,' he answered, bringing the phone to her. 'Don't be all night, this food is nearly ready.'

'I won't. Sorry,' she said, handing Aimee to him. 'Hello, guv. What's up?'

'Are you at home?'

'Yes, why?'

'Is Rob with you?'

'Yes. What's wrong, guv?'

'I don't want you to panic, but someone has posted a photograph of you outside your house with Rob and Aimee. They've posted your address, too.'

'Posted it where?' Laurel's stomach knotted. Rob was listening, a concerned look on his face. He noticed the headlights of a car pulling into their drive.

'On the dark web. Threats are being made.'

'A Niner's site?'

'Yes.'

'What type of threats?'

'Threats to harm you and your family,' Braddick said. He decided not to mention the threat to kidnap Aimee at the next full moon. They hadn't been specific about the relevance of the full moon, but it didn't take a brain surgeon to work out the implication. 'Most of it will be hot air but we have to take it seriously. I've sent an armed response vehicle to your house. They'll be there as long as we perceive there's a credible threat.'

'Who are they?' Laurel asked. 'Making the threats, I mean.'

'We don't know. They might be whackos following the story, but they might be Niners, too, so we'll be cautious. Tell me when the ARU arrive.'

Rob pointed to the police car on their drive and frowned. He shrugged, as if to say: why is there a police car outside?

'They're here,' Laurel said. 'It's okay,' she said to Rob. 'I'll explain in a minute.' Rob rolled his eyes. He didn't look happy. 'Have you been threatened, too?' she asked Braddick.

'Oh yes.' He chuckled, dryly. 'Mine are much worse than yours.'

'Good. I'm glad they're not just picking on me. Do they know you're in charge?' Laurel said, trying to make light of the situation. She felt anything but jovial. 'Can't we trace these idiots?'

'Google has put the tech department on it. They may be able to track some IP addresses, but we'll have to wait and see. Good news about Bruce May being lifted,' he said, changing the subject.

'Fantastic news,' Laurel agreed. 'I believe the snake was trying to burn his wife's body?'

'Yes. On the coal fire in the living room.'

'A cosy night in with the wife,' Laurel said, sarcastically.

'Madness,' Braddick said. 'We'll interview him tomorrow afternoon.'

'Can't wait for that. What is he saying so far?'

'He's pleading innocence. Says he hasn't done anything wrong.'

'No surprise there, I suppose,' Laurel said. 'It should be fun picking him apart.'

'Indeed. We need to coerce with Cheshire before we interview him.' Braddick paused. 'I'm not convinced that he wasn't involved in his wife's murder.'

'You don't think he was in London?'

'All the evidence says he was, but—'

'You don't believe it,' she interrupted. 'Or, you don't trust the Cheshire investigation.'

'I'm not one hundred per cent sure they've analysed his whereabouts thoroughly,' Braddick said. 'I may be way off the mark, but I would rather be certain before we sit down opposite him. He's already proved what a slippery bastard he can be. I don't want to give him any wriggle room again.'

'We can double-check ourselves,' Laurel said. 'How did the search at Metcalfe's place go?'

'I almost forgot to tell you,' Braddick said. 'We've found the missing link that connects them all.'

'Which is what? Don't keep me in suspense.'

'They're trafficking women. African women.'

'What did you find?' Laurel asked, surprised. Suddenly, her need to eat was trumped by her enthusiasm for the job.

'Eight women in a cellar and another twelve in a shipping container,' Braddick said. 'Four of them were dead, the rest in very bad shape. Obviously, Metcalfe couldn't go back to feed them.'

'That's terrible.'

'I think Bruce May was shipping them into the country in containers, and Metcalfe was storing them in his yard. That's what Malcolm Baines said it was about: control. They're trafficking vulnerable women into the country and controlling them by frightening the living daylights out of them. Then, they put them to work.'

'You think they're putting them into the sex industry, don't you?'

'Yes, I do,' Braddick said. 'Those women would be too frightened to try to run away; where could they possibly go?'

'It all adds up,' Laurel said. 'It's a perfect way to make sure they're obedient. And if they disappear, no one knows they were here in the first place. A never-ending stream of victims. Where do you think they're working?'

'My guess would be Victoria May's properties,' Braddick said. 'They're being searched in the morning. We targeted the empty houses first. There's a coordinated breach scheduled for eight o'clock.'

'Who's running the op?'

'Carol Hill from vice. She's working with uniform and armed response. I want them to hit them all at the same time.'

'Makes sense,' Laurel said. 'Do you think they're one operation or run as individual dens?'

'We'll find out in the morning. My guess is, Bruce May brings them in, Fabienne Wilder terrifies them, and then Victoria May puts them to work. Metcalfe is their enforcer; he gets a little too enthusiastic about the occult side of things and starts to believe it – maybe he actually does believe it, he catches prion's disease from an African victim and, bingo, everything starts to unravel.'

'Any sign of Valerie Sykes?'

'Unfortunately, not.'

Rob glared at Laurel and gestured to the kitchen; their food was spoiling.

'Listen, I'll have to go. Thanks for the heads-up. I'll see you tomorrow.'

'No worries,' Braddick said. 'Take care. See you tomorrow.'

They ended the call and Laurel walked to the window. She peered through the blinds at the ARU vehicle on her driveway. The officers gave her a thumbs-up. She returned the greeting.

'Why is there a police car on our driveway?' Rob said, standing close to her.

'Let's eat first,' Laurel said, kissing his cheek. 'Then I'll tell you all about it.'

'Is our family in danger?'

'Not while they're outside, don't worry. Let's eat,' Laurel said. Rob nodded but looked concerned. Laurel squeezed his hand to reassure him, but the doubt didn't leave his eyes. He hated her being in the job, especially now that Aimee had arrived. She planned her words in her head. The ARU on the driveway required an explanation. The words she chose would be vital to how he reacted. She didn't want to give him anything to be overly concerned about, but she had to tell the truth. It was the words that counted, not the message. 'It's just another day at the office,' she said, kissing his forehead.

CHAPTER 27

George woke with a start. It took him a few seconds to remember where he was; it came back to him: they had bedded down in the bin room. He didn't know what had woken him.

'Wake up! George; Ellis; wake up!'

It was Val's voice, echoing round the walls, coming through an air vent at the rear of the bin room. George listened intently to the sounds around him and heard liquid being poured onto the concrete, followed by the click of a lighter. The petrol fumes reached him seconds before the liquid was ignited. There was a whoosh and he heard footsteps running away. Suddenly, the roar of flames was deafening, the fog of sleep was clearing. Searing heat made him cower against a metal skip. Smoke had filled the bin room and it was getting difficult to breathe. He knew they had to stay low, as the toxic smoke was billowing skyward. He looked for an escape, but the doors were ablaze and a wall of fire advanced, climbing towards the bin chute – it was acting as a chimney, sucking the fire upwards. They didn't have much time, so George moved quickly. He grabbed Ellis and rolled him over. Ellis woke up, confused, his eyes were bleary from the alcohol. He used his arms to protect his face from the heat. George could feel the skin on his face blistering and his clothes began to smoulder. They had seconds before they combusted. He half stood, keeping low, and pushed Ellis into the far corner behind the skips. They cowered from the flames while George thought of a plan.

'Ellis,' George shouted

'What?' Ellis was coming around quickly but was confused. 'Where are we?'

'Grab this,' George said, opening the lid of the nearest skip. Ellis pushed it. 'Get in,' George shouted. The stink of rotting refuse mingled with the smoke.

'What do you mean?'

'Get in the skip, quickly!' George linked his hands together. Ellis stood on one foot and, using George's hands as a step, launched himself into the metal skip. 'Pull me in,' George shouted, as he felt his pants starting to burn. He leapt and got one leg over the side. Ellis dragged him in and the lid slammed shut, sealing the choking fumes out.

'That was close,' George panted.

'How did it start?' Ellis asked.

'Well, it wasn't an accident, Ellis,' George said. 'I could smell petrol just before it ignited.'

'We were lucky, George,' Ellis said.

'It's a good job Val shouted,' George said, coughing.

'Was it a fire-starter or were they trying to get us?' Ellis asked.

'I don't know, but we're going to find out,' George said. 'And if someone *has* got it in for us, they've bitten off more than they can chew.' He paused in the darkness; they listened to the crackle of flames. 'Oh, bloody hell,' he moaned.

'Are you all right?' Ellis asked. His eyes were adjusting.

'I think my pants are ruined,' George said.

'Are they burnt?'

'No,' George said. 'I've shit them.'

* * * *

Braddick parked the Evoque on his drive and switched off the headlights. His house was in darkness; it was the place he called home but, tonight, it looked cold and foreboding. He put it down to being tired and the harrowing crime scenes he'd worked recently. It wasn't like him to be disturbed by a crime scene. He had the ability to remove himself from the emotional side of investigating a violent death. Crime scenes had to be analysed with a clinical eye, not a teary one. There was no room for sympathy. Sympathy could colour opinion. There had been plenty of horrific scenes throughout his career, but Stanley House and the May murder were in a league of their own. They were special. Special in a bad way. The reek of the scenes had stayed with him, etched into his memory. He could smell cooked flesh even though it had been days since he'd encountered it. He knew his mind was playing tricks on him. The simple fact was, his brain was telling him he could still sense it. It was a form of post-traumatic shock. The stress the case had invoked was undeniable, and the scale of it wasn't lost on him. It was the horror that intrigued strangers across the globe. The press was running away with the story, adding to the pressure. It was also attracting the attention of the lunatic fringe, and the safety of his officers was being threatened, which was an additional dimension. He wasn't sure how seriously to take the threats. There was no way of knowing if they were coming from harmless crackpots or genuine followers. He had to lean on the side of caution. It was one thing following police officers to their homes, and posting their pictures and addresses online, but they were the actions of a coward – hoping somebody else would complete the job. Could they back it up with violence? That was yet to be seen. The hard core of the group had killed multiple victims, but they would've been incapacitated, probably drugged, and, in some cases, willing to be sacrificed. Preying on a serving police detective was a different animal. He had to take the threats seriously, no matter how difficult it was to grasp. The entire case was madness: an individual capable of killing another human being was disturbing, yet simple to comprehend. Some killed for money, some killed for gain, some killed for belief, and others killed for the thrill. Some individuals were just wired that way. On the other hand, a group of people, with the same mindset, who found killing as easy as ABC, was far more difficult to understand. It was also terrifying. It meant the danger was spread, more difficult to anticipate. Was it group hysteria powered by hallucinogenic drugs, or were they bad people who had stumbled upon each other by chance? Were they only dangerous as a group, or as individuals too? The questions were endless, and the answers slow in coming.

Braddick looked around the garden. The shadows were deep and impenetrable. Yellow light filtered through the bushes from the road, making the grass look fake. He checked the area once more, opened the car door and climbed out. The cold night air touched him, making his skin tingle as if icy fingers had tickled him. A shiver ran down his spine. He looked around again, nervously, searching the shifting shadows for danger. Was someone there, would they dare? He could almost feel eyes staring at him. His composure was shot. He had a very bad feeling about the case. Something evil stalked them. It was unexplainable, yet real. Every branch that creaked was an approaching assassin. He felt more vulnerable than he ever had before. A gust of wind carried dried leaves across the lawn, tumbling and rustling around his ankles. An empty Coke can rattled down the road, making him turn around quickly. He was very edgy.

It was a feeling that had crept up on him over the last few years: the fear of his own mortality. Maybe it was age, maybe it was living alone for so long; it had been too long. He missed the company of a woman in his life and yearned for the touch of a lover, yet he still wasn't over Karin's death. Every time an attractive woman showed any interest, the guilt kicked in and he backed off. He wondered if the feeling would ever pass. It hadn't lessened, that he knew for certain. People lived with grief. They moved on and had relationships, marriages, kids and grandkids, yet he was still stuck at the starting line. The grief had eaten away at him from the inside, and the thought of beginning a new relationship was abhorrent. Courting had been difficult enough as a young man, starting afresh at his age would be a nightmare – trying to be charming, funny and romantic to impress a stranger was beyond his capability now. Being married to the job had become a state of mind. Obsessing over details masked the loneliness; it was easy to become immersed in case after case. He couldn't pinpoint when it had come over him. Everything had been fine and then suddenly, one day, he felt panicked that he might actually be alone for the rest of his life. What would he do all day when the job finished? Play golf, go to the gym, maybe fishing? He didn't do any of those things, never had, never would. Sitting in front of a television, night after night, waiting for old age or illness to kill him, was a terrifying thought. Should he start looking for a partner on the internet? He wouldn't know where to start. The truth was, he had been alone for too long. On reflection, only he could do something about it, but he needed to be in the right frame of mind to begin again, and now wasn't the time.

He locked the Evoque and walked up the path, digging in his pockets for his door key. A rustling sound came from the hedges to his right. He stopped and peered into the night. Something moved. Braddick slipped his keys between each finger, making a spikey knuckleduster, and waited. The lower branches moved, and next door's cat padded out, eyeing him suspiciously. It meowed as it ran back into the undergrowth. He shook his head and took a deep breath, scolding himself for being so jumpy, put the key into the lock and opened the door. Envelopes rustled against the carpet; his post usually consisted of junk mail, council tax and utility bills, nothing exciting arrived anymore. When she was alive, Karin often posted cards and letters. She didn't need a reason; it was usually on a whim. She found it easier to express her feelings in writing, or through the words printed inside a card. He would look through the post in anticipation of something from her, but not anymore, those days had gone. Nowadays his post was functional and unnecessary. He'd promised himself that he would transfer everything to internet billing, but he still hadn't got around to it.

He switched on the light and looked down at the post, which consisted of a frozen-food-store flyer, a reminder for his television licence, a leaflet from his local council and an unmarked envelope. Why would there be an unmarked envelope? Someone was sending a message, that's why. His mind raced. He picked up the envelope by its corner and held it to the light, but he couldn't see what was inside. He felt a rush of adrenalin. It made him feel sick. His instinct told him the envelope was trouble. It was a message he didn't want to read but had to. Whatever was inside was bad – whoever had posted it was equally as bad, but where were they? Were they out there, watching him? He closed the front door and headed into the kitchen, switching on the lights as he went. Reflections turned the windows into mirrors and Braddick closed the blinds; he was nervous. His mind was focused on reading the contents of the envelope, while not compromising any evidence it may contain. He knew who it was from and they were growing bolder. Why risk approaching his house to post something through the letter box? Because it was an invasion of his home; it was done to intimidate, to show how easy it was to reach him. The simple act of pushing a letter through the flap was an assault on the safety of his home. He could feel his stomach knotting with anger. *How dare they cross the line.*

Braddick ripped a square of cling film from the roll and placed it on the worktop. He carefully put the envelope on it, address side down. He opened the bits-and-pieces drawer and took out a tweezer set he'd purchased from Amazon for Karin the week before she'd died. Opening the leather pouch, he took out the tweezers and a small pair of scissors. He held the envelope in place and slid a scissor blade beneath the edge of the flap, working it gently, slicing through the glue with ease. He separated one side and then the other, before lifting the paper flap with the tweezers. Inside was a folded piece of white paper. It wasn't lined and the edges were smooth, not perforated. He took it out and opened it, careful not to touch the paper. The handwriting was neat. He read the words and felt anger boiling inside him, coursing through his veins – anger and confusion, and something else. Fear.

CHAPTER 28

Sara Larkin hadn't slept well. She was frightened to death, despite being locked in a cell, surrounded by high walls, barbed wire and prison officers. It was a relief when morning came, and the lights were turned on; the light chased her demons away. The dark hours were the worst. Her imagination ran wild, torturing and tormenting her. The images from Stanley House wouldn't fade, if anything, they were becoming more vivid. The fear and pain were etched into her mind; the sound of her voice begging was becoming clearer in her memories and her eyes seemed to bore into her soul, condemning her for not helping. Was it because of the blanket news coverage, or was something else bringing it all back? Whatever it was, it was having a profound effect on her mental well-being. It was spreading through her like dry rot through an old house, darkening her perception of the world. She felt tired and frightened all the time. It was a feeling of desperation that she couldn't shift.

When the cell doors opened, she wandered to breakfast with a knot in her stomach and tiredness like fog in her brain. Her food was barely warm, and she picked at it unenthusiastically. The bacon and sausages were undercooked, and the eggs were overcooked; it was a recipe for diarrhoea. The entire wing could be affected. Bouts of mass food poisoning were fairly common, and they made the whole building stink of excrement. She remembered a trip to Chester Zoo as a child, and the eye-watering stink of the monkey house. The smell of urine in there was so powerful it was almost choking. An outbreak of stomach problems on the wing was just as bad. It was times like that she realised prisons were just like zoos, but for humans. All the bleach in the world couldn't mask it.

She sipped her tea and listened to the inane drivel coming from the inmates who shared her landing. It was the same crap she'd listened to every morning: gossip from the other wings; the woman from cell such-and-such was caught fingering the woman from cell so-and-so in the showers, and they're both married to men on the outside – not really earth-shattering news; one of the screws had been lifted for smuggling in contraband up her backside – shock, horror; someone had attacked someone else because someone else had said something they shouldn't have, and so on, and so on, and the feud wasn't finished yet; threats to kill had been made – so what? People made threats every day. It was a prison, full of violent people. What did they expect? She'd heard it all before. It was the same old, same old. Some days it ground her down; the urge to stand up and scream, 'shut up,' was overwhelming, especially when she was tired. Her ability to zone out of conversations was the only way to remain sane. She was drifting into a hazy daydream when one of the screws approached.

'Eat up, Larkin,' she said. 'You've got a visitor.'

'What?' Sara said, checking her watch. 'Who gets a visit at this time in the morning?'

'Naughty hookers who frequented a tower block where people eat their neighbours,' the screw replied, smiling sarcastically. The other inmates laughed. 'Does that ring any bells, Larkin?'

'Is it the police?' Sara felt her chest tighten.

'Yes. But not just the ordinary boys in blue.' She winked. 'You've got a detective sergeant and his mate from the Major Investigation Team, no less. My guess is, you're in the doo-doo,' the screw said. 'Come on. Finish your tea and eat up. They're waiting.'

'Do I need my solicitor?' Sara asked, concerned.

'Apparently not, Larkin,' the screw said. 'Not for now, anyway. Move it.'

Sara left the wing to a cacophony of jibes from the other inmates. Most of them were giving advice on the benefits of giving sexual favours to a police officer, others were just shouting straightforward abuse. The catcalling was deafening. It echoed from the walls. Her mind was racing. What were they going to ask her? Did they know what she'd seen at those flats? Had she actually seen what she thought she had, or was the mushroom tea responsible for her hallucinating? Either way, she couldn't trust herself not to say something stupid. Her mouth was always a few minutes ahead of her brain. She was panicking that she might incriminate herself. The main thing that bothered her was how they knew she'd been there. Had someone already spoken to the police and named her? Maybe one of the other girls had grassed. Her pulse increased and she could feel sweat trickling down her back. The craving to smoke reached monumental levels. She needed a cigarette.

'Have you spoken to them yourself?' Sara asked as they made their way through a series of gates.

'No, Larkin.'

'How do you know what they want to talk to me about?'

'It's my job to know.'

Sara gave up trying to find out what they wanted her for. They reached the visiting area and she was given a blue tabard and ushered in. It was completely empty, except for two men in their thirties; both were doable. They gestured for her to join them at their table. Sara felt like a schoolgirl approaching a disciplinary. She felt their eyes on her, probing her mind, searching for lies. One of them was wearing Boss, the other Creed. She liked both. In a different life she could've dated either of them, maybe even more than dating. Maybe houses, kids, and holidays; who knew what could have been, had she made different choices.

'Hello, Sara,' Ian Barlow said. He pointed to the seat opposite him. 'I'm DS Barlow and this is DC Collins, Merseyside Major Investigation Team.' Sara sat down and looked at the floor, avoiding eye contact. The police had the ability to make her feel guilty even when she wasn't.

'We need to ask you some questions. Do you want some water?' Barlow asked. Sara shook her head. She did want water, but she was nervous. 'Do you know why we're here?' Sara shook her head again. 'You've heard about the murders at Stanley House, haven't you?' She shook her head again. Barlow glared at her. 'You haven't heard about the cannibal murders?'

'I don't think so,' she muttered. Her face blushed red.

'Wow. I find that hard to believe, don't you?' Barlow asked his detective constable.

'Very,' the DC answered. 'The story has been all over the news.'

'Where was it again?' she asked.

'Stanley House,' Barlow said. 'A nine-storey tower block in the Everton Valley. They're calling them the Hannibal murders, the cannibal murders, the satanic murders, all sorts. I don't think I've worked on a case that's had so much attention from the press.' He paused. 'You do have televisions in here, don't you?'

'Yes,' Sara mumbled. 'I might have seen something about it,' she added.

'Might have?' Barlow said.

'I'm not big on the news,' she said, playing with her fingernails.

'You're not big on the news, eh?'

'No.'

'That *is* funny, because, while we were waiting for you, I was talking to one of your POs and she told us you're quite the celebrity in here because you worked in the flats where the murders took place.' Barlow paused for effect. 'Apparently, you told everyone in here you did one of the punters on an altar.' Sara blushed and shrugged, caught out by the very first question. She felt like crawling under the table. 'Do you remember now?'

'Yes.'

'Let's not bullshit each other, Sara, okay?' he said.

'Okay, sorry,' Sara said. 'I'm just nervous.'

'There's no need to be. We just want to talk. This will be much more pleasant if you're straight with us. We're not interested in what you were doing there. That's pretty obvious.'

'It is?' she asked.

'Yes. They had sex parties there and you're a brass. I don't have to be Sherlock to work that one out.'

'How did you know?'

'We know you were there because your fingerprints are there.' Barlow looked into her eyes. 'Look at me, Sara,' he said. 'All we want from you is anything you can tell us about what went on, who attended, and if you saw anything connected to these murders.' He paused again. 'We're not interested in you.'

'I didn't see anything.' Sara said, nervously.

'Nothing?' Barlow sighed. 'Were you blindfolded the entire time?'

'No.'

'Then, you did see other people there, didn't you?'

'I don't know any names. A lot of the men wore masks.'

'Masks?' Barlow frowned. 'What type of masks?'

'Animal masks,' Sara said. 'They were scary.'

'I imagine they were. So, you didn't see any faces at all?'

'Not that I can remember. I was off my face most of the time.' She shrugged again. 'They made everyone drink mushroom tea. That was part of the gig. I can't remember anything.'

Barlow put a photograph of John Metcalfe on the table. Sara glanced at it. Her face reddened and her heartbeat quickened. She folded her arms and looked away.

'It's obvious you recognise him.' Sara looked at her hands. 'You know him, don't you?' Barlow asked. Sara nodded that she did. 'Good. Do you know his name?'

'John, something,' Sara said quietly.

'Does John Metcalfe ring a bell?' Barlow said.

'Not really. I never asked anyone their names.' She sighed. 'You don't in my game.'

'But you knew him as John?' Barlow asked.

Sara nodded.

'His surname is Metcalfe.'

'If you say so. He's a horrible bastard. A real sadist.'

'What makes you say that?' Barlow asked.

'I don't want to talk about it.'

'Okay,' Barlow said, 'we'll come back to him. What about him?' he asked, placing an image of Bruce May on the table. 'Do you recognise him?' Sara nodded that she did. 'You saw both these men, in those flats, while sex parties were going on?'

'Yes, but they weren't sex parties. Not really.'

'What would you call them?' Barlow asked.

'Rituals, ceremonies,' she said, shrugging. 'At no point does the word "party" describe anything that went on there. Party implies it was fun, all about sex; it was far from that.'

'What was it, Sara?'

'I don't know. Some kind of occult shit.'

'Okay. I understand.'

'Do you?' Sara asked. 'Because I don't.'

'How many times did you go there?' Barlow asked.

'I don't know.'

'Roughly, Sara?'

'Four or five,' she mumbled.

'Were they there each time?' Barlow asked, pointing to the photographs.

'John was,' Sara said. 'Bruce wasn't always there. Sometimes there were only a handful of them but that was when the really sick stuff happened. Some of it would make your hair curl.'

'Did you see them hurting anyone?' Barlow asked bluntly.

'Hurting anyone?' Sara snorted. 'That's what it was all about – they're sadists, they hurt each other. Especially him,' she said, pointing to Metcalfe. 'Him and his brother were the worst.'

'Brother?' Barlow asked, trying not to look surprised. His detective constable immediately sent Braddick a text: Metcalfe has a brother.

'Yes. His name was Joe. They always introduced themselves as John and Joe. They weren't twins but they looked alike. Right pair of bastards, they are.'

'What about this woman?' Barlow asked, showing her a photograph of Victoria May.

'She was always there,' Sara said. 'She was one of the more enthusiastic members.'

'Enthusiastic?'

'The stuff she let them do to her is unrepeatable.'

'What do you mean?' Barlow asked.

'I got paid for what I did,' Sara said. 'She did it for the sake of it; a raving masochist if ever I saw one.'

'She liked being hurt?' Barlow asked.

'And then some,' Sara said. 'She liked it a little too much. I think she was trying to impress.'

'Impress who?'

'The black woman who was in charge.'

'Who, her?' Barlow placed a picture of Fabienne Wilder on the table. 'Do you recognise her?'

'That's her. She was the queen bee,' Sara said, looking away. 'The others did everything she said. I'd go as far as to say they worshipped her. Everything revolved around her, but she never joined in. She would wander from room to room, muttering in a foreign language.'

'Did you recognise the language?'

'No. I did a bit of Latin at school and it was similar, but not Latin,' Sara said. 'Who knows what language she speaks, she's a nutter, isn't she?'

'From what we know so far, yes, she is,' Barlow agreed.

'You say they did everything she told them to,' the DC said. 'Did she tell them to hurt people?'

'Yes.'

'And you saw them hurting people?'

'Yes. They got off on it.' Sara shrugged. 'You'll struggle to get anyone to complain about it, though.'

'What do you mean?'

'They were all consenting adults,' Sara said. 'Most of the time. Until ...' she trailed off. A tear ran down her cheek.

'Until what, Sara?' Barlow pushed. 'What did you see?'

'I don't know what I saw. Not really.'

'You saw someone being badly hurt, didn't you?'

'Yes.'

'Who did they hurt?' Barlow asked. Sara looked away and bit her lip. The memory was clearly painful for her. Barlow waited for her to calm down. She was close, he could feel it. There was something she wanted to say. 'Who did they hurt, Sara?' he asked again. 'What did you see in those flats?'

'They hurt each other, they hurt everyone,' she said. 'That's what it was all about.'

'I need you to give me something specific, so we can charge them when we arrest them.'

'Have you arrested any of them?' Sara asked.

'I can't discuss that, but you don't need to worry about them,' Barlow said. 'They can't hurt you anymore.'

'Really?' Sara said. She put her hand into her pocket and took out the hex. It felt nasty to the touch. She dropped it on the table between them, as if it was too hot to hold. 'That was put through my hatch last night.' Barlow recognised it as similar to the one left at Braddick's house. Sara read his expression. 'Have you seen one before?' she asked. Barlow hesitated. 'I thought we weren't going to bullshit each other.' The detectives exchanged glances. 'Have you seen one before? Answer me.'

'We've seen something similar,' Barlow admitted. 'It's something to do with voodoo, we think; probably a warning.'

'A warning? No shit, Sherlock,' Sara said. 'Did you learn that at detective school?'

'We're researching the relevance of it,' Barlow said. It was his turn to blush. He shifted uncomfortably in his chair.

'Researching?' Sara said. 'I'm not a detective, but I have a good idea what it means.' She shook her head. 'I'll tell you what I think, if you tell me what you think.'

'I don't know,' Barlow said. 'Obviously, it's meant to frighten you.'

'You think so?' Sara said, smiling sarcastically. 'No flies on you, are there? If it was meant to frighten me, they achieved just that.' She picked up the small cross and studied it. 'It was put through my door in the middle of the night and I was lying in my bed, crapping myself. Do you know what that says to me?'

'Go on,' Barlow said.

'It says, "shut your mouth, Sara". It says, "we can get to you in prison, Sara, don't talk to the police".'

'Look, Sara,' Barlow said. 'This case has attracted all the lunatics out of the woodwork.'

'Meaning what, exactly?'

'Your PO said everyone on the wing knows who you are. That could have been put through your door by any wannabies who want to be connected to this cult.' Barlow sat back in his chair. He didn't want Sara wiggling off the hook. 'The chances of them actually having members on the inside are slim.'

'*That* tells me different,' Sara said. 'You said you'd seen one similar.'

'We have, but that doesn't mean they're connected.'

'So, you're saying two random nutters have come up with the same idea, at the same time?' Sara said. 'I'm not the brightest bulb on the Christmas tree, but I'm not stupid, either.'

'I'm not saying you're stupid. We'll make sure you're put under observation. You're safe. You have my word on it.'

'I don't think you can make me promises like that,' Sara said. 'You'll be tucked up in bed with the missus tonight. I'm in a cell with my name on a board outside. What if it's one of the screws?' she asked. 'You can't protect me twenty-four hours a day, can you?'

'We can protect you by proxy,' Barlow said. 'I'll speak to the governor myself. Tell us what you've seen, and I'll make sure you're protected.'

'What if there's a trial?' Sara asked. 'I can't go to court.'

'We can protect your identity in a case like this,' Barlow said. 'Because there may be members of this cult outside the investigation, we can apply to the judge for you to testify remotely. You won't even be in the same building as the courtroom.' Sara looked at the table and played with her fingers. Her nails needed painting. It was on the list of things she would do when she sold her story to the press. Testifying in the case would put the price up. It had to. It gave credence to her story. An interview with a key witness would be worth a bundle. It could be her ticket out of the gutter. She looked at Barlow and nodded. 'What do you say, Sara?'

'I can't be specific about much,' she said, shaking her head. 'I told you, I was off my face most of the time.'

'Okay. Tell me what you can be clear about: what about dates?' Barlow asked. 'Can you remember when you were there?'

'Are you kidding me?' Sara said. 'I can't remember what I had for breakfast. One day is much the same as the next to me.'

'Think about it, carefully,' Barlow said. 'Can you remember something that happened in the news, or how close to a holiday it might have been?' he prompted. She frowned.

'What do you mean, "holiday"?' Sara asked.

'Christmas, maybe, or Easter, bonfire night, Halloween?'

'OMG,' she said, sitting up straight. Her eyes were wide with surprise.

'What is it, Sara?' Barlow asked. 'What do you remember?'

'Halloween,' she said. 'The last time we went there was Halloween.' She stopped while the memories played in her mind. 'We should have thought about that, shouldn't we?' Barlow waited. 'Going there at Halloween, we should have realised it was a bad idea. And it was, very bad.'

'Hindsight is a great thing,' Barlow said.

'Isn't it just.'

'Let's start at the beginning,' Barlow said. 'You remember going there on Halloween?'

'Yes.'

'Last year?'

'Yes.'

'Were they all there?' Barlow asked, pointing to the pictures.

'Yes.'

'Bruce May, too?' the DC asked.

'Yes. He was there.'

'Good. Tell me about that night.'

'They were behaving strangely,' Sara said. She chuckled dryly. 'Stranger than usual, anyway.'

'In what way?'

'It's hard to describe. They were acting squirrelly. There was a lot of whispering going on.' Sara's eyes misted over as the memories returned. 'When it started, the atmosphere was intense. She was twitching and shaking and foaming at the mouth.'

'She?'

'Her,' Sara said, pointing to the photographs.

'Fabienne Wilder?'

'Yes. I thought she was having an epileptic fit at one point. The more she fitted, the more excited the rest of them became. Bearing in mind I was tripping on the mushroom tea; I didn't have a clue what was going on. Then they

started on each other, men on men, women on women, really going for it –
hurting each other. It went from bad to worse.'

'Did they hurt you?'

'Yes,' she said.

'What did they do to you?'

'I don't want to talk about it.'

'I think you do,' Barlow pushed. 'What did they do to you?'

'I don't want to talk about it.'

'Come on, Sara,' Barlow said. 'These people dismembered their victims,
ate them, and flushed bits of them down the toilet. They need locking up for the
rest of their lives. I need you to help us do that.' Barlow sighed. He sat forward
and looked into Sara's eyes. 'Tell us what happened. We need your help to lock
them up.'

'Okay.' Sara shook her head as if she'd given in too easily. 'I shouldn't
be doing this. I don't want to be involved.'

'We'll keep your involvement hidden from them,' Barlow said.

'You better had,' Sara said.

'We will. Let's start with a simple question. Did one of them hurt you?'

'Yes,' Sara said, nodding.

'How?'

'They cut me.'

'With a knife?' Barlow asked. Sara nodded and pointed to her breasts.
The constable was rapidly scribbling down notes. 'You're telling us that they cut
you with a knife?' Barlow said.

'Yes.'

'Who did it?'

'John and his brother,' Sara said, pointing to the photograph.

'You're pointing to John Metcalfe.'

'Yes.'

'He cut you on your breasts?'

'Yes.'

'Tell me about it.'

'Joe held my wrists and knelt on my chest so I couldn't move. They took it in turns to make tiny cuts on my nipples,' she whispered. 'They wanted to taste blood. There was always blood.'

'Why on earth did you go back?' Barlow asked.

'It wasn't so bad at first,' Sara said, swallowing hard. 'But it got worse every time we went back. I needed the money and they paid well.'

'We?'

'Sorry?'

'You said, "we".' Barlow said.

'There were always two or three working girls there,' Sara said. 'I was too scared to go alone; none of us would go there alone.'

'Who was there the night they cut you?'

'I'm not giving names,' Sara said.

'Okay, leave that for now. You said you were scared. What were you scared of?' Barlow asked. 'Take your time. In your own words, Sara.'

'You know what I was scared of.' She started crying again.

'I need you to tell me in your own words,' Barlow said.

'The occult stuff,' she said, wiping away another tear. 'It was frightening. Like they said on the television. The satanic stuff was weirding us out. They're nutters. Chanting and praying to whatever she's called.'

'Fabienne Wilder?' the constable asked. Sara nodded. 'Okay, carry on.'

'We were tripping on the mushrooms and that lot were doing whatever it was they were doing, ceremonial nonsense, and then it would get dark – dark and scary. That's when the sex would start. It got worse every time. They pushed the boundaries further and further. Eventually it was all about pain, not sex. And then … the last time I went, that was when they cut me.' Sara began sobbing. 'I screamed and told them to stop, that was going too far, but they didn't stop. The other girls were cut, too.'

'You saw them being assaulted?'

'Yes. It was different to the other times we had been there.'

'How was it different?' Barlow asked.

'It was more intense,' she said. 'They were more excited, almost frenzied. Some of the women were hysterical. It was terrifying. The humming and chanting were deafening at times, and when it reached a high point, someone else was cut.' Sara began to tremble. 'Then they brought in a woman. She was young and black. She didn't speak English very well. They tied her down. She begged them to let her go. I wanted to help her, but I couldn't move. That poor woman.' Sara broke down. Barlow sat back in silence and waited for the sobbing to settle. The seconds turned to minutes; the silence was uncomfortable; she would talk just to fill it. She took a deep breath. 'I'm sorry,' she said. 'It's been on my conscience for a long time.' Barlow nodded that he understood but didn't speak. 'Okay.' Sara folded her fingers into each other. 'I'll tell you what I saw, but I want three things.'

'Which are?' Barlow asked. 'I can't make any promises.'

'I want a brief and I want protection and I want immunity,' Sara said.

'You need to give me some idea what you've got, Sara,' Barlow said, shaking his head. 'Immunity is beyond my pay grade.'

'I witnessed a murder,' she said. 'They murdered two young women that night. I watched them do it.' She paused and wiped tears away from the corners of her eyes. 'I think we were next. We were never meant to get out of there alive that night.'

'You think they were going to kill you?'

'Yes. But…'

'But what?' Barlow asked. 'How did you escape?'

'I started a fire in the bathroom, using a candle and some toilet roll, and we ran.'

'The burnt-out flat at the end of the landing?' Barlow asked. He looked at the DC. It explained how it had caught fire.

'Yes. That was my fault.' Sara wiped her eyes. 'And I can give you two more witnesses who saw it.'

'The girls who went with you?'

'Yes. That's all I'm saying until I get some assurances.' Barlow stood up and took out his phone. 'Make that four things,' she added.

'What's the fourth?' Barlow asked.

'I want a cigarette.'

CHAPTER 29

Carol Hill checked her watch and pushed her black hair behind her ears. She tightened her stab vest and checked the straps were tucked inside. She had been an inspector in the vice squad for three years now. Before that, she'd worked her time as a uniformed officer, walking the beat and driving a patrol car, before becoming part of the Matrix team, working undercover on the grimy streets of Liverpool, identifying, tracking and arresting the city's drug dealers. It was a role she'd cherished and enjoyed until her continued success had put her top of a gangland hit list comprised of officers, judges and barristers who needed eliminated. She was sent on secondment to Cumbria for eighteen months for her own protection, which she hated, before returning to the frontline a year later. By that time, the leaders of the crew that had wanted her executed were banged up, shot dead or in exile. Nowadays, she could go to Tesco or walk around Liverpool One's fashion houses without too much hassle. There was always the odd streetwalker or baghead who might recognise her, but they were too low down the food chain to be of concern – they were more frightened of her than she was of them. A decent pair of sunglasses and a hat were enough to hide behind.

She was glad DS Braddick had brought her into his investigation. Not all officers of his rank would have handed over an operation of this size. He'd been completely honest about the fact that MIT was buckling under the weight of the Hannibal murders; even she'd started using the tag. Braddick was convinced the Mays' properties were an elaborate front for a people trafficking operation, where women were tricked into the sex industry. She had seen her fair share of shakedowns and brothel-busting operations. Coordinating the searches of Victoria May's and John Metcalfe's properties was a simple matter of logistics. It involved forces from Lancashire, Cheshire, and Merseyside to hit them all at the same time so they couldn't warn the others. The plan was simple. Arrest everyone and eliminate them from the investigation or charge them one by one. No one was walking away today. Not while Carol Hill had breath in her lungs. She'd opted to run the operation from the raid on Metcalfe's property in Southport, being carried out by the Lancashire force. She knew MIT would be looking after the properties in Liverpool and Cheshire.

John Metcalfe owned a property at Beechfield Gardens, which was built on a knoll that overlooked the beach and the fairground, Pleasureland, on Southport's seafront. The estate was built in the fifties and was mostly detached houses separated by walls and hedges. It was an aging suburban area that had fallen into disrepair as the wealthy sold up and moved on to newer estates. Carol looked across the dunes towards the sea. It was still dark, but brighter on the horizon as the sun tried to make an impact on the day. The big wheel stood out against the grey sea, making it look closer than it was. The fairground looked desolate in the dull light of a winter morning. She checked her watch again and nodded to the leader of the Trojan Unit. They were set to break down the door with the 'big key' battering ram.

Number thirty-three Beechfield was a three-storey building, with steps leading up to the front door and steps leading down to a basement. There were wrought-iron handrails and spiked railings attached to the sandstone walls. They were rusted, the paint blistered and cracked. Sandstone steps were worn smooth and shiny. The window frames were dark blue, but the grey undercoat was showing through where the paint had fissured and peeled away. There was an asphalt driveway and a double garage to the side, and ivy covered the gable walls. Carol studied the upper windows through binoculars. All the tell-tale signs of a brothel were there. It was shabby on the outside, with no features to attract the eye; people passing by would hardly notice it. It was purposely bland and uninteresting. The neighbours might notice some vehicles coming and going, but most punters would park their vehicles on the beach road and walk to the house to avoid the chance of anyone recognising their car in an unusual place. The windows had thick curtains, which never moved, and no light showed from inside. She knew the windows had probably been covered with stud walling, and decorated over, ensuring total privacy for the punters. Nervous punters wouldn't return if they thought their identity could be compromised. A bedroom with no windows gave them the confidence to do what they'd paid for without concern. Bricking up the windows from the inside also turned a bedroom into a prison – not all the working girls went home every night; some never went home again. Carol had seen enough operations similar to this to know what to expect inside. It should be a simple breach and arrest.

CHAPTER 30

Braddick drove across the city to the M62 and headed towards Warrington. It was barely daylight when he reached the town's main cemetery on Manchester Road. The traffic was heavy, and he slowed down to look for a place to park. He still felt angry, but also a little foolish. Had he driven down the motorway, through the morning rush hour, on a wild goose chase? The letter had stated that the writer knew where his mother and father were buried; it challenged him to meet the writer at the cemetery at midnight to 'chat'. Braddick wasn't stupid enough to accept the challenge alone in the dark, nor was he convinced the writer was genuine. He couldn't risk involving anyone else at this stage. It had crossed his mind to call the uniform division in Cheshire to take a look, but he'd realised how it would look if it was a hoax. Wasting police hours unnecessarily wasn't appreciated. He'd decided to wait it out and take his chances in the morning. His family had been under ground for a long time. They were hardly in any danger.

The cemetery was huge, built in 1857, and his parents were buried in a family plot on the far side of the site, next to the river. It was at least a fifteen-minute walk from the gates, probably more like twenty. Braddick checked his phone. The raids on the May properties would be taking place in half an hour. He knew Laurel and Carol Hill would have everything under control, but the desire to be there was pulling him apart. If there was another way, he would've taken it. This was something he had to do himself. It couldn't be delegated, and it couldn't be postponed. If they'd done something to his parents' grave, he wanted to know. He would be back with the MIT within the hour.

Braddick jogged to the gates and looked around. There was nothing obvious to note. If someone was watching him, they were doing a good job of concealing themselves. There were plenty of places to watch and remain hidden. He didn't think they were likely to have a sniper rifle trained on him, although he couldn't shake the feeling of being watched. The world whizzed by as he debated with himself. The traffic was getting heavier. Dozens of cars and lorries waited at the traffic lights. He checked his mobile and dialled Laurel; it went straight to voicemail. He left a quick message and entered the graveyard. It wouldn't take long to put his mind at rest. He needed to see their grave. If it had been desecrated, he would be distraught, but vandalism could be repaired; not knowing was worse. The fact they could get to him without fronting him up was driving him insane. Threatening Laurel was disgusting, but posting a letter through his letter box, indicating that his parents' resting place was a target, had shifted the investigation up a gear. He had to use protocol and follow the rules, there were lines he couldn't cross, but it seemed there was nothing off limits to them, whoever they were.

Braddick pushed his hands into his coat pockets and walked quickly towards the main pathway. Two men wearing Hi-Viz were standing next to a mound of soil, smoking. They chatted as another worked in a freshly dug hole. The sound of a radio drifted from their van. Braddick nodded a silent hello as he passed. The rest of the graveyard was empty. Ten minutes on, he recognised a huge angel atop a marble headstone, the point where he turned left onto the pathway that led to his family plot. It was another ten-minute walk from there. Braddick looked at the angel. It was beautiful – hewn from a block of marble as tall as he was, shaped and smoothed by the hands of an artist. He wondered who had bought it, like it really mattered; of course, it didn't matter. The purchaser and the sculpture were long dead. Then he wondered if the Niners saw themselves as the opposite of angelic, did they think they were evil angels, perhaps? What was their goal? Was there one, or was it all just for the sake of being bad? Was causing chaos while alive enough to make them happy in the afterlife, or did they just enjoy causing the living pain and suffering? The statue stared blankly back at him, answering no questions and offering no solutions.

Braddick walked on, slowing as he neared the section of the graveyard where his parents lay. A privet hedge separated it from the older areas. He could see the family headstone, fifty yards or so to his left. It was daubed with red paint, but he was too far away to see what it said. There looked to be some words and a star drawn on it: a nine-angled star. He couldn't see the grave itself from there.

Anger flared inside. Braddick jogged down the gravel path then veered off and weaved his way through the headstones to the plot. His foot caught on a stone flower urn, hidden in the long grass, and he tumbled. He fell heavily on his side, cracking his skull on a headstone. He was stunned for a second. A trickle of blood ran from his temple. He took a breath and touched the growing bump, his fingertips sticky with blood. The world began to spin for a moment, and he felt nauseous. He wanted to get up, but his muscles wouldn't work. His vulnerability spiked. He had to get a grip before panic set in.

He took a deep breath and calmed himself a little before taking a tissue from his jacket pocket. He pressed it against the cut and stood up, his legs shaking and weak. The sound of a magpie rattled across the graveyard, turning his attention to the grave. He watched the bird fly down from a tree and land behind the headstone. A moment later it took off, grasping a length of something leathery in its beak. A shiver ran down his spine. As he walked towards the plot, a rotten smell drifted to him. He'd been around enough decomposition to recognise it.

The closer he got, the angrier he became. He could see soil piled to the side of the grave. The corner of a wooden coffin was visible; its brass handles glinted in the dull morning light. Another magpie swooped down, leaving with a strip of something greenish in its beak. He turned a corner and looked at the bizarre scene and realised what they had done. His heart broke; he dropped to his knees and screamed at the brooding clouds.

CHAPTER 31

The Trojan Unit moved into action. An officer wielding the big key struck the door just below the lock, the rest of the team were poised, ready to enter. It made a loud clang, as if he'd hit a brick wall. The door shuddered but didn't give a millimetre. He blushed and swung the ram again, aiming lower this time, but achieved the same result: nothing moved. The commanding officer tensed, sensing something was amiss. The big key struck the door for a third time, but it still didn't budge.

'Help him,' the commanding officer said. 'Double up!'

A second man stepped up and they held a handle each. Swinging the ram as high as they could, using their combined strength, they hammered it into the door. It impacted with a dull thud but caused no damage. Carol Hill felt anxious. This was no ordinary door. Of course, she'd seen fortified front doors before, but the officers in charge had always been aware of them before a breach was attempted and specialised equipment would be deployed. It appeared that either Lancashire hadn't spotted the door was reinforced, or it hadn't been communicated to the Trojan unit. Someone had made a massive oversight. The operation was compromised already. What mattered now, was that the element of surprise had been lost. They needed to gain access to the building quickly. The occupiers would now be well aware that the police were trying to force entry and evidence would be destroyed: drugs would be flushed away, paperwork shredded and burned.

'It's fortified. Get the grinder on it,' Carol ordered. 'Hurry up!'

The sound of the petrol grinder starting shattered the morning silence. It drifted across the dunes to the sea, frightening the seagulls from their perches. A police officer lifted the powerful cutting tool and pulled the trigger. Smoke billowed from the exhaust port. The engine whined and a diamond-tipped disk spun at full throttle. Splinters flew as it connected with the door and ripped through it. It made short work of the wood, but showers of sparks flew as it contacted metal behind it. After cutting in a criss-cross pattern, they used the battering ram to smash the door from the frame. It became apparent why the ram had made no impression on the door: behind it was a second door, forged from steel bars. It was fitted to a steel frame.

'We can't cut through that,' the Trojan officer said. 'We need another way in.' He turned to his men. 'First unit, try the ground floor windows. Second unit, attack the basement door.'

'Is the back door secured?' someone asked.

'There's a security grill fastened to the wall,' Carol said. 'No one is going in or out of that door.'

They smashed the nearest ground floor window and the curtains were pulled down, revealing a breezeblock wall. Carol had expected as much. The sound of more smashing glass came from all directions, but the results were the same each time.

'They're all bricked up, guv,' an officer called.

'This place is like a fortress,' the Trojan commander said, turning to Carol.

'Someone screwed up,' Carol said. 'We should have known that before we attempted the breach.'

'Let's not do this here,' the commander said. 'Any joy down there?' he called to the basement unit.

'We're nearly in, guv,' the answer came. 'A couple of minutes at the most.'

The sound of the grinder was deafening. Through the bars, Carol saw movement in the hallway near the stairs. She tapped the Trojan commander on the shoulder. He followed her gaze. A woman started screaming for help. Her voice was joined by another, and then another, and then more. Some were calling in English, others in foreign tongues. She thought they were coming from upstairs.

'Get some light in there,' he ordered.

Three powerful torches were aimed into the house. There was a man, trudging backwards down the stairs, pouring liquid from a five-gallon container. He reached the bottom and turned to face them, tossing the container down the cellar steps. It clattered out of sight, spraying amber fluid up the walls. The man disappeared through a doorway for a moment and returned with another container. He removed the cap and began to pour the contents onto the hallway carpet.

'Put that down,' Carol ordered. The man looked at her.

His eyes were dark, almost black. He seemed to look beyond her into the distance. A smile touched his lips as if he'd seen someone he liked. Carol looked behind her but there was no one there. The trapped women screamed louder. The sound of them banging on the internal doors echoed from the walls and the smell of petrol reached them. Their voices reached fever-pitch.

'Drop that, now!' Carol shouted. The man ignored her. 'Take him down,' Carol ordered. No one moved. 'Take him down, now!'

An armed response officer shouldered his Heckler and Koch. The man inside didn't seem phased. He lifted the container and poured the liquid over himself.

'Take the shot,' Carol said. The officer fired three times, hitting the man in the chest and shoulder. He staggered backwards, slamming into a wall. His eyes glazed over; he left a bloody smear on the wallpaper as he slid to a sitting position.

'We're in the basement, guv,' a Trojan officer shouted.

'Pull them out,' Carol ordered.

'What?' the unit commander said.

'Pull your men out, now!'

The man inside lifted his head slightly as he flicked a zippo into life. His vest had stopped two bullets, knocking the wind from his lungs. The flame flickered as he tossed it onto the fuel-soaked carpet. He smiled as blue flames engulfed him. They sped along the hallway, up the stairs to the first floor and down the steps into the basement. There was a loud crackling sound as a backdraft was created. Carol was going to shout a warning when something inside exploded. A wall of flames raced down the hallway and through the steel grill, encompassing everyone near the entrance. The basement exploded into flames and the Trojan unit sprinted up the steps, their clothes on fire. She heard the captives screaming in terror but couldn't do a thing to help them. It was a sound she would never forget.

CHAPTER 32

Braddick waited for the first units to attend. Two cars arrived together: one marked, the other unmarked. Three detectives climbed out of the unmarked car to join two uniformed officers and they headed along the narrow path that led to the Braddick family plot. The desecration wouldn't have been obvious to them until they neared. As they took in the scene, their facial expressions varied from disgust, to confusion, and plain shocked.

'DS Braddick?' Braddick nodded and shook his hand. 'I'm DS Blackwell, this is DC Smyth and DC Walsh.' He scanned the scene and shook his head. 'Are you okay?' he asked, seeing the bloody tissue in Braddick's hand.

'I tripped in the long grass and banged my head,' Braddick said.

'Can you tell me what the hell is going on here, please?' Blackwell asked.

'What have you been told?'

'Not much. My governor said that a superintendent from Merseyside was in distress on our patch and needed help,' Blackwell said. 'We got here as soon as we could. I knew it involved the graveyard, but I have to say I didn't expect this.' He read the name on the headstone. 'Are they relations?'

'This is my family plot,' Braddick said. 'That is my grandfather,' he said, pointing to a decomposed corpse dressed in a suit. He pointed to two more corpses. 'They're my mother and father.' The corpses had been placed in seated positions around the open grave, as if they were waiting for him to arrive. His mother and father had skeletal arms on each other's shoulders. The exposed skin had been striped by wildlife. Their bodies were facing together. His grandfather was propped against the headstone, his hands stuffed into the material of his shirt. 'Someone has dug them up, opened their coffins, and taken their skulls. The birds did the rest of the damage.'

'This is sick,' Blackwell said. 'Is it a coincidence you're here? How did you know they'd been dug up?'

'I didn't know until I got here. Last night I had an anonymous note put through my letterbox, stating the address of the plot and asking me to come for a "chat".'

'They wanted you to come to a graveyard for a chat?'

'Yes.'

'Who does that?'

'Stupid people.'

'Why didn't you call us?'

'It was late,' Braddick said. 'I didn't know whether to take it seriously. I wasn't going to waste your time sending a unit out here, just in case it was a hoax. I came this morning to see if the threats had substance and found them like this.'

'Have you had a look for the skulls?' Blackwell asked quietly. He didn't really know what to say. It was like a scene from a Netflix horror.

'Yes,' Braddick said. 'I've looked in the close vicinity. I think they've taken them.'

'What makes you think that?'

'Because they know it will disgust me, that's why,' Braddick said, shrugging. 'They didn't just desecrate my family's grave; they've disrespected their bodies. Beheading them after death and taking their skulls as trophies, it's the ultimate insult. Defiling my family, simply because they can.'

'Do you know who would do this?' Blackwell asked. 'What's it about?'

'It's to do with the Hannibal murders in Liverpool,' Braddick said.

Blackwell opened his mouth and nodded. 'Are you the SIO on that?'

Braddick nodded.

'I see. That explains this, to a degree. Is this retaliation?'

'More like a warning, I think,' Braddick said.

'Warning about what?'

'Catching them, exposing them, spoiling their fun; who knows?' Braddick said. 'Nothing on this case makes sense.'

'I've read some of the reports. It's pretty messed up, isn't it?' Blackwell said.

'That's an understatement.'

'You've found multiple victims in the drains?'

'Pieces of them, yes.'

'Is there any likelihood of identifying them?'

'It's unlikely.'

'Do you know how many victims you have, yet?'

'No.'

'Have you got any more of them in custody?'

'Two of them. One's a cabbage and one's a liar,' Braddick said. 'We'll be interviewing the liar later today.'

'You've got your hands full. This is the last thing you need right now,' Blackwell said. He put his hand on Braddick's shoulder. 'This is disgusting. I'm very sorry for you and your family. Tell me what you want me to do from here.'

'The first thing is to make sure no journalists get near this,' Braddick said. 'If the press get hold of this we'll never hear the end of it.'

'Of course.'

'If you could cover my family up and cover the headstone, so no one sees the family name, I'd be very grateful.'

'No problem,' Blackwell said.

'I need you to get a local undertaker you can trust to take the bodies away. I'll arrange for the headstone to be removed and cleaned up.'

'No problem. I'll have the place sealed off while we deal with it,' Blackwell said. 'Leave it to us.'

'Thank you.'

'Why did they take their skulls?'

'I have no idea,' Braddick said, shaking his head. 'Nothing these people do makes any sense to me. None at all.' He noticed uniformed officers at the gates in the distance. 'Can we get them covered up quickly? It won't take long for someone to get curious. I need to make some calls and get back to the station.'

'Leave it to me,' Blackwell said. 'I'll let you know where they've been taken as soon as I've secured an undertaker.'

'Thanks again,' Braddick said.

CHAPTER 33

Number thirty-three Beechfield Gardens was a smoking shell. The exterior walls were still standing but the interior walls had crumbled beneath the weight of the slate roof, weakened by the inferno. The collapse was caused when the gas main exploded beneath the kitchen. The house had simply collapsed into itself, killing everyone inside. The fire brigade was hosing the smouldering remains from three sides, but it was still too hot and fragile to comb the debris for the dead. There wouldn't be much to find. It was clear that no one could have survived the blaze, and they had no idea how many women had been caged there. DI Carol Hill had heard at least four different voices calling from the upper floor before the fire.

She'd been inundated with calls from the hierarchy from both the Merseyside and Lancashire forces. They were at panic stations. Her ACC sounded like he was going to have a heart attack. He was under pressure from the Stanley House case as it was. The press was in a frenzy and if they connected a fire with multiple deaths to the case, it could tip him over the edge. He was in self-preservation mode, desperately trying to cover his own arse before the news hit the Internet. It was obvious to Carol where the blame should lie: Lancashire had not done their homework. Undercover officers should have entered the building several times, posing as punters, checking the layout and identifying any modifications that had been made. It was a schoolboy error, resulting in multiple fatalities. The top brass from both forces were looking for a scapegoat and she was quite happy to point them in the right direction. The reconnaissance wasn't fit for purpose, and the Trojan unit hadn't completed a thorough enough risk assessment of the information they'd been given. The fact that no undercover officers had been into the building, should have rung alarm bells. No unit commander worth his salt would endanger his men that way. No recon: no entry. Simple.

Her mobile rang. It was Braddick.

'How bad is it,' he asked.

'As bad as it gets,' Carol said. 'No one survived.'

'What happened? Off the record.'

'The recon inside the building wasn't done,' Carol said. 'The place was like a fortress. The only thing left standing is the door. There was no way through it and the windows were bricked up from the inside. They should have expected that as standard.'

'Not everyone has worked in the big, bad city,' Braddick said. He knew she was right. 'The entry unit should have noticed that in the planning. The buck will stop with them in the end.'

'I felt for them, really. You're right though, they didn't do their homework. They were summoned to headquarters at Preston.'

'There'll be a debrief and then someone will get shafted,' Braddick said.

'They're gutted. I could see it on their faces. They were taken in a convoy of minibuses – four of them were taken to the burns unit, two of them are in a serious condition.'

'What would we have found in there?' Braddick asked. 'Did you see anything?'

'I heard at least four female voices shouting for help,' she said. 'They must have been locked in upstairs.'

'Were they foreign?'

'Undoubtably,' she said. 'The guy who set himself on fire looked local, although he didn't speak. He took three in the chest, but he must have had a vest on.'

'There's nothing you could have done,' Braddick said, hearing the tension in her voice.

'There was something about him, Braddick,' Carol said. 'I swear I saw him smiling as he covered himself in petrol.'

'That wouldn't surprise me,' Braddick said. 'This bunch are off the chart, batshit crazy. I'll see you when you get back.'

'Yes. See you later.'

Carol didn't think the unit commander and his direct reporting officer would survive the enquiry. They had been grossly negligent. She had no idea which department had carried out the recon, but heads would roll there, too. Her mobile rang again, and she checked the screen, it was the ACC's office. They would order her back to Canning Place and it would be her role in the operation that would be scrutinised. She felt very sad for the women who had died, and she wished Detective Superintendent Braddick had kept his operation to himself.

CHAPTER 34

Braddick walked into the MIT office and immediately saw the ACC talking with the chief constable and his staff officer. He recognised some other faces from Professional Standards and Legal Services. Seeing them in the MIT department meant the hierarchy was in crisis. It wasn't unexpected. The deaths at Metcalfe's property in Southport had caused panic further up the ranks, and a crisis team had been formed to oversee the case. Braddick sighed and walked towards the gathering. There was no way to avoid their questions.

'Superintendent Braddick,' the ACC said as he approached. The gathering stopped chatting and turned to greet him. 'We've just heard what happened. I want to say how sorry we are about what happened to your family's grave. It's absolutely vile.'

'Thank you, sir.'

'Are you okay?' he asked, concerned. The bruise on Braddick's head was blackening. 'Have you had that seen to?'

'I'm fine, sir,' Braddick said. 'It's just a knock. It looks worse than it is.'

'Have you got time to give us an update while we're waiting for the Lancashire officers to arrive?' the ACC asked. 'The chief and his advisors are meeting with them shortly. The shambles at the Metcalfe property is going to cause a shitstorm. They want to get their stories in order before an enquiry begins.'

'Let me speak to my DS,' Braddick said, waving to Laurel. She waved back and stood up, walking towards them. 'Let's go in my office.' Braddick gestured to the group and they shuffled into the office, Laurel close behind them. Braddick leaned against his desk. He felt weary. Playing politics was the last thing he needed to do. 'We're preparing to interview Bruce May later today. The evidence against him is damning, but we want to nail him for the murder of his wife, too.' Braddick looked at Laurel. 'How are we doing with May's alibi?'

'We've scuppered it, guv,' Laurel said. Braddick felt a wave of relief wash over him. Finally, something had gone their way. 'May claimed to have been in London for three days on business at the time of his wife's murder. He had train receipts and a hotel reservation at the Kennedy Hotel to back up his whereabouts. His debit card activity confirms he bought a return ticket from Chester to Euston, and the hotel confirms that his card was used to book in at reception. It was also used to check out.'

'I don't follow,' the ACC interrupted. 'Doesn't that prove he *was* in London when she was murdered?'

'Yes, sir,' Laurel said, nodding. 'But I checked the CCTV footage of when he checked in and out,' she explained, handing him a photograph. 'The man using his card, clearly isn't Bruce May. We checked the footage from Chester station and this man can be seen boarding the train that Bruce May booked. He never left Chester, sir. He sent someone else to manufacture an alibi for him.'

'Cheshire missed this, sir,' Braddick said. 'Well done, Laurel.'

'Yes. Very well done, detective sergeant,' the ACC said.

'Thank you, sir,' Laurel said.

'Without his alibi,' Braddick said, 'we'll be charging Bruce May with the murder of Victoria May today, along with manslaughter, trafficking, modern-day slavery and living from immoral earnings. That's just to begin with. Bringing in Fabienne Wilder and her cohorts will depend on what he gives us. We still don't know where they are, but when we do we'll lock them up.' He looked around the gathering.

'That sounds encouraging,' the ACC said.

'There's another development,' Braddick added.

'Please share it with us.'

'DS Barlow conducted an informal interview this morning with a potential witness. She claims that she witnessed the murder of two women, probably African migrants, and she can give us two more witnesses who were there. That will give us Fabienne Wilder, Bruce May, Joe Metcalfe, and whoever else we can track down.'

'If we get to court, how reliable are the witnesses?' the ACC asked.

'Rock solid compared to the lunatics in the dock. They cooked their victims and flushed them down the toilet,' Braddick said, shrugging. 'We could bring Billy Liar into court as a witness and the jury would convict.'

'Good work, superintendent,' the chief inspector said. 'Keep us in the loop.'

'Will do, sir. Thank you.'

'Well done, Braddick,' the ACC added as they filed out of his office.

Braddick looked out of the window at the river while he waited for them to go.

'I'm so sorry to hear what happened at the graveyard,' Laurel said. 'It's absolutely disgusting.'

'It's worrying that they're targeting us personally,' Braddick said. 'It's a first for me.'

'Really?' Laurel asked, surprised.

'Oh, I didn't mean it was the first time I've been threatened or attacked,' Braddick said. 'It goes with the job.'

'Rob is giving me earache about working on this case. He's frightened,' Laurel agreed. 'The graveyard thing hasn't helped.'

'There's two ways to look at it,' Braddick said.

'Go on,' Laurel said, curious.

'Firstly, they're resourceful. They looked into my private life, found out my family are dead and found their grave. Clever and creative. They also challenged me to meet them there. What would have happened if I had?' He paused. 'Secondly, they're a bunch of lunatics too scared to face me but brave enough to take a spade to a deserted cemetery. You need to convince Rob they're in the second category, but actually accept they're in the first and they're dangerous, and your family is in danger. Keep your eyes open and lock your doors until we've put them all away.' A knock on the door interrupted them. 'Come in,' Braddick said. Ian Barlow walked in. 'How did it go?'

'Good,' Barlow said. 'Legal are happy to allow Larkin's evidence to be delivered remotely if we need it. I've arranged for a brief to talk to her and I've spoken to the prison governor to organise protection. They'll call me when she's ready to talk.'

'What else did she ask for?'

'Immunity and a cigarette,' Barlow said. 'She wouldn't give me the other names until we've agreed her terms.'

'I think you already have them,' Braddick said.

'What do you mean, guv?'

'The other sets of prints we found.'

'Melissa Walker and Maggie Bennet?' Barlow said. 'They've moved around a lot, guv. We're still trying to find out where they live.'

'Get creative, inspector,' Braddick said. 'Someone on the streets knows where they work and where they live. Find them before someone else does.'

'Are you worried they'll go after our witnesses?'

'They dug up my parents,' Braddick said. 'I wouldn't put anything past them. Find those women and bring them in. Sara Larkin is in the safest place.'

'I'm not so sure about that, guv,' Barlow said. 'Someone put a hex through her door last night. It's exactly the same as the one they left for you.'

'Was it done after lockup?' Braddick asked.

'Yes.'

'Then it must be a guard, or a guard who's turned a blind eye,' Braddick said. 'Did you report it to the governor?'

'Yes,' Barlow said. 'She was annoyed. Apparently, hiring POs she can trust is her number one issue. I stressed how important Larkin is to the case. If she's intimidated again, I think she'll have a sudden case of amnesia.'

'All the more reason to find the other two,' Braddick said. 'Find them, and bring them in.'

CHAPTER 35

Fabienne was cooking; the aroma of garlic and onions filled the air. She sliced up a chicken breast and dropped it into some preheated olive oil, before adding some mushrooms and diced potatoes. The meat sizzled as it browned. She poured boiling water over some chicken stock cubes and added the liquid to the mix. It smelled good already. She stirred it with a wooden spoon and covered it with a lid. It would be ready in an hour or so. The rain hammered against the window and dark clouds raced across the sky. Lightning streaked towards earth; she imagined it striking an oak tree, somewhere to the west. The top branches were sheared in half and the smell of burning wood filled her senses. It was a gift she'd had since she was a child: imagining things she couldn't see, or was it seeing things she couldn't imagine? Whatever it was, it had always been there. She felt the thunder approaching before she heard it. It was a wall of sound, travelling at frightening speed. A few seconds later there was a thunderclap that made the building rattle. Its power made her smile. She loved thunder and lightning. The storms she'd witnessed in the Caribbean as a child were spectacular: light shows performed by the gods. She missed the hot, sticky atmosphere that accompanied them, and the warm torrential rain.

She sensed the car engine before the sound of it reached her, and she looked towards the lane that ran from the house to the road. It was over a mile long; the vehicle wasn't in sight yet. He was coming back, hopefully with news and supplies and trophies. She wanted to see the trophies more than anything. They would take the edge off her craving for a while. The pictures had pleased her, she loved them; being there to see the policeman's expression was the only thing that would have been better – that would have been precious. And he would see the pictures soon, that was exciting too. Very exciting. Then she could toy with him, using the trophies to mess with his mind. That would take planning and thought but it would be a gift that never stopped giving. She could cause grief and agony from afar, with not much effort, until it was time to return to the fold. She would be a wolf amongst the sheep, and she would leave a trail of destruction along the way. Just as she always had.

She lifted the curtain and looked out. The swimming pool was discoloured and full of leaves. It was a while since it had been cleaned. Probably years. The grounds had become dilapidated and unkempt. There was a shift of consciousness, and in her mind's eye she saw three children running around the edge of the pool, laughing and chasing each other. Two girls and a boy, all blond. Their mother watched them play while she crocheted a shawl. Her clothing was Victorian. The little boy was wearing pantaloons. The vision was from the past, a long time ago. She watched the mother as she worked the hook. Fabienne reached out with her mind. The mother looked afraid, as a shiver ran through her. She looked up from her work and their eyes met for a second. The mother took a sharp intake of breath and called the children to her. She gathered all three in her arms. The children followed their mother's gaze and looked up at the window. They began to cry, hiding their faces from the abomination behind the glass. Fabienne smiled as the mother screamed; she closed her eyes for a moment, and when she opened them, the family had gone.

The scene was deserted once more. The patio around the pool was overgrown: thistles and nettles sprouted between the paving slabs. Moss covered the whitewashed walls and the garden furniture was rusted and warped by the weather. A greenhouse as big as a tennis court stood beyond the wall, its windows missing from their frames. Tall trees had grown through the roof. The estate had been left to rack and ruin; decay seeped through the very fibre of it. Once a vibrant space, with a profitable farm and a happy, healthy family residing there, it was now on its way to dereliction. She liked decay. Dereliction was nature's way of showing mankind that their time here is borrowed. The clock started ticking from the moment they were born, tick-tock, tick-tock, tick-tock. Every second could be their last. It was part of the chaos of the universe. Nothing was guaranteed except death.

The vehicle she'd heard turned a corner and came into view. She didn't recognise it; it wasn't him. Her senses became ultra-aware and she knew danger was coming. She peered through the glass as the vehicle approached. It was a black van with a single occupant. The driver was a white male in his fifties. In the back of the van he had a shotgun. It had two barrels, side-by-side, and it was loaded. She sensed dead birds – pheasants – in the back. He was a poacher, almost certainly. Fabienne closed the curtain and went to the back of the kitchen. An adjoining door led into a garage workshop. She looked at the tools on the wall. The choice was irrelevant, as long as it was heavy and sharp.

CHAPTER 36

Braddick and Laurel walked into the interview room at the new Matrix headquarters. The contrast between traditional custody suites and this modern version was startling. They could have been in a meeting room in a big hotel; it was plush, and everything smelled new. Bruce May was sitting next to his solicitor. Braddick didn't recognise him. His previous council had obviously decided this case was too big for him, or Bruce May had decided it was too big for him – it was probably too big for most. The evidence against Bruce was staggering, but someone would make a lot of money defending him, win or lose. Bruce looked twenty years older than the last time he'd sat across the table from them, and he'd obviously taken a punch on the nose – his eyelids were purple and swollen. His stubble was white, aging him significantly. Braddick thought about what he had done and felt anger burning inside him. Just looking at him was difficult. Bruce was obviously anxious and very eager to complain.

'I'm going to sue you, look at what someone did to me. I was attacked for no reason,' Bruce said.

'By a police officer?' Braddick asked, frowning.

'No,' Bruce said. 'Another prisoner.'

'You should sue them then,' Braddick said, matter of fact.

'I will. You lot are supposed to protect me. He punched me for no reason.'

'I think you'll find you were attacked for a reason,' Braddick said. 'Take a good look in the mirror and ask yourself why, honestly, and it might come to you.'

'I didn't kill Victoria,' Bruce said, before the legal necessities had been covered. 'I didn't kill anyone.'

'For the camera,' Braddick said, holding up his hand to silence him. 'Detective Superintendent Braddick and Detective Sergeant Stewart entering the room for the initial interview with Bruce Patrick May. The suspect has been read his rights. Also present is Mr May's solicitor,' Braddick paused. They sat down at the table and opened their files. Laurel had her laptop. 'Please give your name.'

'Alistair Price,' May's solicitor said for the camera.

'Firstly, it's obvious you have been involved in a physical altercation,' Braddick said. 'Have you been seen by a doctor?'

'It wasn't an altercation,' Bruce protested. 'It was an assault.'

'Have you been seen by a doctor?' Braddick repeated.

'Yes.'

'And they cleared you fit to be interviewed?' Braddick asked, looking at Prost. The solicitor nodded. 'Okay, Bruce, the last time we questioned you, you told us a pack of lies. I need you to know that the evidence against you is substantial, and my advice to you is to tell us the truth about everything we ask you.' Bruce shrugged and nodded his head. 'When we last spoke, you denied having been inside the flats on the ninth floor of Stanley House.'

'I did deny it, but I had good reason to lie,' Bruce said. Prost nudged him and shook his head.

'So, you were lying?' Braddick said.

'No comment.'

'We've found your prints and DNA in three of the four flats,' Braddick said. 'You were often there. Along with your wife, John Metcalfe, his brother, Joe, and Fabienne Wilder. We have witnesses and DNA.'

'I should've been honest,' Bruce said. 'I was concerned that I would be set up and framed for killing Victoria. That's what they're trying to do, you know.'

'Who is?' Braddick said.

'Fabienne Wilder and her followers,' Bruce said. 'They'll do or say anything she asks them to.'

'You're saying they're trying to frame you?'

'Yes.'

'By spreading your fingerprints, blood and semen all over the place?' Braddick asked. 'Explain to me, how does that work?'

'That's not what I meant,' Bruce said, blushing. 'I meant in connection to my wife's death.'

'I'm not talking about your wife's *murder* at the moment. I'm talking about the flats on the ninth floor of Stanley House,' Braddick said. 'You were there many times with the others, performing some kind of rituals, right?'

'No comment.'

'Rituals that involved murdering people?' Braddick continued.

'No comment.'

'Rituals that involved killing people and eating parts of them?'

'That's disgusting. I never did anything like that. They're setting me up,' Bruce said. 'I'm nothing to do with any of that.'

'What did you do there?' Laurel asked.

'It was all about sex for me,' Bruce said. 'It's all about sex for most newbies. That's how people get interested. Then it gets more intense as time goes on. I had nothing to do with killing anyone. They're trying to make it look like I did.'

'So, it's a conspiracy against you?'

'Yes.'

'Do you want to expand on your theory?'

'They're trying to make it look as if I killed and disposed of Victoria,' Bruce said. 'I didn't kill her.'

'Explain to us why you were found in possession of her body,' Braddick said.

'They took my wife's body to the cottage in Wales and they put it on the fire to make it look as if I was trying to dispose of her. Then they left, because they knew I was going to turn up. They baited me to go there.'

'Who are "they"?'

'Fabienne and whoever she's got running around for her at the moment.' There was bitterness in Bruce's tone. 'She's good at manipulating people, especially men.'

'So you've said, but your wife's body was found in the boot of your car,' Braddick said. 'You had the keys in your pocket and the only prints on the boot are yours.' Bruce shook his head. 'The only prints inside the house are yours.'

'She's very clever. They're setting me up,' Bruce said.

'Why would they kill your wife, Bruce?' Braddick asked.

'I don't know. I certainly didn't know they were going to kill Victoria, or anyone else for that matter. I knew they were into some weird shit, but I didn't know anyone was being killed.'

'Okay, say I believe you didn't know, tell me what you did know,' Braddick said.

'I knew they were into the occult, but I didn't realise how deep it ran,' Bruce said, looking away. 'They did stuff in the flats, weird stuff. It started with sex and turned into madness. It wasn't for me, so I didn't go again.'

'What kind of weird stuff?' Braddick asked.

'They studied dark arts. Victoria was obsessed with it.'

'Your blood and semen were found there, Bruce,' Braddick said. 'You were doing some weird stuff yourself.' Bruce blushed again. 'Your DNA says you were there.'

'I've admitted being there,' Bruce said. 'I had sex with my wife during the rituals. Things got rough. I told you how it works.'

'How many times did you go there?'

'I can't remember exactly, a few.'

'You need to realise, whatever went on there will be put on you unless you tell us otherwise. Your DNA has been found at a crime scene where multiple victims were murdered, Bruce. You will take the wrap.'

'What do you want from me?' Bruce asked. 'I had sex with my wife during some of the meetings. She was obsessed with Fabienne and her religion. I went along with it sometimes, but I wasn't involved in the heavy stuff. I wasn't even invited to the serious rituals.'

'Why not?' Braddick asked.

'I wasn't trusted,' Bruce said. 'I think Fabienne knew that I thought it was all bullshit. She didn't trust me to be in the inner circle. I only had sex with my wife. Fabienne wants everyone to go with everyone else, no holds barred, but there were lines I wouldn't cross. I don't go near other men for anyone. It's just not for me. But they would do everything she said, no questions asked.'

'Would they kill for her?' Laurel asked.

'They would do absolutely anything she said. They killed those people, not me,' Bruce insisted.

'You never saw anyone being hurt during the rituals?' Laurel asked.

'Hurt. Yes, of course I did. The rituals were all about pain and sex and hurting each other. It's all about negative energy, dark thoughts, evil acts.' He shrugged. 'I told you, it's all bullshit.'

'But your wife didn't think so?' Braddick said.

'She was obsessed with it. It consumed her completely.'

'Was she in the inner circle?'

'Yes. Too far in,' Bruce said, looking at his hands. 'It took over her. I warned her that it would end in tears, but I never expected them to kill her. That never crossed my mind.'

'Did she tell you what they did when you weren't invited?' Laurel asked.

'No.'

'Did you ask?' Laurel pushed.

'Of course, I did,' Bruce said. 'I asked her until I was blue in the face. We argued about it all the time. It ruined our marriage in the end.'

'The Metcalfe brothers,' Braddick interrupted, 'were they in the inner circle?'

'Yes.'

'So, when you weren't there, your wife would have sex with the other men in the group?' Laurel asked. Bruce nodded and glared at her. 'That must have been difficult for you, knowing that?'

'It was. I thought about leaving her a million times, but I loved her, you see,' Bruce said. His eyes filled up. 'We'd been married eighteen years before that woman turned up. She ruined our lives with her hocus-pocus.'

'You met Fabienne Wilder two years ago?' Laurel asked.

'My wife did,' Bruce said. 'I didn't meet her until six months or so later.'

'When did she meet John Metcalfe?' Braddick asked.

'I don't remember,' Bruce said. His eyes flickered up and right: a lie.

'Roughly?'

'Ten or fifteen years ago, something like that,' Bruce said. 'She employed him to do some building work on a property.'

'When did she start having sex with him?' Laurel asked.

'What?' Bruce asked, shocked.

'I'm curious if she was sleeping with him before Fabienne Wilder arrived on the scene.'

'I don't think that's relevant,' Prost said. 'What has that got to do with anything?'

'It's very relevant,' Laurel said. 'It goes to motive – a man who knows his wife has been cheating on him for fifteen years at least, has motive. Add on that he knows she has sex with multiple partners on a regular basis, he has motive to murder her, don't you think?' Prost nodded and made a note. She turned back to Bruce. 'Answer the question, Mr May. Was she sleeping with Metcalfe before she met Wilder?'

'I don't know,' Bruce said. 'Probably. Hindsight is a wonderful thing. I should have left her years ago.'

'Did you kill her instead?' Braddick asked.

'No,' Bruce snapped. 'I loved Victoria. They killed her and they're trying to frame me.'

'I don't think anyone would be surprised if you did,' Laurel added.

'I didn't kill my wife,' Bruce insisted.

'The evidence looks damning,' Braddick pushed. 'You were arrested next to some bin bags that contained your wife's dismembered body. The rest of her was in the boot of your Porsche.'

'Plus, a bit in a saucepan, cooking on the stove,' Laurel said. Prost looked at her and shook his head. Laurel looked him in the eye. 'What is your issue with that, are the cold, hard facts too much for you?'

'My client has explained how he came to be there,' Prost said. 'He's denied being involved in her death.'

'Your client has lied before,' Laurel countered. 'I think he's lying now.'

'I'm not lying to you,' Bruce said. 'Fabienne took her body there, I lent her my car. I didn't even know she was going to the cottage until I called her. I made my way there by train and in a taxi. She baited me.'

'Baited you how?'

'Fabienne lied to me,' Bruce said.

'She lied to you about what?'

'She said we could be together,' Bruce said quietly. 'That's why she killed Victoria.'

'You're telling us that Fabienne Wilder killed your wife so she could be with you?' Laurel asked. 'I've heard it all now.'

'Yes. In a roundabout way,' Bruce nodded. 'I love Fabienne, you see. I know she's much younger than me, but you can't help who you fall in love with. She knows that and she used me.'

'I'm not sure I follow,' Braddick said. 'She used you for what?'

'She knows I have a lot of money and Victoria owned property,' Bruce said. 'She wanted Victoria out of the way so she could step into her shoes. Everything is about money with Fabienne.'

'It doesn't explain why she dismembered her and cooked her, does it?' Laurel asked. 'That's nothing to do with money.'

'That's to do with her beliefs,' Bruce said. 'She has a very dark side to her personality.'

'Do you think so?' Laurel asked sarcastically. 'Did she know about your trafficking and prostitution businesses?' Braddick shot her a glance. He wanted to keep their cards close to their chest. Laurel frowned. 'I'm assuming she did.'

Prost leaned closer to Bruce and whispered in his ear.

'No comment,' Bruce said. His solicitor cleared his throat but didn't speak. He was poised to interrupt but decided to keep his powder dry.

'Oh, come on, Bruce,' Braddick said. 'Your wife and you and the Metcalfe brothers have been shipping migrants into this country and prostituting them for nearly fifteen years, haven't you?'

'No comment.'

'Making a no comment interview at this stage will damage your case when you get to court,' Braddick said. 'The evidence is overwhelming. We raided all your wife's properties and we've recovered over thirty women from Africa who all claim they've been forced into prostitution.'

'I don't know anything about what goes on at her properties,' Bruce said.

'They were slaves, but do you know what they are now, Bruce?' Braddick asked. Bruce shook his head. 'They're witnesses, Bruce. So are the women found at Metcalfe's garage. There were dead bodies removed from your containers.' Bruce looked at his solicitor. The solicitor shook his head. 'Can you see where this is going, Bruce?' Bruce looked at the table but didn't speak. 'Your wife is dead, and John Metcalfe is dying, you're at the centre of the entire operation. The burden of guilt will be on you. You will get the hard time for this.'

'I'm not in charge of anything. I never have been,' Bruce said. Prost whispered in his ear. 'I don't care what your advice is,' he snapped at his solicitor. 'I'm not some kind of criminal mastermind. I just went along with it all until Fabienne arrived on the scene. Then I realised I didn't want anything to do with it. I tried to fit in by going along a few times, but it wasn't for me. As for the trafficking, that's nonsense.'

'You're saying you had nothing to do with it?' Braddick said.

'I knew they were up to no good, but I didn't pry,' Bruce said.

'They were trafficked in your containers,' Braddick said.

'I have over a thousand containers,' Bruce countered. 'I have a big company. I don't know what's in them. How could I possibly know what's in them?'

'So, it's a coincidence that your containers were found at the Metcalfe's property with migrants in them?' Braddick asked.

'No comment.'

'You're not making yourself clear by saying "no comment", Bruce,' Braddick said. 'Are you denying being involved, is this all news to you? What are you trying to say?'

'I didn't want to be involved in any of it.' Bruce put his head in his hands and rocked back and forth. 'I should have put my foot down years ago, but I was too weak. Victoria bullied me and manipulated me from day one. It was all her idea, her and John. I said it was madness. My business was legitimate until they meddled in it.'

'So, you did know about the trafficking operation?' Braddick asked.

'I knew it happened occasionally, but I turned a blind eye to it,' Bruce said. 'I didn't realise the scale of it.'

'It's amazing what went on without your knowledge,' Laurel said.

'You'd better start at the beginning, Bruce,' Braddick said.

'I reiterate my advice not to answer any questions on this subject,' Prost interrupted.

'Stuff your advice where the sun doesn't shine,' Bruce said. 'I'm sick of being told what to do. That's why I'm here, listening to other people.'

'If you need to talk to your solicitor, we can take a break,' Braddick said. Laurel looked surprised. He tapped her foot under the table.

'I think that's advisable,' Prost said. Bruce shrugged and shook his head. 'If we can have five minutes, please, Superintendent Braddick.'

'Fine,' Braddick said, standing. He opened the door and walked into the corridor. Laurel followed him, an angry expression on her face. 'Stop stressing,' Braddick said.

'We've hardly got going. What are you doing?' Laurel asked.

'This is going to be a marathon, not a sprint,' Braddick said. He smiled to disarm her. 'Bruce May is a puppy dog. He's trying to convince us he's a victim in all this and he's dying to spill his guts. He has no idea yet that we know he didn't go to London. His alibi is shot, but the more he denies it, the worse it will be. All he needs is a little encouragement and he'll talk himself into a life sentence. What I want to be sure of, is that he can't recant later – saying we pushed him against the advice of his brief. If he wants to make a statement, it has to be seen to be his choice. Trust me on this. He'll put his own head in the noose, I guarantee it.'

'Okay,' Laurel said. 'You're the boss.'

'Superintendent Braddick?' A detective from the Matrix division approached them. Braddick turned to greet him. 'MIT are trying to get hold of you. They said it's urgent.'

'Thanks,' Braddick said. He took out his mobile and checked the screen: five missed calls and a voicemail. He dialled Google's extension. 'Google,' Braddick said when he answered. 'What's the emergency?'

'Malcolm Baines called,' Google said. 'He's been watching the Niners' sites on the dark web and he's found some images that were uploaded this morning.'

'Images of what?' Braddick said. His stomach tightened. He knew the answer before it came.

'They filmed themselves digging up your family. It's being shared all over the net.'

CHAPTER 37

Maggie pulled her coat around her to fend off the wind. It was a cold afternoon and business had been slow. Times were hard on the streets and she knew the reasons why; every time she looked in the mirror, they stared her in the face. Old Father Time had taken his toll on her. She was getting too old to be first choice for a punter, especially when there were a dozen younger girls working the same area. Competition was fierce but the younger girls had the advantage. Youth always won. Maggie was forced to take any punter who made her an offer. The days of being picky were long gone. She used to be able to choose, but not anymore. It made the hours longer and the job harder, and, ultimately, less safe. It was the slide in income that had led to them taking the gig at Stanley House. That and the shitty weather. Working inside was always preferable to freezing on the streets, but it wasn't always the safest option. Many times, a normal punter had changed, from charming to nutcase, once the front door was locked. She'd had a few close calls.

Maggie took out her cigarettes and shook the last one from the box, lighting it with practised ease despite the wind. She needed to buy some more so waited for a gap in the traffic to cross the road. The corner shop was more like a supermarket nowadays, which didn't help her waistline. It was difficult to resist buying something to eat; every time she went in there, she came out munching on something. She avoided the chilled aisle and went straight to the till and ordered twenty cigarettes, picking up a bar of Cadbury chocolate and a packet of chewing gum. The shop assistant served her with the minimum courtesy required. He recognised her as a working girl from the surrounding streets and talking to her was beneath him. Judgemental arsehole. She made her way back across the road to her spot and took up her pose.

A black saloon approached and slowed down to proposition a woman nearby. Maggie knew her as Carla. She leaned in the window and words were exchanged, then she looked over her shoulder and waved to Maggie. Maggie walked over, confused. She couldn't imagine any punter would knock back Carla in favour of her. Carla was a stunner, but she hadn't been on the game for long. Her looks would fade along with her hopes and dreams.

'He's asking for you,' Carla said, scowling as she walked away. 'Wasting my time, man,' she mumbled.

'What does he want?' Maggie asked as she neared the car.

'I don't know, ask him,' Carla said irritably.

Maggie moved in towards the passenger window and the man leaned over to speak to her. She could smell Armani on him. It was one of her favourites.

'What do you want?' she asked suspiciously. He looked normal and smelled clean. That was always a bonus.

'Are you Maggie Bennet?' he asked, glancing in the mirror to check he wasn't blocking the traffic.

'Who's asking?'

'Detective Allen,' the man said. 'Vice squad. I need a word with you, jump in.'

'What's it about?'

'Nothing to worry about. I just need a chat.'

'A vice squad detective wants a chat, that's not normal. What's this about?' Maggie asked suspiciously.

'Stanley House,' the man said.

'I don't know anything about it,' Maggie lied. She turned to walk away.

'Sara Larkin said you were there when a woman was murdered,' he called after her. 'Lying to me could get you in trouble.' Maggie stopped and walked back to the vehicle. 'That's better. It won't take long. Get in.'

'Let me see your warrant card first,' Maggie said. The detective rolled his eyes and reached into his pocket. He took out his wallet and opened it, leaning over the seat.

Maggie leaned closer to read his ID. She realised it was fake too late. The man grabbed Maggie by the lapels of her coat, dragging her head and shoulders into the car. Maggie screamed for help, but the man punched her in the face hard, silencing her cries. She felt her nose break and blood ran from her nostrils. He hit her again and she felt blinding pain shoot through her brain. Two of the other girls ran to help her, grabbing her clothes to pull her out. The man pressed the window button, trapping her upper body inside, and put the car in gear. He accelerated, dragging the girls with him until they couldn't hold on to Maggie any longer. They fell onto the pavement with a thump, screaming and shouting for help. Pedestrians stopped to watch, and several cars slowed down, their drivers rubber-necking the action. A man from the shop ran across the road to help while another took out his phone and filmed it.

'Get the number plate!' someone shouted.

'I've got it on my phone.'

The driver aimed the vehicle at a lamppost and accelerated. He steered the front wheel up the pavement. Maggie looked up through the windscreen, blood and tears blurred her vision. She could see the line he was taking and grabbed the wheel to stop him from smashing her body against the lamppost, but he was too strong. The vehicle was travelling at thirty miles an hour when it hit. The wing scraped against the lamppost, causing sparks to fly, then Maggie's body hit it. The impact was powerful enough to catapult her from the vehicle. She landed on the pavement, almost broken in half, and the black saloon sped away. Blood trickled from her ears and mouth. When help arrived, her eyes were still open, but the light was fading from them.

'Call an ambulance,' a man said, although he didn't think anyone could have survived such a catastrophic impact. He took off his coat and placed it over her to keep her warm.

'Melissa,' Maggie whispered.

'What's she saying?' someone asked.

'My friend, Melissa, is in danger,' Maggie murmured before her eyes closed.

* * * *

Melissa watched her punter leave; he was moving like a scalded cat. Some of them were like that; they couldn't get away quick enough. He'd paid fifty pounds for the grand total of thirty-five seconds of sex. It had taken him longer to get undressed and put the condom on than to do the act itself. Probably not value for money, in the true context of the word value, but fast and easy suited Melissa. He was obviously a quick draw – the quicker the better, although his wife probably didn't think so. If that was the best he could do, little wonder he wasn't getting any at home.

She heard his footsteps going downstairs and the sound of the front door being closed. It was on the latch when she was working. She looked out of the window and shivered. It was freezing out there. The sky was dark grey and moody, threatening to rain any moment. She thought about Maggie standing on the street and felt sorry for her. It was her own choice. Maggie wanted to work outside for a few months until things had settled down. She'd become claustrophobic since witnessing the murders at Stanley House and she couldn't go inside with a punter without having a panic attack. Some of her regulars had stopped using her because of it. As if things weren't bad enough. The experience had affected her badly. She pretended to be as tough as old boots, but she wasn't. It was different for Melissa: she felt safer indoors than out, although she understood how Maggie felt. Each to their own. It was warm inside and, on days like that, warm was a massive bonus. Warm almost trumped safe. Almost, but not quite. Safe was top of the list.

Melissa heard the front door open and footsteps on the stairs. Another punter already. He wasn't booked in, but she had a free slot or two. The extra cash would come in handy. She waited for him to reach the landing before looking through the security hole. The man was looking around the hallway, inspecting everything. He looked very dodgy. Dodgy wasn't good. The man pressed the buzzer.

'Hello?' Melissa said through the intercom. She didn't give him any sign of who lived there.

'I'm looking for Melissa Walker,' the man said.

'Sorry, wrong address,' she said. The man looked angry. He sighed and put his hands in his pockets.

'I've been told she works here,' the man said.

'She doesn't.'

'Are you sure?'

'Positive.'

'Can you give her a message for me?'

'No. I've never heard of her.'

'Tell her that her friend, Maggie Bennet, was attacked an hour ago,' the man said. 'She's in a critical condition at the Royal hospital. It's touch and go if she makes it.'

'What?' Melissa said, panicked.

'You heard me. Your friend Maggie Bennet is in hospital.'

'Who are you?' Mel could feel her heart pounding in her chest. She wanted to rip open the door and run to the hospital as fast as she could.

'Detective Sergeant Ian Barlow,' the man said. 'I need to talk to you about what happened at Stanley House.'

'I don't know anything about it,' Melissa said.

'Sara Larkin mentioned your name to us. She said you were there.'

'Sara Larkin has got a big mouth.'

'She's very frightened and she's decided to do something about it,' Barlow said. 'You can't blame her for that.'

'Who attacked Maggie?'

'We don't know but, because of what you saw, we know you're in danger, Melissa,' Barlow said. 'You are Melissa Walker, aren't you?'

'Yes,' Melissa said. She was suddenly frightened. 'Do you think she'll be alright?'

'I don't know, she's in a bad way,' Barlow said. 'Open the door and we can have a chat. You need to come in and speak to us on the record. We can protect you then.'

'Show me your ID,' Melissa said. Barlow took out his warrant card and showed it to her. She could tell immediately that it was real. 'Okay,' she said, unlocking the door and letting him in. 'How did you find me?'

'Fifty quid,' Barlow said, grinning. 'No one could remember where you worked at first, but it's amazing how people's memories return when there's money involved.'

'Who told you where I was working for fifty quid?' Mel asked, offended. 'Wait until I see them next, cheeky buggers.'

'I can't give my source away,' Barlow joked. 'Gather your stuff together while we chat. I want to get you out of here. If I found you, someone else can.'

'Don't say that,' Mel said, 'you're frightening me.' She went into the bedroom and returned with a sports bag and her coat. 'I can't believe Maggie was attacked. Do you know what happened?'

'We're not sure, but someone tried to abduct her,' Barlow said. 'It was a bungled attempt and she was badly injured when the vehicle hit a lamppost.'

'Poor Maggie, I hope she's okay. Do you think it's connected to Stanley House?'

'It would be a massive coincidence that someone else would want to shut her up,' Barlow said. 'We can't be a hundred per cent positive, but we have to assume it is for now. Better to be on the safe side.'

'Okay,' Melissa said. 'I'll grab my phone and my handbag. Can I see her on the way?'

'I don't know if the doctors will let anyone in. The last I heard, she was in theatre,' Barlow said, shaking his head. He checked his watch. 'Maybe tomorrow.'

'You said she might not make it. I'd never forgive myself if I didn't say goodbye. Please, just for a minute?'

'I'll call the hospital on the way in. If she's out of theatre, we could pop in quickly. But it will have to be quick, okay?' Barlow looked out of the window and checked the street outside. Everything looked normal.

'Yes, thanks.'

'Sara Larkin told me that you and Maggie witnessed a murder at Stanley House,' Barlow said. 'Is that true?'

'Yes. Two actually,' Melissa said. 'It was horrible. I couldn't believe it was happening. I knew they were lunatics, but I never expected them to go that far.'

'It must have been frightening for all of you,' Barlow said.

'It was terrifying. If it wasn't for Sara, we wouldn't have got out that night. I was convinced they were going to kill us next.' Mel was starting to fill up; the memories were upsetting. 'I'm sorry. I try to blank it out but sometimes it gets to me.'

'Okay, don't worry. We'll take a proper statement at the station. Can you remember any of the men who were there that night?'

'Yes,' Melissa said.

'Can you remember their names?'

'Some of them. There was Bruce, John, Joe and George. They were always there, although Bruce not so much.' Her forehead creased in concentration. 'And there were two others. One was Clive, I never knew the other man's name, but he was with Clive. They arrived together.'

'Was anyone else there?'

'Not that I can remember.'

'How well did you know them?'

'Not well at all. We weren't there to have a conversation – you know what I mean.'

'I've heard all of those names except George.' Barlow looked out of the window again. 'What do you know about him?'

'I know he was a jeweller in the city. He was minted, always tipped well.'

'Do you know his second name?'

'No, but I know where one of his shops is,' Melissa said. 'I saw him parked up one day outside it. Then he went in with one of those jeweller briefcases.'

'Where was that?' Barlow asked.

'Queens Drive, near Mossley Hill,' she said. 'There's a lot of money around there.'

'Was it the parade of shops near the synagogue?'

'Yes. Next to Greggs.'

'I know where you mean,' Barlow said. 'Are you ready?'

'Yes.'

'Do you need to let anyone know you're leaving for the day?' Barlow asked.

'No. It's a new gaff. I'm setting up on my own,' Melissa said, grabbing her handbag under her arm. 'I'm sick of being ripped off. This way, I keep what I earn.'

'Good for you,' Barlow said. 'Let's go.'

Melissa had one last check around and reached for the door. Barlow grabbed her hair at the back of her head and smashed her face into the wall. She felt her lips split and the impact stunned her. He pushed her head again, this time with more force. The skin on her forehead split open from her nose to her hairline. Her legs buckled beneath her. He pulled her head back and thrust it into the wall again. And again. And a fourth time, crushing her skull. Melissa's body went limp. He slipped his hands around her throat and squeezed his thumbs into her larynx, crushing her windpipe. Her eyes rolled back as the life was squeezed from her. He watched her feet twitching and kept the pressure on until they were still.

CHAPTER 38

Fabienne watched as the van approached the front of the house. It slowed down to a crawl and followed the road round to the rear, stopping near a row of dilapidated outhouses. The driver turned off the engine and climbed out, reaching into the back of the van to retrieve his shotgun. She knew he had one. She'd seen it in her mind's eye. He broke the gun and thumbed a cartridge into each barrel while studying the windows for any sign of life. She wondered what he was doing there; if he was a poacher, why was he so interested in the house? A poacher would have been more interested in the grounds and the surrounding woods. Maybe he hunted there regularly and was used to the house being empty. The place had hardly been used for over a decade, so he could be forgiven for thinking someone was there today. She had opened some of the upstairs windows and curtains to let in some fresh air. If he'd been there before he would have noticed there was something different. She waited and watched.

The man looked jumpy. He walked to the back door of the house and tried the handle: it was locked from the inside. He stood back and looked at the upper windows before walking a full circuit of the building, checking the doors and windows. Satisfied they were secure, he walked towards the garage where Fabienne was waiting. Fabienne gripped the handle of the pitchfork and watched the man through a crack in the wood. The sound of another vehicle came to her. He was coming back. The man heard it too and stopped in his tracks. He turned to look at the approaching vehicle, his back to Fabienne. She opened the door quietly and took two steps before thrusting the pitchfork between his shoulders. The spikes went between his ribs, deep into the chest cavity. He dropped the shotgun and fell to his knees, desperately trying to reach behind him. His fingers couldn't touch the fork, let alone pull it out. Fabienne watched his frantic efforts fade and he crumbled to the ground, lying on his side. His eyes met hers and he tried to speak but no sound came out. His mouth opened and flecks of blood sprayed from his lips. He lay writhing on the grass, his efforts becoming weaker and weaker. Fabienne smiled.

A black saloon came into view and drove around the house, coming to a stop next to the van. Joe Metcalfe climbed out, he looked confused. He was wearing green combats and a beanie hat. His stubble was a few days old.

'What took so long?' Fabienne asked.

'It was a long night,' Joe replied. 'I've brought you something.' He lifted up a plastic rubble bag. There were three spheres inside it.

'Their skulls?' she asked.

'Yes. Have you seen the pictures?'

'Yes,' she said, nodding. 'Very entertaining.'

'Who's that?' Joe asked, pointing to the man on the floor.

'I've got no idea,' Fabienne said. 'Caretaker, gamekeeper, poacher; who cares? He was snooping around with a loaded shotgun. We need to get rid of him.'

'I'll take him into the woods,' Joe said. 'I'll do it now. It will be dark soon.'

* * * *

Ian Barlow filled the bathroom sink with hot water and bleach and dipped a towel into it. He wiped some spots of blood from his gloves, face and neck and rinsed the towel, turning the water pink. He pulled the plug and let it drain away, pouring more bleach after it. The reflection in the mirror looked back at him, accusingly. He'd had no choice. He'd always thought of himself as a good copper – until a few years ago – but nowadays he could hardly look himself in the eye. His own reflection made him feel ashamed. He'd broken every vow he'd made and gone against everything he held dear. It was a slippery slope he was on and he was finding it difficult to apply the brakes. Where his fall from grace would end, he didn't know. He was in too deep and he could see no way back; how could he come back from murder?

He stepped out of the bathroom and went into the living room, standing on the settee to remove a digital camera from the architrave. It was the type that sent images directly to a laptop or smart phone. He put it in his pocket and wiped where it had been with the bleach-soaked towel. Melissa's phone was in her handbag, visible at the top. He took it out and smashed the back off, taking the SIM card from it and disposing of it down the toilet. He stuffed her handbag into the sports bag. He could dispose of them later, far away from her body. She was looking at him through bloodshot eyes, they were dead and lifeless. He touched her face in apology and looked through her bag, taking out her cigarettes and lighter. They were the brand he'd preferred when he used to smoke. He lit one and drew deeply on it, releasing the soothing smoke through his nose. He took Melissa's keys and locked the flat, turning the deadbolt on the downstairs door too. He kept his head down as he walked back to his car.

Melissa Walker was one less witness. He felt sorry for her, but he would face a life sentence if he made any mistakes – although prison was the least of his worries. Fabienne Wilder and her acolytes were far more frightening than prison. What she could do to him was worse than anything the penal system threatened. He wished he'd never met her, but it was too late for regret. Regrets were the things lifers dwelled on in their eight-by-four cells, and he had no intention of being locked up in one of those.

CHAPTER 39

Joe Metcalfe grabbed the man's hands and dragged him face down across the grass towards the woods. He could feel the pulse in his wrists. The man's heart was still beating. When they got into the treeline, he knelt and felt the pulse in his neck, rolling him on to his side.

'Listen to me,' Joe said. The man's eyes flickered open. Blood streaked saliva dribbled from the corner of his mouth. 'If I take this thing out of you, you'll bleed to death in minutes. You need to keep still until I get help.' The man's eyes watched Joe's lips as he spoke. 'You stupid bastard. I warned you that she's perceptive, and you drove straight up to the house. What were you thinking? She knew you were coming before you did, idiot. All you had to do was pull the trigger and blow her head off and we could all walk away from the bitch.' The man closed his eyes and a tear ran from the corner. 'I'll drag you further in and cover you to keep you warm. Don't shout for help, whatever you do, understand?' The man nodded. Joe dragged him another twenty yards and dropped him near a rhododendron bush. He scooped up dry leaves and covered his legs and hips to keep in some heat. 'I'll be as quick as I can,' Joe said. The man looked like he was fading. 'We can't do this alone anymore. I'm going to call the police; I'll tell them where you are. She can't get to us easily if she's banged up.' The injured man shook his head. 'There's no other way. You're not going to live through this. It's the only choice we have.'

Joe Metcalfe took out his phone, dialled 999, and made an anonymous tip-off giving the whereabouts of the fugitive, Fabienne Wilder. He gave the location of his friend in the woods and told them that Fabienne had a loaded shotgun. All he had to do now was get away before the police arrived. Everything had turned to shit. The import business; the sex trade; everything had been raided and shut down. It was every man for himself, now. Fabienne had poisoned them all with her black magic. She'd all but killed his younger brother. His deterioration into madness had been scary to witness. She was to blame. Fabienne was evil and twisted; he hadn't realised the extent of her abilities at first, but now he did. It was time to get as far away from her as he could. He needed to move – and keep moving. If Fabienne didn't find him, the police might. He guessed it would take the police a while, following his tip-off, to organise a raid on the estate.

He waited as long as he dared before making his way back to the house and heading towards his car. The light was beginning to fade. There was no sign of Fabienne. He slowed his step as he neared the vehicle. The hairs on the back of his neck tingled. He knew what she was capable of. If she got a sniff of his betrayal, he would wish he'd never been born. There would be nowhere to run to and nowhere to hide. There were hundreds of them out there, hanging on her every word, and she would send them to find him. Tracking him down would be harder to orchestrate from a prison cell, but she wouldn't rest until he'd been found. Joe treaded carefully as he reached his car.

'Where are you going?' Fabienne asked, climbing out of the intruder's van.

'Nowhere,' Joe said, trying to remain calm. 'I think I've left my wallet in my car.'

'It's in your pocket,' she said. Her eyes darkened. 'Your right-hand pocket.'

'So it is.' Joe patted his jeans. 'I thought that was my phone. I've left that in my car. I knew it was one or the other,' he said, rolling his eyes. He opened his car door and reached in, fishing for his phone. It was a spare he kept away from her. 'Here it is.' He closed the door and walked towards her. 'Don't worry about him, they'll never find him in there.'

'Who was he?' Fabienne asked, gesturing towards the trees. Her eyes searched his face. She was suspicious, always suspicious.

'Who knows?' Joe shrugged. 'Doesn't matter who he was any more. He's in the ground.'

'He had a shotgun.' Fabienne was holding it, both barrels pointing at Joe. 'And he had a phone.' Joe looked worried. 'He was texting someone about coming here to "blow her head off and make sure she's dead",' she said, reading from the screen. 'Do you think they meant me?'

'I doubt it,' Joe said, shaking his head. 'How would he know you were here?'

'How would a stranger know anyone was here at all?' she asked. Joe didn't speak. 'Only two people know where I am.' She pointed the gun at his groin. 'Me, and you.'

'I would never betray you, Fabienne,' Joe said, raising his hands. 'Not in a million years. You know John and I were loyal.' Fabienne pressed dial on the man's phone. 'You've got this all wrong.' Joe's voice was shaking. His mobile began to ring.

'He was texting your phone, Joe,' Fabienne said. She sensed a vibration on the horizon. It was moving towards them, quickly. The thrumming of helicopter blades reached her before the sound did. She glared at him, searching his eyes for the truth. There was nothing there but guilt.

'Did you call the police, Joe?' she asked, frowning. She seemed to be genuinely disappointed. 'After everything I've shown you? I took you to places you could never have seen, and you turn on me so easily. How could you do that?'

'I didn't call the police, Fabienne,' Joe stammered. 'He must have, before you stabbed him.'

'Do you think I'm stupid, Joe?' she asked.

'No. Of course not.'

'You must do,' she said.

Police sirens blared and blue flashing lights appeared around the bend in the road. The helicopter hovered above the estate. She watched the vehicles racing towards them, keeping one eye on Joe. There were four vehicles in the front group – an armed unit. Another four cars hung back until the armed units called it safe to approach. Fabienne waited until they were close enough to witness what was going on. She wanted them to see what she was going to do.

'Did you call them?' she asked. 'Tell me the truth.'

'No.'

'You're a liar,' she said. Her eyes darkened to almost black as she pulled the triggers. Both barrels roared. The buckshot ripped a bloody hole in Joe's crotch. His combats turned red with blood. He doubled over in agony, grabbing the jagged rent where his genitals had been. 'I think you'll survive, Joe,' she said, smiling. 'You'll spend the rest of your life as a cockless gimp in prison. I'll send some of my friends to visit you in your cell. You take care of yourself, won't you?' Joe collapsed to the ground. 'I'll see you in hell, Joe.'

The police screeched to a halt and deployed quickly. Armed men surrounded Fabienne and Joe, shouting orders. Fabienne dropped the shotgun and raised her hands. She smiled as they led her away.

CHAPTER 40

Braddick and Laurel sat down opposite Bruce May and his solicitor, Prost. There was a deep sadness inside Braddick and an unexplainable anger. He'd watched the footage of his family being exhumed, their coffins being opened, and their corpses defiled. It was one of the most distressing things he'd ever seen. He wasn't sure why he was so distressed, they were dead, after all; but it was just wrong. They reiterated the legal requirements for the camera.

'Are you ready to restart?' Braddick asked. His tone was cold and measured. Bruce nodded that he was. 'I want to move on from where we were before the break, okay?'

'You're in charge,' Bruce said.

'There's been a development,' Braddick said. 'Fabienne Wilder has been arrested at an estate in Cheshire. They're bringing her in now. She'll be processed and interviewed as soon as she's had time with her solicitor.'

'Are they bringing her here?' Bruce asked, nervously. His eyes darted from one to the other. 'To this building?'

'Yes. She'll be here until we charge her and then she'll be shipped out to a remand prison.' Braddick leaned forward and put his elbows on the table. 'You need to stop worrying about her and think about how long you want to go away for, Bruce. There's no question that you're going down; it's when, and for how long?'

'I'm—' Bruce tried to interrupt.

'Shut up,' Braddick snapped. Bruce looked put out. 'Where were you when your wife was murdered?' Laurel looked at Braddick. His softly-softly approach had been abandoned, for now. She understood why.

'I was on business in London,' Bruce said. 'Victoria was supposed to pick me up at the station. She wasn't answering her phone, so I took a taxi home. You know all this.'

'We know you didn't get on the train to Euston, Bruce, and the man who checked in at the Kennedy Hotel, using your debit card, wasn't you,' Braddick said, coldly. Bruce looked stunned. 'The man who checked *out* of the Kennedy Hotel, using *your* debit card, wasn't you either.'

Bruce blushed and tried to speak. 'Be quiet,' Braddick said. 'The next words out of your mouth need to be well thought out, because when we speak to Fabienne Wilder, I have a feeling she's going to try to shift the blame wherever she can, to lessen her time in jail.' Bruce swallowed hard. 'So, I'll repeat my question to you once more: where were you when your wife was murdered?'

Bruce looked at his solicitor. Prost looked like he'd been punched in the stomach and had the wind knocked out of him. He shook his head.

'No comment,' Bruce said.

'That was your last chance, Bruce,' Braddick said, standing up. 'We're not playing your games. Bruce May, I'm charging you with the murder of your wife, Victoria Theresa May. You don't have to say anything, but anything you do say may be used in evidence—'

'Wait, wait,' Bruce said, panicked. 'I'll tell you what happened.'

'Don't say anything else,' Prost said.

'I wasn't in London.' Bruce looked pained as he spoke, like a child about to cry. 'I was there, but I didn't kill her. She wanted them to do it and I watched, but I swear I didn't know they were going to kill her. Victoria didn't know they were going to kill her either.'

'Bullshit,' Braddick said.

'Detective Superintendent Braddick,' Prost protested.

'Why fabricate an alibi if you didn't know what was going on?' Braddick asked. Bruce started to weep. 'I'll tell you what happened, and you can tell me if I'm wrong. You were in cahoots with Fabienne Wilder. Your wife was a masochist, and she'd been drawn so far in that she believed whatever Wilder said. She thought it was just another ritual, something that would endear her even more to Fabienne, but you all knew it would end with her murder, that's why you fabricated an alibi to cover your tracks before the event.' Braddick paused as Bruce sobbed. 'How am I doing so far, Bruce?'

'I didn't kill her,' he moaned.

'You'd had enough of her. She was in the inner circle, screwing whoever she wanted to, while you sat in your car waiting for the lights to go out. Fabienne tired of her and saw a way to inherit her money and property, the illegal businesses – the lot. She fed you a load of bull about being together, you swallowed it and went along with killing your wife.' Braddick shook his head. He despised the tears Bruce was crying. There was no pity in him, just anger. 'Then Fabienne betrayed you and left you there to take the wrap. Did you really think a woman like that would want to be with you?'

'You've got this all wrong,' Bruce cried.

'Were you at Stanley House on Halloween last year?' Braddick changed tack. Bruce wiped his nose and looked up. 'I'll rephrase that: you *were* at Stanley House on Halloween last year. We have a witness who puts you there when two young black women were murdered.'

'I don't know what you're talking about,' Bruce murmured.

'You do. I can see it in your eyes. They were foreign women, Bruce, and I'll wager they'd been trafficked into the country in one of your containers, put to work as prostitutes to pay off their fares for smuggling them in, and then they became fodder for your sick games at Stanley House. You could kill them without impunity because they didn't exist in the first place.' Braddick glared at Bruce, pushing for a reaction. Bruce seemed to shrink into himself. 'Have we still got you all wrong, Bruce, or were you an innocent bystander at those murders, too?'

'You don't understand what she can do,' Bruce said, his voice almost a whisper. He wiped tears from his eyes.

Braddick stood up. 'I've heard enough of your snivelling, Bruce. Charge him,' he said, leaving the room.

* * * *

DS Barlow parked up and took Melissa's sports bag from the boot. He opened it and searched through her handbag inside again just to be sure, there was nothing incriminating. He stuffed it back into the sports bag and zipped it up. The road was quiet. He crossed it, walked towards the bridge, and trotted down some steps to the riverbank. There was no one around when he filled the bag with stones and tossed it into the flowing water. It floated for a while, and he was beginning to think he hadn't put enough weight in it: the handles poked above the surface, refusing to go under. Disposing of the evidence was supposed to be a relief. He considered wading out to push the bag under, but he wasn't sure how deep it was in the middle. He looked around and saw a house brick on the path; he picked it up and hurled it at the bag. It was a direct hit. It lessened his paranoia a little and he watched as the bag disappeared. He pulled up his hood as he crossed the road and jogged back to the car. As he got in, a passing lorry made the vehicle vibrate, but the driver didn't notice him. There was nothing out of the ordinary to see. He started the engine and drove away from the river, through the city to the Royal hospital. The roads were quiet, but it still took forty minutes to get there. He parked in an emergency vehicle bay, leaving a police identity disk on the dashboard, and walked to the reception. The high-dependency wards were on the top floor, at the rear of the building. He made his way to the elevators but there was a crowd of people waiting so he took the stairs instead. The fewer people who saw his face, the better. He was taking a risk coming to the hospital at all, despite his superior insisting that he found their witnesses quickly. There was no guarantee that the connection between their witness, Maggie Bennet, and the woman brought into ICU, had been made outside his contacts. He was fairly certain that Braddick wouldn't yet know she'd been targeted, although, it wouldn't be long before he did. If Maggie had regained consciousness, she may well have already asked for MIT to protect her. He had to hope she would die on the operating table or be rendered comatose and never recover. It was a lottery and his chances of winning this one was slim, getting slimmer all the time.

When Barlow reached the top floor, he was surprised to see three uniformed officers standing in the corridor. They looked at him as he approached. He couldn't turn and walk away, it was too late, they'd seen him. One them, a sergeant, knew him and said hello.

'That was quick, I've only just spoken to Laurel at MIT. She said she would send you over,' the sergeant said. 'Were you in the area?'

'About a half mile away, tops,' Barlow replied. He didn't have a clue what the sergeant was talking about but had to pretend that he had a reason to be there. His phone rang, it was Laurel. He waved in excuse to the uniformed officers. 'Excuse me, I need to take this,' he said. He pushed through some double doors into a quiet corridor. 'Hi, Laurel.' He walked further along, out of earshot. 'What's happening at your end?'

'One of your witnesses, Maggie Bennet, is in the Royal ICU. She's in a bad way,' Laurel said. 'Someone tried to kill her this morning.'

'What happened?' Barlow asked, trying to sound surprised.

'We're not a hundred per cent certain yet, but the gist of it is, someone tried to drag her into a car, and she was badly injured as it drove away. Can you get over there and speak to her?'

'Yes. No worries,' Barlow said, relieved that he had an excuse to be there.

'She came around after surgery and asked a uniformed officer to contact MIT with regards to witnessing a murder at Stanley House,' Laurel said. 'It looks like we've got a witness to back up Sara Larkin. We need a statement from her.'

'That's brilliant,' Barlow said. A Tannoy announcement started, echoing down the corridor. 'I'm not far away. I'll get over there now.'

'What was that, where are you now?' Laurel asked. She could hear the Tannoy announcement asking for Dr Chisolm to go to ICU. 'You're in a hospital, aren't you?'

'You should be a detective,' Barlow joked, nervously, feeling trapped. 'I'm at Broadgreen Hospital, funnily enough. I've been chasing down a lead on Melissa Walker.'

'Oh, right. Any joy?' Laurel wondered why he sounded so shady.

'I've got an address where she might be working,' Barlow said. 'Can you get uniform to knock on the door and see if it's legit?'

'Yes. Let me have it,' Laurel said. 'How reliable is the source?'

'I'm confident he's telling the truth,' Barlow said. 'He's a client of hers, a doctor. I squeezed him a little and he gave me the address: 27 Allerton Road. It's above a newsagent.'

'I'll get someone over there and bring her in,' Laurel said. 'Call in when you've spoken to Maggie Bennet.'

'I will do,' Barlow said. 'Is there an armed unit on her yet?'

'It's on the way. There should be a uniformed unit there when you arrive, they followed the ambulance in from the incident.'

'Okay. Talk later,' Barlow said, ending the call.

He walked to the window and put his head on the glass. It felt cool against his skin. Had he heard uncertainty in Laurel's voice? The Tannoy announcement couldn't have been made at a worse time. He wondered if she'd believed his explanation about the doctor at Broadgreen. It was plausible, on the spur of the moment, and he could stand his ground about keeping his informer's identity anonymous because of the damage it may cause to his professional career. Maybe he was being paranoid. He had every reason to be paranoid. There were a million reasons to be paranoid. He tried to compose himself before returning to the corridor. The uniformed officers were talking to two members of the ARU, and the group turned to say hello as he approached. Their sergeant was talking on his mobile. He eyed Barlow awkwardly and frowned.

'DS Barlow will be here soon? He's here now, Laurel,' he said, looking at Barlow, confused. 'Laurel wants a word.' He handed him the phone.

'You got there quickly,' she said. Barlow didn't answer. 'I forgot to mention that Fabienne Wilder was arrested earlier.' Barlow remained silent. He could feel cold sweat forming on his skin. 'She was with Joe Metcalfe.'

'That's great news,' Barlow said. His throat was dry. 'Did they bring him in, too?'

'No. Fabienne blasted him with a shotgun, right in front of the ARU. She blew his bollocks off.' Barlow felt his breathing increase. 'He's in hospital, along with another man who's got a pitchfork in his back.'

'Bloody hell,' Barlow said. 'This case goes from bad to worse. It's a result bringing her in. Great news.' He tried to sound positive but felt like a ten-ton weight was pushing him down. 'I'll let Maggie Bennet know we've got them. It might make her more talkative.'

'Yes. Do that,' Laurel said. 'Oh, by the way,' she added. 'Why are you lying about being at the Royal?'

'I got a tip from an informer here,' Barlow lied. 'He told me Maggie Bennet had been admitted. I didn't want to drop him in the shit for telling me. He's security here. That's all. Nothing to worry about.'

'I'm not worried about it,' Laurel said. 'I'm confused as to why one of my colleagues feels the need to lie to me. When people tell lies, they're usually up to no good.' She paused and waited for him to respond. She expected him to react angrily, but he didn't. 'You're not up to no good, are you, Ian?'

'No, don't be ridiculous. I'll call you when I've spoken to Maggie,' Barlow said, hanging up. He handed the mobile back to the sergeant. 'Thanks,' he said. The uniformed officer nodded and took the phone from him. 'I'm going to speak to Maggie Bennet. You guys can get off now ARU are here.'

'DS Stewart asked me to hang around for a few hours, until she calls back,' the sergeant said.

'Did she?' Barlow said under his breath. He turned and walked towards ICU. Things were beginning to unravel, not least in his mind. He walked through the sealed doors and flashed his warrant card to a nurse. The nurse took him into an anteroom where Maggie Bennet was recovering. She had cannulas in both hands and an oxygen mask over her nose and mouth. 'What's her condition?'

'She has internal injuries and multiple fractures to her legs and hips,' the nurse said. 'The orthopaedic surgeons think she'll need her pelvis screwed together. We're prepping her now.'

'Can I have two minutes with her?' Barlow asked. 'I literally need to ask her one question.'

'You can try. She's pretty out of it,' the nurse said. 'I'll be back in one minute.'

'Thanks,' Barlow said. He walked over to Maggie and watched her chest rise and fall. She was struggling. He leaned close to her ear. 'Maggie,' he whispered. Her eyes flickered open. She looked at him and her eyes widened in terror. 'You recognise me, don't you, Maggie?' She blinked but couldn't answer him. 'Good. I need you to listen to me because I have a message from Fabienne.' He leaned closer and whispered in her ear. Maggie closed her eyes and started to cry.

CHAPTER 41

Laurel met the uniformed unit that had been sent to 27 Allerton Road. One of the constables was guarding the front door, the other was on the landing upstairs. She said hello and climbed the stairs, feeling anxious. The unit had been despatched within minutes of Laurel making the call and they'd arrived ten minutes later. When they couldn't get an answer, but noticed the lights were on, they'd called MIT for instructions. A ladder was brought and one of the constables looked in through the front window. There was a single shoe in the middle of the room. It looked out of place in the tidy flat. Laurel had given authorisation for a locksmith to be called to the scene to open the outer door. She wanted to be there when they opened the second door.

'Sarge,' the uniformed officer greeted her. 'I've told the locksmith to stay in his van for now,' he said. 'I knelt down to see if there was a gap under the door and I got a whiff.' He lowered his voice. 'It doesn't smell good, sarge.'

'You think someone lost control of their insides in there?' Laurel asked.

'I do, sarge. I didn't want the guy opening the door and finding a stiff on the other side.' He rattled the door with his hand. 'There's nothing to this door. I can open it with my shoulder, if you want me to?'

'Do it,' Laurel said. The constable grabbed the handle and slammed his shoulder against the door. It catapulted open and clattered against the wall. Melissa Walker was lying on her back, eyes open, staring into eternity. Laurel didn't need to check if she was dead. She'd been dead a few hours. The pallor of her skin and stink of her bowels emptying told her all she needed to know.

'Let's get CSI in here,' Laurel said. She thought about calling Ian Barlow, and asking him who his information had come from, but decided against it. She wanted to speak to Braddick about it first. Something wasn't right. Barlow had failed to find both witnesses and suddenly, one was dead and the other was close to being dead. Coincidences like that didn't happen, not unless they were manufactured by someone. Someone desperate enough to risk killing two people in daylight. Desperate people were dangerous. She looked around the room from the doorway, looking for something, anything, that would indicate who had killed Melissa. There was nothing obvious. Then, something beneath the settee caught her eye. It was a laptop. 'Tell them to get that laptop to forensics sharpish,' she said. CSI might unearth something for them to go on. The killer wasn't far away, she knew that. She guesstimated how long it would take to drive from the flat to the hospital – not very long. Barlow had lied about being at the Royal. People who lie are up to no good.

CHAPTER 42

Braddick and Laurel waited in a private visiting booth. Sara Larkin was being brought down from the landing to make a formal statement. They'd spoken about Barlow's odd behaviour and decided not to send him back to interview her. There was an unusual pattern to his behaviour, nothing Braddick could put his finger on, just a wishy-washy attitude to finding the witnesses. Barlow was never wishy-washy about anything, that's what made it unusual. It would be dealt with, but not right now. Braddick wanted to talk to Sara himself and he'd sent Barlow on another information-gathering mission, one important enough not to raise his suspicion.

Sara's solicitor was already there but she wasn't the most talkative woman. She was there as a witness rather than a legal advisor. Braddick reckoned she wasn't far from retirement and had little to no interest in the case. The door opened and Sara Larkin was shown in by a male PO.

'Take a seat, Sara,' Laurel said. They'd already decided she would lead the interview. 'I'm Detective Sergeant Stewart and this is Detective Superintendent Braddick,' she said. 'We want you to tell us everything you can remember about the night of Halloween last year.'

'Okay,' Sara said. 'I'm ready.'

'We're going to ask you questions as you talk, and when we're done, we'll go back to the beginning and write it all down for you to sign, okay?' Laurel said.

'That's fine,' Sara said. 'As long as I don't have to see that woman in court.'

'Don't worry about that. You'll never have to see her again,' Laurel said. 'Start at the beginning; tell us what you remember about that night.'

'Where shall I start?' Sara said, shifting uncomfortably in her chair.

'Tell us how you got there,' Laurel said, trying to put her at ease.

'Okay, let me think. Maggie got a taxi from hers and picked me and Melissa up on the way. We stopped at the shop and bought a half bottle of vodka and got there about ten o'clock and knocked on number ninety. John opened the door and showed us along the landing to the end flat. He took us into the living room, which was set up as usual.'

'That was this man, John Metcalfe?' Laurel said, showing her an image. Laurel nodded that it was. 'You said it was set up. Can you explain to us what you mean by that?'

'There was a big circle on the floor and one on the ceiling, writing all over the walls, and candles everywhere. There were mattresses scattered around, and some of them were already there, drinking the mushroom tea. Incense sticks were burning. The atmosphere was overpowering before we had any tea.'

'Who was there, Sara?' Laurel asked.

'Bruce, Victoria, and a man I hadn't seen before,' Sara said.

'Bruce May and his wife, Victoria May?' Laurel asked, showing her their images.

'Yes.'

'Okay, then what happened?'

'We stripped to our underwear, as usual, then sat down and Victoria came over with some tea for us. It was stronger than usual; it didn't taste the same. I remember it hit me like a bus. The room was warping in and out within twenty minutes. Then the others came in. Fabienne was first, and she sat in the circle and began to hum. She always hummed and mumbled stuff I couldn't understand. John and Joe were there too. There were others there, in animal masks. Men and women. They were all excited. The atmosphere was oppressive. I would have gone home then if I didn't need the money.'

'How many people were there?'

'Thirteen,' Sara said. 'There were always thirteen. If any more came, they used another flat. There were never more than thirteen in each gathering. It was a rule.'

'How often did that happen?' Laurel asked.

'What?'

'Them using more than one flat.'

'Most of the time,' Sara said. 'There were always lots of people there, but that night was different.'

'Tell me why it was different?'

'The build-up was different. She was rambling more than usual, tripping like I'd never seen her before. She was in a trance-like state. When she signalled them to join in, they were all like rabid dogs. It was so intense; I thought my head was going to explode. I knew we were in trouble from the first minute. The next few hours are a jumble of images, and then, as it approached midnight, they brought the foreign women in. Two of them, scared to death they were.'

'Who brought them in?' Laurel asked.

'Bruce and Joe,' Sara said. 'They were tied up. The others went wild. They were on them like a pack of animals. I watched them and it wasn't normal. I had a feeling something really bad was going to happen. Then he turned one of them over and slit her throat.' She had to stop; the memory was difficult to recount. 'The blood sprayed everywhere. I didn't think it was real at first, I thought it was staged, but the smell got to me. I knew it was real blood and it sent them into a frenzy. They were at her neck like vampires, and all the while he was still having sex with her. I've never seen anything like it. He was like an animal. It was all I could do to look away. He was in a frenzy, they all were.'

'Who was in a frenzy, Sara?' Laurel asked. Sara faltered. 'Who cut her throat?'

'Bruce May,' Sara said.

'Bruce May killed her?' Braddick interrupted. 'You're absolutely sure it was him?'

'Yes. Joe held them down, but Bruce used the knife.'

'Then what happened?' Braddick asked.

'We knew it had gone way too far and I had the feeling it wasn't over by a long chalk; there was worse to come, I could feel it in my bones. I wanted out but she was at the door.'

'She?' Laurel said. 'Fabienne Wilder?'

'Yes. She was so frightening when she got going. Her eyes were black like coal and there were times when she would shake like she was fitting, other times she'd scream like a banshee. I can't explain it, but she terrified me. She's evil. When the first woman had stopped moving, and the pack began to calm, he did the same thing to the other one.' Sara sobbed. 'She knew what they were going to do … she was so scared, begging for her life. He laughed at her. They went loopy as she bled to death. Some of them were smearing her blood all over themselves.'

'Bruce killed them both?' Braddick asked.

'Yes.'

'Carry on,' Laurel said.

'When the second woman was dead, I looked at the door and Fabienne had left the room. I heard the front door closing; I think she went to another flat. She flitted in and out from one to the other. Even the regulars were in shock. There were people crying while others were laughing like hyenas. I was convinced we were next, so I used an old trick to get out of the room,' Sara said, lowering her voice. 'I pissed on the floor. It's amazing how people move when you wet yourself. I pretended it was an accident and took a candle into the toilet. The other girls knew what I was doing, and they grabbed our clothes. I set fire to the shower curtain and we ran. We got dressed on the stairs and we didn't stop running until we were near the town centre and there were plenty of people around. I've never been so frightened in my life. That was the last time we went there.'

'You've done very well. That must have been difficult to recount,' Laurel said. 'Thank you for being so frank.'

'I wish I'd done it sooner, but I was frightened, and the next day when the mushrooms had worn off, it didn't seem real anymore. It was flashes of a nightmare. I couldn't decide if it had happened or not. It was only when the murders hit the news that I realised it was all real.' Sara stopped talking, as if something had occurred to her. 'Have you spoken to Maggie and Melissa yet?'

'We will be later today,' Braddick lied. 'Okay, we need to get all that down in writing.' Laurel looked at him. 'Start again, at the beginning.'

CHAPTER 43

Braddick drove out of the prison car park. It was dark and raining. They'd been quiet since leaving the prison, both mulling over the terrible details of Sara Larkin's story. It was a difficult story to envisage and even more difficult to comprehend. He turned down the radio, oblivious to what was playing.

'What are your thoughts?' Laurel asked. She looked out of the passenger window, watching the world go by in a haze of headlights.

'I'm lost for words, to be honest,' Braddick said. 'I don't know why I'm surprised but I am.'

'What about?'

'Bruce May. Bruce May is a Jekyll and Hyde character. You wouldn't think he had the bottle for any of this. I've underestimated some criminals in my time, but this is out of the ether. He can sit across the table and look me in the eye, crying for his dead wife, when he knows we have witnesses who watched him slit the throats of two women he trafficked into the sex industry.' Braddick shrugged and pulled the Evoque into the traffic. 'I'm numb, to be honest. Why am I so surprised? They dug up my parents,' he added, shaking his head. 'What the hell is that all about?'

'I'm worried Sara will withdraw her statement when she finds out Melissa Walker was murdered and Maggie Bennet is in ICU,' Laurel said.

'Me too,' Braddick replied. 'I wonder what Maggie Bennet will say when she comes around and has had time to think about it. She could decide not to make a statement, and we'd be left with DNA and speculation as to how it got there. We need more, Laurel.'

'Until her arrest, we had nothing on Fabienne,' Laurel said. 'She could have slipped the net. How did she manage to not leave her prints anywhere?'

'She left them on a pitchfork,' Braddick said. 'And she left them on a shotgun. We've got her nailed for shooting Joe Metcalfe and murdering Harry Alsop. I'd be more comfortable if we had irrefutable evidence of her involvement at Stanley House.'

'Like what?'

'I've been thinking about the pictures they've uploaded to the net.'

'From the graveyard?'

'Yes. They like filming stuff. They filmed us at home, they filmed the desecration, and they filmed us talking to witnesses in the tower block. That makes me wonder if they filmed any of their meetings at Stanley House – I think they would have.'

'It makes sense. There's a chance they did,' Laurel said, 'but they wouldn't tell us where they're stored.'

'I know one of them who might,' Braddick said.

'Who?'

'Joe Metcalfe. He must be pretty pissed off with Fabienne Wilder. They traced the tip-off to her whereabouts to his mobile,' Braddick said. 'He turned her in before she shot him. She blew his genitals off; now, if that was me, I'd be pretty angry. I think if we speak to him and offer him protection, he'll spill. He's going to be inside for life, and we could make things a bit more comfortable in return for something concrete to go to court with.'

'Might be worth a try,' Laurel said, nodding. 'I'll call Google and put him on Bluetooth.' She dialled the number and connected it to the speaker.

'Hello, Google, it's Laurel.'

'Hiya, Laurel. How did the Larkin interview go?'

'Good, but we think both her and Maggie Bennet's evidence is vulnerable. Maggie Bennet hasn't made a statement yet. Even if she does, they could both recant them at any time.'

'Okay,' Google said. 'What do you need me to do?'

'We need to do an update on Metcalfe's condition,' Braddick said. 'I want to talk to him before we interview Wilder. He might be able to give us something solid to challenge her with.'

'The last thing I heard, he was in surgery up to an hour ago,' Google said. 'I'll call the ward and ask them to contact us when he comes around.'

'No. We need to have men there when he comes around. He might wake up but not make the distance. If he comes to, we need to ask him for solid evidence, something that can't be withdrawn,' Braddick said. 'And tell forensics to re-examine everything we found at Stanley House, the Metcalfe property and the May home.'

'What are we looking for?'

'A memory stick, SIM card, laptop, handheld camera – something they can store images on of their rituals. I think the temptation to film themselves would be too great to resist,' Braddick said. 'If we can find footage of them, it will make keeping them inside easier. I'm worried they'll get some of their goons on the outside to put pressure on our witnesses. If they withdraw their evidence – at any point – they could be let out on appeal.'

'I agree,' Google said. 'You could be on to something there. Malcolm Baines found the graveyard footage on the dark web. He stumbled on it by accident, but he seems to be finding his way around their platforms. I wouldn't be surprised if there was more on there somewhere and, if there is, he might be the man to find it.'

'Contact him and ask him to search the sites he's been looking at for any footage of the ceremonies at Stanley House,' Braddick said. 'Tell him this could be the evidence that locks them all up and gets them off his back, too.'

'I'll give him a call. It's worth a try,' Google said. He was about to speak again when the sound of Laurel screaming pierced his ears. It was high-pitched and cut short by a deafening crash. The noise of metal crushing metal, tyres squealing, and glass shattering filled his senses. He looked at the handset in horror. There was an explosion, and the line went dead.

CHAPTER 44

TWO WEEKS LATER

Detective Superintendent Jo Jones waited impatiently for the doctors to ascertain whether Joe Metcalfe was fit to be spoken to. Two uniformed officers stood guard at the door. The doctors made their decision and stepped out into the corridor.

'He's very drowsy but knows what's going on,' one of them said. 'In light of the seriousness of the case, I'm comfortable allowing you five minutes. Please bear in mind he's very weak indeed. The sepsis nearly killed him and, while he's on the mend, he's not out of the woods yet.'

'Thanks,' Jo said, walking into the room. Barlow followed her. She stood to the right of the bed, in Metcalfe's line of sight. Barlow lingered behind her, where he couldn't be seen. 'I'm Detective Superintendent Jones. I want to ask you a few questions about the events at Stanley House. Before I begin, I want you to know you're safe. Fabienne Wilder is in isolation, in a high-security wing of a women's prison. She has no access to visitors, the Internet or a telephone. Whatever you say to me might help your own position when it comes to sentencing. Do you understand me?'

'Yes. I understand,' Metcalfe said weakly.

'We've seen lots of videos online, uploaded by your group. Did you film the rituals at Stanley House?' Jo asked. She saw a flicker of recognition in Metcalfe's eyes. 'We want to make sure Fabienne Wilder doesn't get out of prison alive. If there's film footage of those rituals, I can guarantee you'll be safe. She'll never know which prison you're in and she'll never know we spoke.' Joe shook his head. He looked weak and vulnerable. 'Come on, Joe, help me to help you.'

Joe Metcalfe licked his lips and closed his eyes, deep in thought. When he opened them, he tried to focus on the man standing behind the superintendent, but he was out of range. There was something about his aura that disturbed him, it made him feel unsafe. Fabienne haunted his dreams, taunting him, threatening him. It was probably the cocktail of drugs in his veins, allowing his imagination to run away from him, but he knew better than that. She had a gift. Her gift was being able to get inside your head. He tried and tried not to let her in, but she wouldn't leave him alone.

'You have no idea what you're dealing with, have you?' Metcalfe said. His voice was hoarse. 'Don't underestimate that woman. She knows where I am. She knows everything. She has eyes and ears in places you wouldn't believe.'

'I'm not underestimating anyone. I'm dealing with the facts, and the fact is, she's banged up in one of the most secure prisons in the world. She can't get out.'

'You don't understand,' Joe said, shaking his head.

'I understand she's a nutter and she's never going to be let out of jail, Joe. You might be. Did they film the rituals?'

'Yes,' he said, nodding. 'Every single one.'

'Where can we find them?'

'I don't know,' Metcalfe said.

'You must have some idea. Give me somewhere to look.'

'I can tell you she spent hours on the dark web uploading stuff. That's how she attracted new recruits: the promise of unbridled sex with strangers. It suckers them in in their droves. If those films are anywhere, it's there.'

'You're telling me Wilder uploaded them, each time?' Jo asked.

'Maybe not every time. I'm telling you she spent hours on the dark web uploading shit. I never really bought into the Internet. It's not my forte.'

'Do you know which sites she used the most?'

'Her own,' Metcalfe said. 'She was self-obsessed. I know she had her own site, but it was well hidden. You'll never find them unless she tells you where to look.'

'There must be something solid you can give me, Joe?'

Metcalfe shook his head. Jo Jones sighed and turned to walk out. Metcalfe got a glimpse of Barlow's face.

'Superintendent?' Metcalfe said. Jo turned around. 'Can you see the scar on my shoulder?' Jo approached and looked closely. There was an h-shaped scar etched into his skin. It would have been a deep, painful wound. 'She marked her conquests, dead or alive. This was her mark.' Metcalfe stared at Barlow, who shuffled his feet uncomfortably. 'Keep it mind. It might help you find what you're looking for.'

'Okay,' Jo said, nodding. She'd noticed the hard stare between the two men. 'Do you two know each other?' They both shook their heads. Barlow couldn't look her in the eye. 'Thank you. Let's go,' she said. Barlow opened the door and left the room in a hurry. She looked at Metcalfe one last time as she closed the door. His eyes were closed, and his lips were moving, as if in silent prayer. She wondered who he was praying to.

CHAPTER 45

Rob Stewart held Aimee to his chest while he watched the nurses change Laurel's dressings. The burns on her arms and neck were sticky and raw. They dabbed at them gently, peeling old dressings away and reapplying new. Laurel was in pain. It was etched on her face. This was his worst nightmare. He had feared her being hurt or killed every day since they had met, but from the day her pregnancy was confirmed, his angst had increased tenfold. She was lucky to be alive. The first five days following the crash were touch and go; she was on the edge between life and death. Those days had gone by in a blur for Rob, looking after Aimee was the only thing keeping him sane. Laurel opened her eyes and focused on him through the glass. She smiled but the pain didn't leave her eyes. Rob waved and spoke to Aimee, taking her tiny hand and waving it at her mother. The nurses finished and came out of the room.

'How is she?' Rob asked.

'Sore,' the nurse said. 'She's been looking forward to seeing Aimee. Go in, don't keep her waiting.'

'Thank you,' Rob said. He carried Aimee into the room and took her to Laurel. Her eyes watered.

'I want to hold her so much,' Laurel said. 'Do you think she knows I can't?'

'She can see you and hear your voice,' Rob said. 'She's a baby, don't stress. We need to concentrate on getting you better. What have the doctors said?'

'I'm going to need a lot of skin grafts over the next few years,' Laurel said. 'Any news on Braddick?'

'No,' Rob said, shaking his head. 'He's still in an induced coma.'

'I'm so gutted, Rob,' she said, holding back her tears. 'The ACC told me the woman who drove into us was employed by Bruce May. It wasn't an accident. She died yesterday. I feel so guilty about Braddick.'

'He wouldn't want you to,' Rob said. 'He pulled you out of that fire because that's who he is and he would do it a hundred times over, and I'm glad he did, Laurel. It means my daughter will grow up with her mother there.'

'I know,' Laurel said. 'I just can't stop thinking about him.'

'You've been given a second chance, Laurel,' Rob said. 'Enough is enough. I don't want to feel sick every time you go to work, wondering if you're going to come home.'

Laurel looked at Aimee and let the tears go. She knew he was right, and she knew this was the end. Enough was enough. It was time to take a different path, a longer path with a happy ending. Aimee smiled and dribbled; her eyes sparkled as if she knew what her mother was thinking.

CHAPTER 46

Detective Superintendent Jones was standing behind Google, who was on the telephone to Malcolm Baines. He had spent days on end trying to find Fabienne Wilder's dark website with nothing to show for it. He was calling to tell Google the route he had taken and how far he'd progressed before he'd hit a brick wall. Google thanked him and hung up.

'What do you think?' Jo asked. She shook her dark hair from her shoulders. Google typed away on his laptop, following Malcolm's directions. Within a few minutes he had accessed the dark web and logged into an O9A site.

'I think they're a bunch of very disturbed individuals,' Google said, scrolling down the content pages. 'This is a step-by-step guide to living the life of a Niner, including instructions on how to identify and capture victims for sacrifice.'

'How very convenient,' Jo said sarcastically. 'Joe Metcalfe was convinced they filmed the rituals and he was adamant Wilder had her own site where she uploaded stuff.'

'Look here,' Google said. He clicked on a content link. 'I remember Braddick talking about a female goddess, Baphomet. This site is dedicated to her.' He scrolled through pages and pages of script that made little to no sense to them. 'No wonder Malcolm couldn't get any further. This is a maze of absolute madness.' He shook his head. 'Did Metcalfe say anything specific?'

'He showed me a scar on his shoulder,' Jo said. 'It was h-shaped and very deep. He said Wilder marked her conquests and it might help us find what we're looking for. What that means, I have no idea.'

'Guv,' Miles called over from another desk. 'Dr Libby is on line one. He said it's urgent and it's private.'

'Bloody hell,' Jo muttered as she went to Braddick's office. She walked in and closed the door behind her. One of his overcoats was hanging behind the door. There was a faint smell of his aftershave in the air: Armani. It was distinctive and always reminded her of him. She paused at the window as she picked up the phone. A cruise ship had docked on the Pier Head, the choppy water around her was deep grey. 'Dr Libby,' she said.

'Hello, Jo,' he said. He sounded panicked. 'Are you alone?'

'Yes,' she said. 'What on earth has got you so rattled?'

'We've been ploughing through the electronic devices involved in the case. There was a laptop recovered from the property where Melissa Walker was murdered. We've only just got around to it.'

'I'm familiar with the scene,' Jo said, confused. They were searching for images connected to the Niners, not the witnesses. 'What have you found?'

'There was a security camera in the flat, which must have been removed after the murder. It was the type that transmits to an electronic device – a mobile phone, or a computer or the like.'

'Okay,' Jo said, following.

'This was programmed to do both. It captured Melissa Walker being attacked,' he said. He was flustered. 'It filmed her being murdered.'

'Can we identify the attacker from the images?'

'We've already done that,' the doctor said. 'It's Detective Sergeant Barlow.'

'Detective Sergeant Ian Barlow?' Jo said, looking through the window in the door. Barlow was sitting at his desk, talking on the telephone.

'Yes. It's absolutely clear. One hundred per cent. Barlow killed Melissa Walker.'

'I'll need that sending over to me,' Jo said. 'Keep it under your hat, please, Dr Libby. Once we've locked him up, I'll contact the ACC.'

'No problem.'

Jo made a call to the custody suite and requested for a couple of uniformed officers to be sent upstairs. She watched Barlow working at his desk and wondered why a decorated detective had murdered a prostitute in cold blood. She decided not to dwell on it. Nothing about this case made sense.

CHAPTER 47

It was late when Jo arrived home that night. Barlow had been arrested and was led away without a fight. He made a no comment interview and looked washed out, exhausted and numb. The MIT were stunned. A silence had descended on the office. If it hadn't been for the images of the murder on the laptop, no one in the team would have believed it possible. The team was rocked: Laurel was badly burned and didn't look like returning any time soon, and Braddick was in a coma. Now Barlow had been lifted for murdering a witness who was vital to the case they'd been battling against for weeks – the biggest case on record. It had been dumped in Jo Jones' lap because she'd worked closely with MIT when she was with vice. She knew the detectives well, including Ian Barlow. Replacing Braddick was impossible but she could fill the gap until he was fit enough to return to his desk.

She kicked off her shoes and opened a bottle of Pinot, filling a glass. The television was on, but she had no desire to hear any more about Brexit, she couldn't care less about it. The CPS were happy to progress with prosecuting Joe Metcalfe, Bruce May and Fabienne Wilder with the evidence they had. Sara Larkin and Maggie Bennet were reluctant eyewitnesses, but eyewitnesses, nonetheless. The press was still in a whirl about the story. It was flavour of the month. The attempted assassination of the senior investigating officers had further fuelled the flames. It was a journalist's wet dream: multiple murder victims; cannibals; the occult; the desecration of a grave; and a murderous attack on serving detectives. They could milk it for years. The ramifications for people affected by the case were like ripples in a pond, spreading wider and wider as DNA from the drains was identified. Relatives of the victims were being interviewed and paraded by the press. It seemed endless, with no clear boundaries.

Jo plonked herself on the settee and closed her eyes. She wanted to drift as far away from the case as she possibly could, but it was impossible to escape it. When her mobile buzzed, she considered ignoring it.

'Hello, Google,' she said, yawning. 'What are you doing up so late?'

'We've found them, guv,' Google said. Jo couldn't speak. She sat upright and nearly spilled her wine. 'You were right about that h-shaped scar. I kept trawling the Baphomet pages and found an image of a tattoo of the Goddess on someone's leg. I scrolled past it a few times but then I noticed a scar on the flesh above the tattoo. I clicked on it and it took me into Wilder's content – the scar was the portal into her content. She's even more dangerous than we thought, guv. I've never seen anything like it. There are hundreds of videos there. I've only looked at a few but there's enough to put them away and keep them away.'

'That's great news. Well done, Google.' Jo felt a massive wave of relief wash over her. 'Have you identified anyone?'

'Yes: Wilder, the Mays and the Metcalfe brothers, and there's plenty more faces to work on. We can match up the prints Dr Libby found, with facial recognition. It will identify a few more of them.'

'I'll go to the hospital tomorrow and tell Braddick. He might be asleep, but I think he'd want to know.'

'Good idea. There's something else,' Google said. 'Ian Barlow is on them too, guv. He's one of them. I wouldn't have believed it if I hadn't seen it with my own eyes.'

'Oh, no,' Jo said. 'I was hoping there was no connection.'

'Me too,' Google said. 'I'll see you in the morning, guv. Goodnight.'

'Goodnight, Google. See you tomorrow.' Jo put down the phone and emptied her glass in one long glug. It would take the entire bottle for her to sleep that night.

CHAPTER 48

Fabienne was under close observation and had been placed on suicide watch. Her behaviour was concerning the medical staff. They were considering transferring her to a secure psychiatric hospital, but the police and CPS were highly agitated by the prospect. Any talk of moving her met protest. She hadn't spoken since being arrested and had refused to eat or drink. She spent her time rocking and humming strange tunes, mumbling to herself. It appeared she had retreated to the furthest corners of her mind and refused to come back to reality.

On the inside, Fabienne was rebuilding. She could sense where the others were and she logged it for future reference – they could be dealt with later, when she'd thought of a way out of prison. It would be difficult, but she had every confidence she would. Someone would help her, they always did. She would bring them in close to her, where she could work her magic and sink her hooks in. Then they would do anything she asked, including helping her to escape. She wouldn't be in high security for ever. They would let their guard down eventually, they always did. In the meantime, she would feed off the darkness in her mind. It would make her stronger until the time came.

CHAPTER 49

Laurel had made her way to the ICU where Braddick was being treated. Jo Jones had called in to see her after visiting Braddick to tell him about their discovery; he hadn't responded but Jo hoped he had heard her. Laurel wanted to see him herself. She pushed an IV stand alongside her. The doctors said she would need to be on IV fluids for a long time yet. Her hands and arms were wrapped, and she still couldn't use them with any expertise, it was too painful. She had years of painful grafts and treatment to look forward to. When she reached Braddick's room, she sensed his distress. Doctors and nurses were rushing in and out. She stood, frozen, and watched through the glass. His body had been burned from head to toe and he made a pitiful sight. A scrum of doctors was working on him, concern on their faces. The monitors were detached from him, so the doctors had more room to work. Plasma and antibiotics were attached to the intravenous drips and a nurse squeezed them into the tubes towards the cannula, desperate to get fluids into him. She saw his eyes flicker open for a moment. He looked distressed. His eyebrows and lashes were gone, blisters in their place. His fingers twitched against the sheets as if he was trying to grasp something. One leg began to tremble, bending at the knee. She thought he was trying to get out of bed. The doctors and nurses held him still, doing their best to calm him while the drugs entered his veins. He struggled against them for a few seconds and then he relaxed. The doctors talked over him. Braddick started to spasm, his entire body twitched violently until suddenly, his body became still. Laurel was stunned, her legs wouldn't move. Braddick was gone, his fight for life was over.

CHAPTER 50

Valerie Sykes watched George and Ellis bedding down for the night. They had given their version of the story of the murders at Stanley House to a national newspaper and made a few thousand pounds. Neither of them wanted to go back to the rat race, they were happy on the streets, so they used some of the money to buy decent coats and sleeping bags. They ate a hot meal every day and they were making an effort to stay off the booze together. It made her happy that they were warm, and their bellies were full. Things were calming down at Stanley House and there were fewer ghouls every day. There was nothing to see any more: the flats on the ninth floor had been boarded up and the steps to the landing were sealed from the eighth floor. All access had been blocked. Even the press had bored of the story. They thought everyone involved was dead, dying, or locked up, but Val knew differently. Fabienne was still there, although her power was weaker, she still stalked the walkways. Val felt her walking along the landings, but she avoided her and hid until she'd moved on. So far, Fabienne had failed to detect her presence and Val wanted to keep it that way. She felt a little bit safer as time went by; her confidence was improving all the time.

She moved up the stairway to the ninth floor and looked across the city to the east. In the distance she could see the lights of suburbia, and the satellite towns where she'd been dragged up. Her family had moved from St Helens to Widnes, then Runcorn, Warrington, Earlstown and, finally, Prescott. Social Services and the child protection units were always hot on their tails. Her father was an alcoholic, aggressive and abusive, her mother a prescription drug addict who couldn't fend for herself, let alone her children. When Val and her siblings were finally removed and taken into care, they were separated, which broke her heart. She'd mothered her younger brother and sister, protecting them from their father and replacing their malfunctioning mother. She'd cooked, washed, and cleaned the house. Losing them had tipped her over the edge. They had been her purpose in life, and so, she'd run away and found a haven at Stanley House. She was very young and made the wrong choices and she'd paid dearly. Maxine and Wanda had tried to guide her, but even the best advice can be useless when it falls on young ears.

There had been a time when she'd hated her parents and couldn't wait to be away from them, but now, she'd give anything to be back there, cuddled up to her siblings. Her heart longed to go home, but this was her home now, until she was ready to let go and move into the light. Remembering the terrible nature of her death made her sad. No one would ever know she'd been slaughtered, a week to the day before Wanda. No one would ever find her body or know for certain she was actually dead. She would be on the missing persons list forever and a day. There would be no funeral and nowhere for her family to visit. That made her sad, and that made her hang around, drifting from landing to landing, trying to gain the strength to pass over properly. She'd tried to warn Wanda not to go to the ninth floor. She'd walked alongside her, while she spoke to Maxine, and talked until she was tired, but Wanda couldn't hear her. No one could anymore. She'd tried to stop them killing Wanda, but she had no effect on the living any more. And then suddenly, Fabienne had been aware she was there and screamed at her. Val had felt darkness reaching for her; evil had surrounded her and tried to drag her to an evil place. It was a place of torment and anguish. She'd fled and hid in the stairwells until it was all over. She'd tried to help people since then – sometimes she was successful, sometimes she wasn't. One day, she would leave this place and pass over to the other side; until then, she was doomed to haunt it. She had to build up the courage to let go of her mortal coil and travel somewhere Fabienne Wilder would never find her. One day she would pass, and she hoped it would be one day soon.

EPILOGUE

Fabienne Wilder is real. I encountered her in the writing of another novel, and she is as evil as she is portrayed in *Deliver Us from Evil*. During a long spell in captivity, she changed her name to Jennifer Booth and dedicated her energy to find Malcolm Baines and to wreak revenge on him for highlighting the Niners in his writings. Her focus then changed to other authors, me included. You can read about what happened in *A Child for the Devil*.

https://www.amazon.co.uk/Child-Devil-Nine-Angels-Books-ebook/dp/B009OIVDZK

Or the box set is;

https://www.amazon.co.uk/Hunting-Angels-Box-Set-ebook/dp/B00GZ0TH7G

Printed in Great Britain
by Amazon

84295492R00146